One Drunkin' Monkee

W.C. Beattie

Contents

To Mom and Dad,

...many thanks for moving us to South Florida.

Acknowledgment

Sending acknowledgement to the USCG. Protecting us on the sea around the world. Thanks for being a large inspiration to this novel.

About the Author

W.C. moved to South Florida with his family in 1971, at the age of fifteen. Growing up and coming of age during this time was an experience he would never have had in his home state of N.J. Owning his own boat was the ultimate, fishing all day, booze cursing with the waitresses enjoying the go-fast boats and luxury yachts as they pass by, only enhanced living the lifestyle. Occasional interaction with the Coast Guard and other law enforcement agencies on the water provided him with some of the material for the stories and descriptions in his new book.

Prologue

Pedro "Pepe" Largo just celebrates his 16th birthday. The celebration isn't what you'd expect for a typical sixteen-year-old's birthday party—no DJ playing the latest hits, no bevy of good friends, cake, or ice cream. No, Pepe's party consists of him laboring in the midday Cuban heat on a makeshift dock near the fringe of a rainforest, physically unloading cargo from a Russian freighter. His frail brown body sweats profusely as he works under the scorching sun, his saturated white cotton shirt clinging to his skin as if glued there. Even his handmade straw hat oozes perspiration, making it feel heavier than it actually is. The eighty-pound bags of cement are more than half his body weight, yet he refuses to let that slow him down. He works just as hard as men twice his size.

Despite his age and build, he gets no slack from the unforgiving taskmaster. If he can't keep up, he'll be sent away, replaced without a second thought. Pepe needs this job. He's grateful for it, earning the equivalent of five U.S. dollars a day—the only source of income for his family since his father boarded a raft for America and was never heard from again. This reality weighs heavily on Pepe. He is now the head of the household, responsible for providing while his mother tends to the family garden and cares for his two-year-old twin brothers.

Pepe works tirelessly, day or night, rain or shine. Whenever ships arrive, the men must be ready. Loading or off-loading, he never complains. For three months, the work is steady—two ships per week. Now, the ships are many, two ships per day. The heavy cargo moves into makeshift warehouses, their ragged camouflage netting barely providing shelter. No one asked questioned about what they are unloading or why it's here. Pepe doesn't care. He only knows that each load he carries keeps food on his family's table.

He pauses briefly, wiping the glistening sweat from his brow. His mind drifts, as it often does, to the dream of leaving for America, where he can build a better life for himself and his family. He thinks about what a wonderful country Cuba could be—the Pearl of the Caribbean—if only things were different. An agricultural dreamland with fertile fields and miles of beautiful beaches, waiting for the first generation of free Cubans. A free Cuba, he imagines, would thrive with an influx of American businesses and a healthy international trade.

Standing in the cool shade of a palm tree, Pepe listens to the rustling fronds swaying in the soft breeze, the sound reminiscent of a light warm rain. As he tilts his head back, covering his face with his red neckerchief, the sudden loud shouted of nearby men startle him. Ripping the damp cloth from his face, Pepe freezes, his eyes locked on the chaos unfolding before him.

His last vision is of a breaking cargo net and one hundred bags of cement plummeting toward him. In an instant, Pepe Largo and three of his fellow workers are crushed beneath the weight of the falling cargo.

"Rapido! Rapido!" yelled the hardened foreman. "Get those bodies out of here and get back to work! You've seen dead men before! Rapido!" He dismisses the fallen men as if they were nothing more than debris blocking his way.

Pepe's mother receives the news of her son's death from a man who works on the docks. There is no wrongful death lawsuit, no settlement, not even an apology from those in charge. That's just the way it is.

Tears spill from her eyes as she grieves over her son's poorly marked grave in the city cemetery. Then, as always, she moves on. She has to. She still has two sons to care for. She prays for the day when communism is gone, when Cuba is finally free. But for Maria Largo, as with the rest of Cuba, life is cheap.

Chapter 1

"Buckle your seat belt," read the handmade sign taped to the partition inside the taxi. MacShane just fluffs it off as someone trying to get his compliances in order for any safety inspection. He did not even consider it a premonition.

Enjoying the ride from the Fort Lauderdale International airport, MacShane gawked at the tropical scenery, the manicured lush green lawns and beautiful mega yachts docked along Las Olas Blvd. The lawns gave way to low level apartment buildings before making a slight turn to revel the sky scrapers of downtown Fort Lauderdale. Not skyscrapers to a New Yorkers point of view but big enough for the locals. Arriving at his destination MacShane heard

"Dat ill be 12.50 Mon," muttered the cab driver in a thick Caribbean accent.

Morgan MacShane steps out of the cab and into the sweltering mid-day heat. The tall middle aged black man looks at the picture in his hand again and verifies the address. 300 New River public docks. Right location, but the vessel in his picture isn't anywhere to be found.

"Every ting ahrite Mon?" asked the cabbie.

"Yeah, it's *perfect*. The guy I'm meeting must be running late," answered MacShane as he peels a twenty off his bankroll and hands it to the driver. "Keep the change; I might need you again real soon."

"Tanks Mon! E'res me card. You call Pierre and I be dere!" said the cabbie taking the bill and rolling up his window.

As MacShane watches cab's number 075 roll away, and with it goes his chance for a quick getaway.

Lifting his duffle to his shoulder MacShane started to walk down the docks when a familiar voice stops him. "Hey Mac! Over here!" MacShane turns and see his old army buddy T.C. Allen waving and smiling, walking off the gang plank of an old beat up coastal freighter registered out of Panama, under the chipped paint is a barely readable name "Sequoia."

MacShane sees his good friend and started to laugh. "Hey T.C.! real funny, you coming off that rust bucket. How the hell does that son of a bitch even stay afloat?" remarked MacShane. "I was beginning to think I was at the wrong place."

"No Mac, this is the right place," said T.C. giving his old friend a half hug and a firm handshake.

"Let's get to our boat, this heat is brutal. Where's she tied up?" asked MacShane.

"Not far bro. Here give me your gear." T.C. leans over and grabs MacShane's duffle bag slinging it over his shoulder and said, "Follow me."

T.C. started to walk up the same gang plank he had just come off of. MacShane now feeling a little apprehensive started to follow a few paces slower as the gangplank flexed and groaned with the weight of the two men. Arriving on deck T.C. rests the duffle on the rusted hulk and said, "Welcome home partner!"

"Yeah, right. Come on take me to our boat and quit fooling around, it's way too hot for this crap," said MacShane looking around at what had the appearance of left over inventory from a marine flea market. Wooden crates, cargo nets and several pieces of machinery covered with oil stained tarps were littered about the deck; one thing for certain paint appeared to be a commodity in short supply.

"Lock jaw central! Comon' quit screwin' around, it's hot out here."

"No really, this is it. This is the boat I bought with our money," answered T.C.

"What! This... this Shit Storm! You used my money to buy this!? This isn't the boat you sent me the picture of! Are you smokin' crack? You psycho son of a bitch. The only thing holding this toilet together is your fuckin' warped imagination!" MacShane was coming unglued; the veins in his neck were bulging out. T.C. had anticipated it and was taking a defensive stance by holding up the duffle bag as a shield.

"No! Mac! Wait! Come look inside, calm down!" T.C. tries to explain but MacShane was now swinging punches at his own gear trying to get a shot through to T.C. Again T.C. spoke, "Relax Mac, calm down give it a few minutes, you'll love her I swear! Believe me looking like this definitely has its advantages. If she was all fixed up I would be afraid of getting her dirty, and what good is a salvage ship without a little dirt."

Morgan was starting to simmer down, either from T.C's pleading but more than likely the heat was beginning to take its toll. Mac lowered his hands and decides to hear T.C. out.

Mac never could stay mad at T.C. for very long any way. T.C.'s big Hollywood smile and easy going laid back South Florida style always amazed Morgan. For a moment Mac got a flashback of another time when they were in the service detached to special ops. MacShane's team was ready to do a low level jump out of an old DC-3 into some sand dune, flea ridden domain. Everyone was eager to do their duty for God and Country and there was T.C. sound asleep on a wooden seat in full jump gear.

T.C. knew from the look on his friend's face that he was zoning out. Putting a hand on Mac's shoulder he started to offer up an apology, "You're right dude, I owe you an explanation, let's go inside and grab a cold beer and I'll give you the whole story." T.C. and Mac walk towards the water tight hatch when T.C. spots the mail man. "Mac you go on in, the galley is to the right. I need to catch up with the mail man. Go ahead I'll be right behind you." As he walks away T.C. added, "This old girl will really grow on ya... honest."

"Yeah, and so will jungle rot!" utters MacShane under his breath.

Morgan eyed up the rusted latches and hinges of the old scow and estimated how much strength he would need to pry it open. His guess was far off the mark, the hatch with its well-oiled hinges flew open effortlessly. If Morgan hadn't moved his hand, it would have been smashed against the bulkhead. "Damn who would have think?"

Ice cold air engulfed Morgan's body as he entered the aged vessel, a welcome relief from the hot and humid tropical July weather he experienced outside. Now the old tub was starting to look and feel a tad bit better.

Proceeding down a passageway Morgan noticed the beautiful mahogany paneling, the raised wooden molding giving the corridor a grandeur that reminded Mac Shane of the cruise ships of a by-gone era. He envisioned some foreign craftsman laboring for hours outfitting this old girl into her present condition. Morgan proceeded along, getting a feel for his new surroundings, walking up to the first stateroom he happened upon he opens the door to check it out. Inside, bent over at the waist with her back to him, was an incredibly fit naked woman combing out her long flaming red hair. MacShane being a typical inquisitive American male, checked to see if she was indeed a natural red head; however, the area of his inspection was as clean shaven as a baby's behind.

Without missing a stroke of her hair she asked, "Did your friend arrive yet?"

"Oh yeah, and I'm so glad he did," responded Morgan.

Hearing the unfamiliar voice the woman snapped up and started to scream, "Who the hell are you! T.C.! T.C.!"

Morgan was ducking a flying shoe when T.C. came running down the passageway laughing. "Holly, that's no way to treat our new partner!"

Holly in cat like fashion moved across the cabin and donned her robe before continuing her tirade. "YOU! You're Morgan? You're really not what I expected. T.C. never mentioned..."

"What? That I'm a big black guy?" said Morgan finishing her sentence. "Miss White breed got's a problem wit dat?" Morgan graduated in the top ten percentile at West Point, was fluent in both Spanish and French, but if need be, he could always drop back to communicating with a ghetto attitude when the need arose.

"No, of course not! What I was about to say was T.C. never mentioned that you were so young!! All I kept hearing about was that 'his good old friend Morgan finally retired from the Military. When Morgan retires, we'll get him to join us…' from the way T.C. described you I was expecting someone who rode with General Custer. And by the way Morgan, don't you ever try to finish a sentence of mine again! You copy that, Soldier!" Holly was making herself quite clear that she wasn't your typical bimbo, having grown up with three brothers with her being the youngest of the lot made her one opinionated, strong-willed individual. A total opposite of the low key T.C. but that's what makes them so right for each other.

"AND YOU!" said Holly pointing to T.C., "I should have known you'd pull something like this, letting a guest show himself around!" still upset about the past few minutes.

"Hey lady, I wasn't showing myself to anyone, that category was already taken," laughs Morgan.

"Look the shows over! T.C. take Morgan to the galley and fix us something to eat before I leave for work." More of an order then a request.

"Yes dear," said T.C. mockingly in a mousy voice. "Let's go Morgan the star needs her space. I'll give you the guided tour myself." The two men left the stateroom and walked toward the galley. Along the way T.C. started to explain some of the nuances of the old vessel. Entering the dining room MacShane stopped to stare at the luxurious surroundings, a crystal chandelier, solid cherry wood dining room table that seats eight, side credenza and china cabinet of matching wood. Most impressive for such a rust bucket, he thought to himself.

"This tub gets more incredible with every step," commented Morgan.

"Like I told ya bro, this old girl is something very special. And like Momma used to say, 'T.C., never judge a book by its cover,' smart lady that Mrs. Allen," replied T.C. now beaming with pride. "The galley's behind this bulkhead, step right in."

"Un-friggin-belivable!" were the only words Morgan could spit out as T.C. turns on the lights in the galley. This from a man with twenty plus years of active military service. Who's been around the world twice, witnessed a public hanging in Morocco and toured the back streets of Bangkok, MacShane thought he had seen it all.

"Nice uh? I know some chef's that would give their right nut for a kitchen like this," boasts T.C now standing in his pride and joy. Out of all the places on the Sequoia this is his favorite.

Being a half way decent cook himself (T.C. refuses to use the word chef, since all the chefs he had ever met or worked for had been dicks, except for one. He was a humble man as he was a great cook, and when asked about his skills he would only say he was the old pot washer. This was the philosophy T.C. was to adopt for himself.)

The sight of this galley always gets T.C.'s potatoes boiling. Anxiously he shows off his galley to his friend. Pots and pans of every shape and size, all hung in their proper place. The stainless steel equipment was as shiny as the day it was made. With matching Hobart reach-in cooler and freezer, Panasonic microwave, Vulcan 6 burner stove with a convection oven, Pitco deep fat fryer and a Hoshizaki 1500lbs ice maker, this kitchen was laid out for someone who liked to party and eat, T.C. fit the bill to the letter.

"How about a brew? I sure could use a coldie," asked T.C. Not waiting for a reply T.C. had two bottles of ice-cold Becks opened and in his hand before Morgan knew what was happening.

"This is just incredible!" Morgan was suffering a bit of culture shock and was at a loss for words. He was beginning to experience what a third world refugee would feel like walking into a Radio Shack for the first time. The unsightly exterior of this scow was fading from his memory and the prospect of actually living on this smoke and mirror show was becoming more and more appealing.

"Well captain, what's for lunch?" asked MacShane, now starting to take it all in stride.

"Lobsters! Got some from one of my neighbors. He went out diving the other day and threw me a couple. Guy feels kind of sorry for me living on this 'rat trap,'" laughs T.C.

"What, he's never been aboard?" questioned Morgan.

"Hell No! But that's the beauty of this whole thing bro. Low-key elegance, I like to call it. By keeping the outside looking the way it is, no one ever bothers you. If the outside was all fixed up every asshole in town would be crawling all over it, trying to sell me everything from Encyclopedias to water softeners. Screw 'em!" explained T.C. chugging down half the ice-cold golden liquid in one gulp.

"Man, you never change, the master of subterfuge. David Cooperfield's got nothing on you," MacShane's smile growing wider with each sip of brew.

T.C. grabbed the pre-cooked lobsters and twisted off the tails in a well-practiced maneuver. Taking an 8" Hinkle chefs' knife he make short work of the lobster meat, cutting them into bite size pieces. "Hand me the mayo, will ya bud?"

Next to the cutting board were a couple of red peppers, tomatoes, celery stalks and a Vidalia onion. "Hey Mac watch this," blurts T.C. as he expertly dissected the tomato making each half look like a king's crown. "Neat huh? Learned that from watching TV, Iron Chef I think." But Morgan knew better, after T.C. had fifteen years of an army life, he decided to withdraw from the military and use his G.I loan to attend culinary school. Since there was one in his home town of Fort Lauderdale, T.C. signed himself up for some classes.

The lobster salad came together quite well. In fact, the dish could have been used as a cover photo for a food magazine.

"Voila! We'll get Holly up here and then we'll eat." T.C. places his masterpieces on the spacious table and pressed the intercom button. "Com-on babe, lunch's up."

"On my way," was the answer from deep below deck. In a few minutes Holly came walking into the galley wearing a pair of cut-off jeans and a Shirttail Charlie's Restaurant tee shirt.

"Got time to eat?" asked T.C.

"Yes chef! Don't want to miss out on that lobster!" Holly is now in a much better mood.

"Something special going on at work or do you always get so dolled up?" asked Morgan in a sarcastic tone.

"I'll have to, you know I keep all my costumes at work. I might as well be comfortable getting there," shot back Holly.

"And where exactly do you work Miss Holly?" inquired Mac.

"At 'Snappers on the Bay!' I'm one of the featured dancers. My stage name is Seventies Suzie," Holly answered in a proud voice

"Well if this ain't a day for surprises!" remarked Morgan.

"Don't tell me let me guess... T.C. never mentioned I was a dancer, right?" Holly knew the answer, Morgan didn't have to speak. "Does that make you uncomfortable Morgie?" Holly was trying hard to push MacShane's buttons, but he was too smart to let that happen.

"Lady, until I stepped on board this vessel, I thought I had seen it all. And in your case, I actually have. And believe me it doesn't make me the least bit uncomfortable," answered Morgan sitting back, smiling, crossing his arms behind his head.

"Good! Because I use the fly bridge for sun bathing and I'm not ready to stop now. I need to keep from getting tan lines; guys go crazy for chicks without tan lines you know," Holly responding as if she just gave her closing argument in a high-profile jury trial.

Morgan looked at T.C. and said, "And what the hell are you grinning about?"

"Nothin', I was just thinking, we're becoming like one big happy family."

That was all it took to alleviate any hostilities that may have been building up. The rest of the lunch was spent with Mac and T.C. catching up on old times and reliving some of their exploits. Holly only sat back and shook her head at some of the stories she was privileged to hear. Getting up from the table she had gained a whole new respect for their new partner.

Chapter 2

With lunch over, Holly picked up the dishes and placed them in the sink, knowing damn well that they would still be there when she got home. After Holly left, MacShane and T.C. grabbed a couple more beers and headed to the bridge.

"Man, this tub is phenomenal!" said Mac, looking around the bridge.

"Check out this hi-tech stuff, a Garmin GPS system, radar, sonar, color depth finder with current and water temp, chart plotter, single side band radio, Icom VHF radio, Satcom telephone, night vision scopes and the all-important kick-ass stereo system." T.C. gave Mac a few moments to let everything sink in.

"Damn! This tub is better equipped than some military craft I've been on," remarked Morgan, still flabbergasted.

"Well, the guys that had this tub built didn't have to get government approval for anything." laughed T.C.

"Alright what gives... what's the real story on this thing," demands MacShane.

T.C. sits in the helm chair and begins to come clean. "Well remember when I called you and said I had this great deal for us?"

"Yeah, go on."

"Well, the truth is I was watching a Sea Hunt marathon on an old-time TV channel and I thought that it would be great to get into the salvage business," explained T.C.

"And!"

"And I was reading the paper the next day and saw that the government was having an auction of confiscated boats, cars and stuff, so I thought I would check it out. When I got there and picked up a program, I noticed the Sequoia was listed as a coastal freighter, so I decided to take a look-see. When I get to the dock where she's tied up, there are a number of people milling about. I walk up on deck and overhear a discussion between two guys who are putting a bit together estimating how much she would fetch as scrap."

"Keep going, I'm listening."

"Well, I start walking around the deck and notice no one has gone inside her. So, I open the door and start to look around and can't believe what I see! The outside was such a wreck no one wanted to go inside. That's when I knew I couldn't let her go for scrap and I had to have her. In fact I called you from right here in this chair." T.C. had Mac's full attention.

"So what's with all the fancy? Who owned her?"

"This is the best part; the Sequoia is an old mother ship that was used for hauling dope! Story goes that she would be loaded in Columbia and then head off to South Florida to meet the smaller dope boats out at sea. From there her crew would offload the pot and cocaine to the go-fast boats. They said a good crew could load a boat with up to 2000 pound of the illegal weed in fifty to eighty-pound bales and be gone within fifteen to twenty minutes. You know the type of boat, long and sleek with plenty of horsepower and large square grouper hatches in their decks. Back in the day, nine out of the ten boats would get through. If one got caught, sunk or blew up, no one cared because they were making so much money on the rest of the boats, and replacement crews were easy to find. South Florida nightclubs and bars were filled with plenty of people willing to take a chance for some quick, easy money."

"And this is when your dream of becoming a salvage man came into being?" interjectedMacShane still paying attention to this tall tale.

"With all the history associated with her, I knew I had to own her. At the auction I was the only other bidder besides the scrap man. But when the gavel fell, it was all me bro!" T.C. was standing now, stretching his arms out in a P.T. Barnum grandiose style.

"You mean all us!" answered MacShane. "But why the Sequoia? Isn't that a redwood tree or something?"

"Yeah, it is. But I researched it and found out that that used to be the name of the Presidential Yacht before Carter sold it off. Guess they thought it would be funny to name a dope boat after the Presidential Yacht. Now the laughs on them!"

"And what next, Captain Chaos? What wonderful salvage jobs do you have in mind or am I here for some cheap labor?" asked MacShane.

"Come into the dining room and I'll show you our goal. Now, get ready to see why I really called you down here!" said T.C. with more seriousness in his voice than Morgan had heard all day.

"Ya, what you got bro?" half mocking T.C.'s style of speech.

Ignoring the slam, Morgan and T.C. make their way into the dining room and as they enter T.C. flips a bank of switches, transforming the area into a stylish meeting room. The crystal chandelier retracted into the ceiling, one wall panel slid over revealing a projection screen for an audio-video system and the indirect lighting kicked on. Something Morgan never noticed while the room was still in its dining room mode.

"Man, the guys that set this friggin' place up were amazing. Those dopers spared no expense when it came to living well... what a shock jail must have been to their system." Snickered MacShane.

While Morgan was ogling about, T.C. pulled a pile of old maps, ship's logs and notes out of a well-hidden wall safe. As T.C. was laying out the fragile papers, an awful alarm sounded.

"What the Fuck! Is this tub sinking!?" Morgan asked less than half joking.

"No, it's the boarding alarm. Let me know when someone steps on the gangplank. A real handy gadget," answered T.C. as he scans the monitor above the main display screen. "Shit! He wasn't supposed to be back until the day after tomorrow!"

"Who's not?"

"Benson, the dockmaster. He's here for the rent," said T.C.

"Well let me guess... you're late and don't have the money. How unusual!" scoffs Morgan in a less then jovial mood.

"Morgan.. Buddy... Partner...! We just require another small capital investment right now. All you have to do is come up with this month's rent... and maybe a little of last month's," told T.C.

"Good God, man! I must be out of my friggin' mind to invest any more money with you." Morgan took a deep breath, stepped back and gave T.C. a very hard stare. T.C. knew Morgan well enough to know not to push or prod MacShane at a point like this; it was best to let Morgan find his own Zen. Finally, after what seemed like the longest twenty seconds, T.C. could remember Morgan's stone-cold stare slowly turned to a slight grin as his eyes began to ease up on their death to everyone's appearance.

"Well..." MacShane begins, "Everyone has to be somewhere, and I might as well be here, at least for a while. Let's go meet Benson... partner!"

Benson was just about on board when the two men stepped through the hatch onto the cluttered deck.

"Benson! My Man! Didn't expect to see you back so soon; how was the vacation?" spouts T.C. with a renewed vigor in his voice.

"This rust bucket still floating?" answered Benson, getting in the first dig. A tall, slender black man who was born and raised in Fort Lauderdale, Benson Todd was a natural for this job.

Known to his long-time friends as Backwards Benson because more than once, he's been called Todd Benson by the uninformed. His big round eyes always had a warm glow to them when he flashed that broad smile at you. Add a friendly, outgoing personality and with more stories to tell than the Brothers Grimm, you have a man perfect for dealing with the yachties.

"Whad-ya expect this baby's a bute. How dare you disrespect this proud girl," teased T.C., gesturing his arms spread out wide.

"They always say beauty is in the eye of the beholder, but MAN you need some glasses," banters Benson.

"Oh, com'on Benson step inside and look around, you'll be quite amazed, I guarantee it," answered T.C. as he opened a different hatch for the dock master to enter than the one the two men came out of.

Benson stepped over to the entrance, took one look inside and decided to forgo the inspection. With a look of disbelief on his face he decided to change the subject.

"T.C., the real reason I came over is that you owe the city some rent money, and I need to collect, or I'll have to move you out," informed Benson preparing himself for the usual line of crap he hears month after month.

"No problem, Backwards. Morgan, will you please pay this nice man," told T.C. most congenially.

"Jesus man! You're actually going to pay me!? What do I owe this honor to?" Benson was still in shock, he would have bet these months' pay he would have been leaving with another bad i.o.u.

"Backwards Benson, I would like to introduce you to my new partner, Morgan MacShane."

"New partner? Man, you must be the slickest snake oil salesman of all time," chortles Benson as he shakes Morgan's hand.

"Nice to meet you, Bassakwards!" Morgan smiled back, squeezing Benson's hand harder than he needed to, letting Benson know he didn't take kindly to being called a chump.

"No offence Morgan," signaling to MacShane that he got the message by rubbing his right hand. "Just seems like you're a much smarter man than what I'm used to seeing hanging around this guy."

"None taken Benson, we're just old Army buddies trying to catch up on old times," added Morgan, being as vague as possible with his answer. Benson Todd's been around long enough to know a brush-off when he hears one.

"Nice to meet you Morgan, be seeing you around," he said, turning to leave. "Oh, and T.C., thanks for the rent; I'll probably run into you at Snappers later tonight. Holly's working, isn't she?"

"Yea, and it's a good thing that's the city's money or I'd be getting it back from Holly!" jokes T.C., laughing. "See you later... but not for long." The last part T.C. said under his breath so only Morgan could hear.

The two men were alone, leaning on the rail beside the gangplank as they watched Backwards Benson drive away.

"What did you mean by that crack?" asked Morgan.

"Come on. I'll show you if we don't get any more interruptions," told T.C. with a somber tone.

The men entered the dining room, and T.C. resumed setting out his old charts and notes.

As MacShane started to look at the old papers, he got a flashback of being nine years old. He was on a family vacation, and they were at Gettysburg, Penn. Standing in a gift shop watching his brother go through a pile of "parchment papers" of General Lee's letters to and from his sister.

Morgan will always remember, with a fond memory, that pungent smell of vinegar permeating the pseudo parchment paper and a family vacation that would shape his future for years to come. It was at Gettysburg, with its deep sense of history and visions of soldiers fighting and dying at Hell's Gate and the farmers' fields, that became the sight of massive slaughters. Brother fighting brother for what each one thought just and fair, these images of honor and loyalty would shape the impressionable mind of young Morgan MacShane.

"Morgan, you listening?" asked T.C., snapping MacShane back from his trip down memory lane.

"Sorry, just getting a flashback. Go ahead," replied MacShane.

"Look here. These maps show the exact location of the sunken city of Port Royale!" explained T.C., trying to contain his excitement.

As T.C. moved around the delicate papers on the polished tabletop Morgan just stood there with a confused look on his seasoned face, waiting for more information. "And what five and dime did you pick these up in?" questioned Morgan sarcastically, still smiling from his flashback.

T.C. could tell that his statement fell on uneducated ears. "Dude, these papers are authentic; lots of research went into obtaining them. For Christ's sake man, it's Port Royale! Do you know what that means!" exclaimed T.C., getting all excited.

"Sorry, maybe you should take me to school," replied Morgan dryly.

"Let me spell it out for you P-O-R-T R-O-Y-A-L-E. The Fort Knox of the Caribbean? Sunk during an earthquake on its hay day? Tell me you've never heard of it," stated T.C. in a condensing voice.

"Get real bud, you've been watching too many Errol Flynn movies," said MacShane, shaking his head.

Morgan started to actually study the documents a little closer now, the old crinkled texture of the fragile yellow documents with their creases, tares and stains from past centuries, the handwriting that looked like it came right off the pages of the Declaration of Independence, all began to give T.C.s story more validity. This, along with T.C.'s overzealous demeanor had Morgan MacShane starting to find he was now eager to hear more. It can't hurt to let the fool go a little further with his story, besides MacShane had nowhere else to go, and the beer is good and cold.

"Right here, Port Royale, the pirate stronghold of the Caribbean, a safe harborage for cutthroats, privateers, and Spanish gold," continued T.C., pointing to an old chart.

"JAMAICA!!! That place is so developed that there can't possibly be anything left!" commented Morgan , looking at T.C. as if he really was crazy.

"Well partner, I guess it is time for a history lesson." Beamed T.C., he was always ready for a chance to spout forth knowledge, most times if you wanted to hear it or not.

Morgan still wasn't quite accustomed to T.C. referring to him as a partner, and it gave him a slight pain deep inside his gut, a feeling he's come to depend on, a feeling that kept him alive during his tours of duty in Vietnam, Panama and countless other conflicts. A feeling that he would never doubt nor ignore.

To separate his thoughts from his emotions, Morgan stood up and said, "If I'm going to school, I might as well be comfortable." With that remark, he gets up and left the room, leaving T.C. standing there wondering whether he was coming back or not.

T.C. didn't have long to wait as Morgan returns from the galley and handed T.C. a cold Beck's. "Here, you long winded bastard, now just let me get set before you begin, O.K. teach?" told Morgan as he arranges two chairs so that he could prop his feet up on one and recline on the other as he sipped his ice-cold brew. He knew how T.C. can be, once he gets rolling, and this was going to be a grand performance.

With a raise of the clear bottle dripping with condensation, as if making a toast, T.C. acknowledged the thoughtfulness of his old buddy and slugged down a good part of the gold liquid.

"Now pay close attention, there will be a test directly following the lecture." This is about all T.C. could remember from his days at Broward Community College, but he wanted to sound official.

"Now Port Royale was a sort of a Sodom and Gomorrah of the Caribbean; anything went, booze, wild women, the place was lawless. But the best part was that it was the storehouse for Numerous pirates such as Calico Jack, Black Bart, Captain Kidd and other less famous outlaws, they all kept their gold at Port Royale," spouts T.C.

"Exactly what does that mean for us? 99% of the Jamaican coast is made up of resorts," interjectedMorgan, shaking his head.

"Patience class." T.C. was now getting into the role. "Port Royale was a real hoppin spot, everything was going smooth, except for a few raids by the British, but they were unable to penetrate the stronghold. Then one day, a huge earthquake hits and sends Port Royale into the sea. Some believe it was God sending his wrath upon the unholy, and with it, all the pirates' gold and goodies were sent to the bottom." T.C.'s eyes were wide open and sparkling as Morgan had never seen before.

"And no one's ever thought to dive on it?" mocks Morgan, always the pessimist

"Oh sure, people have dove on it before... but none with this map," repliec T.C. confidently, pointing to an antique relic.

"So why is your map so special?" queried Morgan, taking another swig off his beer.

"This map is of the city just before the earthquake; it was commissioned by the pirate governor at the time, and this one was penned just after the quake; it was commissioned by the English government. Now take into account natural erosion, tidal drift and commercial development and we have a very good idea where all this gold is located," concludes T.C.

"And just where in the hell did you get this wonderful bit of information, mister? The History Channel?" Morgan was being a tough sell.

"Miami," replied T.C. cooly.

Morgan having just taken a swallow of beer, shot it out of his mouth as he sprang up from the chair. "MIAMI!! What kind of crazed fool are you? Miami! Shit! The home of fake passports, Counterfeit money, dope dealers and all other kinds of low lives who manufacture fake IDs for the purpose of defrauding government officials. Shit man, they can't even run a straight election down there!" Morgan took a breath and continued. "Exactly what street corner bar were you drinking at when you bought this, Indiana Jones." It was now Morgan's turn to be on a roll.

"No dude, it's nothing like that. These papers came from an old Spanish Monastery," said T.C. all too calmly.

"What from the rummage sale?" questioned Morgan sarcastically.

"No Listen… the old Priest—" T.C. stopped and collected his thoughts. He could tell that he was losing Morgan's attention quickly; he knew that the next bit of information would either make or break the deal. So, he took a deep breath, cleared his head and spoke, "Morgan, let me start from the beginning, just sit back and try not to interrupt. O.K.? O.K., here we go. A few months back I was starting my research based on what I had read in the paper, just a small blurb about Jamaica, something about an archaeological team that couldn't get funding for a dig they were going to do around the old city. I then remembered about a book I had read that Port Royale was the sin city of the Caribbean, but I had completely forgotten about it until I saw that article," T.C. pauses, takes a sip to wet his whistle and continued again.

"While I was in the library, I found a book that showed the old trade routes between Cuba and Jamaica. The old plantation owners would trade sugar cane for rum, and textiles, you know the deal. The author of the book was trying to show how close the two countries were while still remaining totally different even though they were in such close proximity. It delved into the tales of two families who were the major players back then, one family in Cuba, the other in Jamaica. The book goes on to explain basically the life and times of the two families right up to the year 1920, which is when the book was published. The book ended with the continuing tale of a cousin, Juan Carlos Hernandez, who just finished schooling to be a priest and was going to spread the word of Christianity to the Indian tribes around Miami! So, I got on the internet and finally found some of his relatives, still living in Miami. I called them up, and I explained about how I found them and they agreed to meet with me." T.C. knew he would have Morgan hooked, gutted, and filleted after he told this story.

"You're incredible," was all Morgan could get out.

"Well, are you ready for more?" asked T.C., not waiting for a reply. "After I drove to Miami, I was able to speak with the granddaughter of the author of the book, Estella Gonzalez, who told me about how her family escaped from Cuba after Castro took over and of a monastery her family came to for help upon arriving in the United Stated. The monastery was an old Spanish outpost left over from Spain's occupation of Florida. It remains standing to this day, but you'd never see it as it's surrounded by a hammock of Gumbo Limbo trees planted over 100 years ago, and the order of Monks keep mainly to themselves. Estella's family knew of this order because it was there that her distant cousin Juan Carlos was sent to in order to help bring the word of Christianity to the heathen Seminole and Miccosukee Indians, or so the story goes." T.C. could tell Morgan was softening.

"When the family arrived back in the early fifties and asked to see Juan Carlos, who would have been in his late sixties by then, they were told of an unfortunate accident that occurred while Juan Carlos was traveling in a dugout canoe going to see a Seminole chief shortly after he arrived. The dugout canoe he was riding in... and here is where the story becomes a tad fuzzy," said T.C.

"A tad fuzzy... this thing is starting to sound like the damn Twilight Zone," exclaimed Morgan.

"The dugout tipped over and..."

"Oh! Let me finish. He was eaten by alligators!" blurts Morgan, trying to hold back his laughter.

"He was bitten by water moccasins, a lot of moccasins, about a dozen or so. He fell into a nest of them, and he was bitten underwater, something the Indians never saw happen before. With that much venom, Juan Carlos was dead before he knew what bit him. The Seminoles taking this as a bad omen from their gods, righted the canoe, put the dead body into it and gave it a pushback east. It wasn't until four days later that, a local farm boy was fishing way off from his usual hunting grounds that Juan Carlos's body was discovered. You can just imagine the condition of the body after four days in the tropical heat with a million insects feasting on him," T.C. pauses for effect as he saw the grimaced look on MacShane's face at the thought of the rotting body.

Morgan was sitting up straight in his chair by now. He really didn't know whether T.C. was making this up as he went along or that there was some semblance of truth to it. Morgan just stared at T.C. and finished the rest of his beer.

"Alright," he said shifting his weight to a more comfortable position. "Let's hear the rest; this shit is just too bizarre to be fake. Even you couldn't make up something this far-fetched."

"Morgan, I swear this is exactly how it came down," T.C. continued on to explain. "I spoke to Estella and she was happy to divulge her family history, such as how her ancestors had a big plantation in Cuba and they had a trading relationship with another group of plantation owners on the island of Jamaica. She also went on to explain how, in the old days, monasteries were often used to house important papers. The Monks would often make handwritten copies of important documents, charts and official notices. It was during this 'copying' process that the maps were together for the sake of duplicating when a massive storm, a hurricane, came ashore and devastated most of the island.

The Monks thought the important documents would be safer in Cuba since they didn't sustain as much damage. The two maps, as well as most of the other important papers of the day were shipped to a monastery in Cuba accompanied by several of the members of the Jamaican sect.

As the story goes on, years pass, the politics of the church get involved and the documents get put on the back burner for more important local works. And there they sat in a sideboard cabinet for years, that is until Castro started his rebellion up in the hills and began to gain more power. The head Priest of the monastery decides that he didn't like what was about to happen to his beloved Cuba and calls upon a family that has always been there for the brothers, a local plantation owner, Estella's family. Estella's grandfather now sees the writing on the wall: the rebels are gaining support from all sides of the island. Castro's takeover is now inevitable, and Grandpa decides to take his family to the safety of the United Stated." T.C. picks up on old chart to use as a visual aid.

"As he goes by the monastery to wish them well and ask for the blessing of Saint Christopher for their journey. The old Priest brings Grandpa into the old copying room and opens the sideboard cabinet. The priest knew that these papers would be destroyed by the heathens during the overthrow and wanted them to remain safe, so he packed them into an oilskin pouch and blessed the grandfather for his kindness and the support he provided in the past and wished them well on their journey to America. 'Vaya con dios mi amigo,' said the priest as he hustled the old man out the front gate. The short version is that the maps and other papers came to America with Estella's family and ended up in the old mission in Miami." T.C. ended his history dissertation and asked his 'class' for questioned.

"Oh professor. I have a question," told Morgan.

"Yes?" replied T.C.

"Just how the HELL did you end up with this pot of gold? You just happened to leave that part out," quizzed MacShane.

"Me? I just paid a visit to the old Mission with Estella and made, how shall we say, a 'small' contribution to the order for the use of 'borrowing' them for a while," grinned T.C.

"Exactly how much was this 'little' contribution of ours?" asked Morgan not really knowing if he wanted the answer.

"Well it's a mere pittance, well worth the investment," responded T.C.

"How much!?" Came a sterner request.

"Not much. Don't worry," dismisses T.C.

Morgan now understanding that it must have been substantial, demands again, "How much?"

"Only five thousand dollars." Was the hasty reply.

"What! Five grand! For some old map that could be useless, what the hell are you smoking down here? You've gone completely mad! Five Grand, Damn!" Morgan was not happy with T.C.'s answer.

"You wait bro, this is going to be the best investment we ever made." guaranteed T.C.

All Morgan could do was roll his eyes and head off for another beer.

Chapter 3

An intermittent rattle of a loose wheel on the bottom of the janitor's fifty-five-gallon gray plastic garbage can was the only sound that echoed off the Pentagon's deserted hallway as it was being pushed down the highly polished floor.

All was quiet, at 11:56 p.m. Monday night, 95% of the building was empty, allowing the cleaning crew to make the building ready for the next day. The only occupied office in this part of the building belonged to General Andrew Kane.

Bent over his work table with a magnifying glass were the General and two members of his staff. The object of their fascination was a satellite photo of the southwestern side of Cuba.

"Looks like some sort of half-assed docking area," remarked Kane to his staff members.

"Why do you think Castro needs this facility out in the middle of nowhere? It's miles from any developed road or even the smallest town," shot back Major Anthony Chandler.

"Sure, not for tourist development," threw in Colonel Sam Stone.

"This area could be buildings covered over with camouflage, but with the shadows from this angle, it's tough to say. Our job tonight is to give the best guess scenario for my upcoming briefing," said Kane as he moves the magnifying glass across the photo to view another area.

Chandler motioned to General Kane, saying that he wanted the imagine enhancer. Having worked with the General for some time now, Stone and Chandler could get away with a more informal approach but only when they were alone and never in the presence of others.

"What do you see Tony?" questioned Kane.

"Could be something..." he pauses for a moment, then said. "These tracks are heading to the area. If there was heavy equipment moving in and out unloading these ships, the roads would be more pronounced. Now they look like they're starting to grow over. Sure, doesn't look like there's much traffic on it."

"Good call, Tony. We need more reconnaissance over this area. Sam make a call to McDill and tell them to get the U-2 airborne for a few passes over Cuba. Let's shoot for first light," ordered Kane.

General Kane was an intuitive old duck. He just felt that something was afoot but couldn't put a finger on it, but he trusted his inner voice and knew when to go with it.

"Roger that General," replied Stone. With that confirmation of the order, Colonel Stone made the call.

"General, McDill will have the bird up and over the targeted area by first light," reports Stone after he hung up the phone.

"Very good Sam. Well gentleman, there's not much else to do until the U-2 returns. I'll contact Sargeant Crawford to finalize the arrangements for the film. Let's call a general staff briefing for Wednesday at 07 hundred to bring everyone else up to speed. Until then, I've got to do some schmoozing on Capital Hill."

More of a solider than a diplomat General Kane had a love/hate relationship with his feelings when dealing with politicians. On one hand, he loved to play the mind games and sift through the lies and on the other, he thought how much more efficient the system would be if everyone would act like the words of an old Jimmy Buffet song and just, 'mean what they say and say what they mean.'

Chapter 4

Steel gray smoke from a Monte Cristo # 2 exhaled through the big man's pursed lips. Smoke surrounded his crew cut head and followed along with him as he entered the futuristic conference room; as he did, six men jumped to attention.

"As you were gentleman!" barks General Andrew Kane, proceeding to the head of the large, hi-glossed burlwood oval table. This was his ballpark, and he wasn't the type of man to let anyone forget it. The meeting was called for 07:00 and every officer knew that they had better be there at least fifteen minutes early, be wide awake and ready to function. The general had no time for excuses or for, as he would put it 'inept people.' Legendry was the story of the last officer to arrive late for a briefing. Captain Tret Lomax showed up two minutes after the general. The meeting went on as scheduled, and that was the last time anyone on his staff saw or heard of Captain Lomax, and they all knew better than to ask. Rumor has it that his transfer papers were approved and processed twenty minutes after the meeting. His desk, personal belongings and his ass were on a plane to a weather station in Greenland before lunch. You didn't want to piss off the General.

"Let's get to it. After my visit to the Hill yesterday, we were briefed that intel has been monitoring Cuba and picked up that Castro is active and is using Cuba as a Free Trade zone for brokering deals with hostile governments. There's a makeshift port on the south side of the island. The satellite recon photos showed some construction going on that resembled the baby formula factories of Iraq. Now no one is saying for certain but chemical or biological weapons could be under way for development there. Castro is getting old and might try making a final statement to the *decadent West*." the general overly emphasizing the last two words.

The barely audible buzz from the monitor in front of the general interrupted his briefing. "Yes" was the general's brief response.

"Sir, Staff Sergeant Crawford is here," informed the secretary.

"Send him right in, Lieutenant."

"Now gentleman, we will see what that bastard is up to," said Kane.

Sergeant Thomas Crawford entered the room and proceeded to the head of the table presenting Kane with a package labeled 'Top Secret.' With a nod of recognition, Kane opened the package and spread out the pictures taken from a U-2 spy plane on the slick surface of the conference table. General Kane was still an old-fashioned kind of guy. Even with all of the most modern technology known to man at his disposal, he still wanted to do things the 'old-fashioned' way. His reasoning was simple and direct, he wanted his surveillance done his way and to run under his security. Sergeant Crawford was an old-time companion who's been with Kane since

Viet Nam, unfortunately, Crawford shall we say veered from the promotional path, having twice been promoted to captain but having been busted down for imbibing a bit too often. General Kane's first order, when he became General, was to have Crawford transferred to his personal staff and placed him in charge of all his top-secret reconnaissance. Crawford might drink a bit off duty, but when he's on an assignment, he's all Army and there is no one the general trusts more or who is as resourceful. Crawford's assignment was to meet the U-2 when it landed and take the film pack to the lab. Crawford didn't leave that film's side for one second. He was in the lab with the techs while it was being developed, printed and sealed in its top-secret bag. He knows how tight the chest the general likes to keep things. Too many times copies of secret photos show up around the base or happen to end up on internet websites. Crawford was there to make certain that nothing like that ever happened to the general's photo's, not now, not ever, for Sargeant Crawford owed General Kane his life a few times over.

"Here they are gentleman, fresh off the press, now we shall see if we can find out what that bearded prick is up to. You know, things would have been so different if only the Pittsburgh Pirates scouts thought enough of Castro to give him that pitching job back in the fifties," Kane spoke out loud, not really addressing his second statement to anyone in particular. Knowing deep down that if it wasn't Castro leading the revolution, it would have been some other unemployed intellectual, ignorant masses love an educated rabble-rouser.

"They're on the south side of the Zapata Peninsula in Cayo Matahmbre. That's the area Intel said, 'is heating up.' Look at this; they dredged out a canal that branches off of the Monterrey passage that leads right into the bay of Matahmbre. Check out the number of ships anchored off waiting to get in and unload. Vessels from all over, friendlies and hostile alike." The general put his photos on the monitor so his staff could see what he was talking about.

"The latest reports say that the un-flagged vessel Spain boarded in international waters off the coast of Yemen in the Arabian Sea, the *SO SAN,* was found to contain fifteen Scud missiles sold by North Korea to Syria. When our boys joined up with the Spaniards, they found the missiles hiding under sacks of concrete. Spain was tracking this ship since she left Cuba. Our Intel thinks Castro has set up some sort of Free Trade Zone for terrorists and is taking a percentage for allowing them to broker the deals in Cuba!" the general pauses for a moment, letting this information sink in.

"A terrorist free trade zone ninety miles from the United Stated, what a set of balls," commented Major Anthony Chandler. Chandler has been a member of Kane's staff and the General respected his opinion and liked the fact Chandler always spoke his mind, a habit that didn't always work entirely in Chandler's favor at times. "How long have we known about this General?"

"Within the last three weeks, but this just confirmed what was only conjecture. When I was on Capital Hill yesterday I sat in on a briefing about the last boatload of refugees who landed on Haulover beach in Miami. There was a guy on board who worked on the construction of the docks and warehouses. He thought he could make a few extra dinero to help him bring his wife, sixteen-year-old son and twin boys to the Stated and jump-start living the American Dream by turning over what he knew to the local F.B.I. agents in Miami. Took the poor bastard over three weeks for any of the INS people would take him seriously," the General said, shaking his head.

Chapter 5

Out on deck, Morgan was starting to feel the buzz of a few brews. He attributed it to the South Florida heat and the overwhelming amount of what he thought was bullshit spewing from T.C.'s mouth.

The downtown buildings of Fort Lauderdale were starting to change color with the setting sun. The high-rise buildings with their glass sides were reflecting the orange and pink hues of another beautiful sunset in the Sunshine State. The only noise was coming from a flock of African green parrots flying overhead going back to their nests. The two men had left the air-conditioned comfort of the dining/conference area and moved to the bridge to enjoy the view and plan their next move.

"What a magnificent sight," said Morgan.

"Yeah buddy, this city takes on a whole different look around sunset. How about getting something to eat? Holly won't be back for a while, com'on I'll take you to where I used to cook when I was in high school," offered T.C.

"That place still open? I thought you told me it burnt down?" asked Morgan.

"No dude, you didn't listen, I said they had a fire," replied T.C.

"To me, fire equates with burning down," huffed Morgan.

"No, no I told you that I said it was in all the papers, long time landmark restaurant catches on fire... Man I have some great memories of that place," said T.C.

"And they're still willing to let you back in after some of the things you told me?" asked Morgan.

"Man you have to remember that it's the restaurant business and what is normal to those people would seem totally bizarre to most regular folk," answered T.C.

T.C. went on to explain to Morgan that working in a restaurant was kind of like the army only much more fun and profitable. The bonds you make with other cooks and servers form a relationship that can last for many years. It's like a second family, and in a family-run business if you were a good employee, you could always get a job if you were on the shorts for cash.

"Morgan give me a hand, and we'll take the Mako over to the restaurant," said T.C.

The 21' Mako, center console boat had much more eye appeal than the rest of the Sequoia. A polished black Mercury 225 hp engine hung on the transom in stark contrast to the bright white hull and golden teak trim in the cockpit. T.C. gave a few pumps to the in-line fuel primer bulb, twisted the key in the ignition, and the big Mercury sputtered, coughed, and sneezed to life. T.C. then flipped on the switches for the navigation lights. The bow lights came on immediately; however, the stern light stayed dark.

"Damn!" was all T.C. said.

Morgan should have expected as much; he knew the boat couldn't go anywhere without a full set of nav lights. Just when Morgan was ready to step back onto the dock, T.C. told him to have a seat.

"What, you gonna run this river without a stern light?" asked Morgan at T.C.'s insistence that he stay on board.

"Happens a lot; just watch and learn, my man," said T.C.

T.C., in a most practiced move, stepped over to the stern light, unscrewed the connection, lifted the aluminum shaft out of the base, and proceeded to rub the contacts on the leg of his shorts.

"All you have to do is clean the corrosion off the contacts, and we'll be on our way." T.C.'s carefree self was coming back. "Hand me that can of W-D 40, will ya Mac? Never leave the dock without one," he said, mocking the American Express ad. "Now, let's go eat!"

T.C. returned the stern light to its proper position, and the light popped on.

"Shirttails, here we come!" T.C. said out loud.

The Mako pulled away from the dock and headed with the current to the restaurant. Morgan was standing next to T.C. at the helm, grabbing hold of the stainless-steel handrail that went around the windshield and just marveled at the sights. Multimillion-dollar homes lined the banks of the New River, everywhere the eyes looked were houses that belonged in a filming of the rich and famous.

"Whose shack is that?" asked Morgan over the sounds of Jimmy Buffets 'A Pirate Looks at Forty" gushing out of the waterproof Polyplanner speakers.

"I made enough money to buy Miami, but pissed it away so fast, never meant to last," T.C. answered, singing with the CD. "Real appropriate that song coming on just now, that house used to belong to a guy that shafted people over an Internet pyramid scheme. Now he's living in a bigger house with many, many roommates," laughed T.C.

"You for real?" asked Morgan not ready to believe T.C.

"Sure enough, feds busted him when he closed on the joint, paid seven million... CASH!! When that much money is on the table, you can bet your ass, the feds will be nosing around asking about it. Now, it just sits there, waiting for the right person to buy it and call it home. Yep, two bowling lanes, ice cream polar, movie theater the place has got it all," replied T.C.

Morgan was just giving T.C. the look and knew Morgan didn't believe him.

"No seriously Mac, the place has all those things in it. Lauderdale is a strange place; people from all over the world come here to play, have a good time, and spend money. The rich ones buy houses and pimp them out, trying to outdo the neighbors. The houses they keep here are totally different from the houses they live in up north. Up north, things all have to be conservative and straight. In Lauderdale, there are more hidden boats, houses, and girlfriends' apartments than you would ever believe." Then T.C. went on to tell Morgan about this boat that he kept an eye on for this guy who lived in Montana. "An eighty-foot Hatteras that his wife nor his company knew anything about. Every time I called to check in, I always had to tell his secretary that I was a golfing buddy."

Morgan was starting to realize that this place and the people in it just ain't right. "What happened to that guy and his boat?" asked Morgan.

"Typical shit that usually happens to them all, he comes down one time, picks up some bimbos at a bar, hooks up with them all weekend, takes the boat to Bimini, and when he comes back to port, customs pull him over and boards the boat, standard stuff when you've been out of the country. Customs checks their I.D.s and finds out one of the girls is wanted for a possessions charge, and when she's searched, they find a pound of marijuana in her bag. They impound the boat, take everyone to lock-up, and he's left with a shit load of lawyer bills and a ton of explaining to do. Last I heard, his boat was up for sale, his wife and kids left him, and his partners filed lawsuits up the ass. Never saw him again, but he was always a real nice guy to me," T.C. added with a chuckle.

"No shit, this stuff happens often you say?" asked Morgan.

"Yea, it happens so much it never even makes the papers anymore. The only sure way to find out what the real story is, is to hang out at some of the boat yards or get to know the captains of the local water taxis, now those guys get around!" said T.C.

"Didn't you write me once that you ran one of those rigs?" said Morgan, vaguely remembering a story T.C. had written to him.

"Sure did, and I'll tell you what, the money wasn't that great but the fun I had working with those other captains really made up for it. I still keep in touch with some of them, always try to keep my ear to the coconut telegraph, never know what you might pick up," laughed T.C.

The Mako glided along the New River at idle speed, leaving a smooth, small wake as it proceeded to the restaurant, "Man, just look at those buildings; sure has changed a lot since I was a kid," remarked T.C. Even though he lived on the river, the amount of change taking place in downtown Fort Lauderdale always amazed him. "See that one going up there? That one's going to be forty-two stories tall," informed T.C. as he went back to giving his narrated tour.

"Christ, how is that going to put up with a category V Hurricane?" Morgan wondered aloud.

T.C., in his infinite wisdom said it all, "Time will tell dude, but I don't want to be on the top floor to find out! Get the lines ready; we're almost there. I can smell the burgers cooking from here."

T.C. handled that Mako like a real pro. As the vessel approached the dock, he headed to the slip closest to the bar, cut the throttle, coasted a few feet, spun the wheel in the opposite direction, hit the reverse throttle a bit, and the Mako came to rest with the slightest kiss of the padded piling.

"Not bad, even if I do say so myself," gloated T.C.

On the dock was the restaurant deck hand Samson, waiting to be of assistance with the line handling, but when he noticed that it was T.C., he just waved and smiled. He knew his assistance wouldn't be needed. It was a busy night and he already had his share of "weekend warriors," the type of people who can afford a large boat but weren't blessed with the intelligence it required to handle one. That's why the restaurant hired him, to make the people look good with their docking. If he could do that, he would make a few bucks, and the boat owner would look like a star to his guests. If the boat owner was really bad and had to try a few times to get docked up, the deckhand would take the blame, and he would still get a few bucks. The most important thing was to make the captain look good, whatever it took. T.C. has seen Samson get verbally chastised for everything from lost sunglasses to stalled engines, and he always managed to keep a smiling good attitude. T.C. threw him five bucks anyway; he can relate to what it's like to deal with the public.

"Hello my friend," greeted Samson. "What you do tonight?" he said with his Creole accent and bright island smile, you could tell he was truly glad to see him. Samson had worked at Shirttail's when T.C. had, and the short Haitian always liked him. T.C. treated his fellow employees with respect no matter what language they spoke or where they came from.

"Como Sa Vous Samson, this is my good friend Morgan. Got a table for us?"

"Any time my friend, I tell them to make you one right now." Samson went off to tell the busboy to re-set a table and be quick about it. It was never mentioned but T.C. knew there was some sort of pecking order within the Haitian workers. He just couldn't get it no matter how he tried to understand. Most were related family members, and if one of them did a bad job, the rest thought it would disgrace the lot of them, so they all kept close tabs on each other's work performance.

"Come on, come on, my friend! We make nice table for you and your noir," said Samson, waving to T.C. and Morgan. Motioning them towards a wooden picnic table out on the dock directly over the water.

"Your WHAT!! Did he just call me what I think he did?" said Morgan, looking at T.C., not knowing how to take the comment.

"Chill dude, that's just his way of saying you are my black friend. He usually calls me Blanc; it's just their way of saying he's accepted you as a friend because you're a friend of mine. Nothing else," explained T.C. to a confused Morgan.

Morgan still wasn't convinced, and he wasn't sure if T.C. had set this whole thing up as some sort of practical joke, so he decided to go with it and see where it lead. "Okay Samson, what's up my noir?" asked Morgan, his mouth smiling, but his eyes were not.

Samson shook hands with the two men as soon as they were on the dock, "Hey noir, you got big power!" he said as Morgan released his hand. Morgan just smiled; it was the same the world over, everybody judges you by your handshake. A soft, weak one, and they start to get ideas that you're a pushover, a firm strong one, and they think twice about screwing with you.

Samson walked the two men over to the table, laughing and talking all the way. Just as they sat down, a thirty-six-foot Searay cruiser took a bearing on one of the empty slips in the restaurant.

Samson could tell from the way the boat was trying to dock with the current that the captain was an inexperienced operator. He stood up, shook his head, muttering something in Creole about the crazy white guy operating the boat and said, "Got to go and help this blanc, tie up his boat, order the Mahi; it's fresh today, very nice," and with that he was off to save the struggling captain signaling directions as he walked down the dock.

"What a kook!" said Morgan after he left. The two men watched in amazement as Samson gave ordered to the people on the Searay to try to tie them up, doing as little damage as possible to the boat or Samson's dock.

"So much money, so little brains," was all T.C. said and went back to reading the menu.

"Let me order Mac, okay?" asked T.C. as the waitress came over.

"Go ahead, it's your show." Morgan was starting to lay back a little and was content to take in the sights of the busy river traffic.

"We'll start with an order of conch fritters and then have two blackened dolphin sandwiches with Monterey Jack cheese melted on top, a slice of red onion, and a side of fries, extra crispy, with two Red Stripes," T.C. ordered like an expert, the waitress gave him a slight smile and a nod and was off to fetch the beers.

"Sound like you've had that before," said Morgan.

"All the time dude, best sandwich on the whole river, it's a treat not to be missed."

"So, now that you are wining and dining me, is this when you're going to hit me with the closing," asked Morgan.

"What! Can't two old friends go out and have a good time without talking business," said T.C., almost acting insulted at the thought.

"Common man, I've known you for too long; let's hear the pitch," prodded Morgan.

"Not now, here comes the food, and it's way too good to mix with business, besides too many ears in the area." The last part of T.C.'s comment was delivered in a low whisper that was uncommon for him and sounded like he was more worried than anything.

The old friends sat and reminisced about their army days, MacShane's first marriage, stories of fishing, and MacShane's retirement. The food was devoured, and another round of Red Stripes was ordered. MacShane was actually starting to enjoy himself and, for the first time in a long time, was feeling relaxed.

Darkness encapsulated the men on the ride back to the Sequoia, the river taking on a whole different look at night. The black water absorbing the light instead of reflecting it, making for the captain of a vessel to pay close attention. All the multi-million-dollar mansions were aglow in the harsh glare of incandescent flood lights.

"Man, I'd like to have the money that guy spends on just lighting up his palm trees," quipped MacShane.

"Yes Sir, Florida Power and Light really love these people," answered T.C., now speaking slow even for him. "By the way, Mac keep a lookout for 2x4s and palm fronds. You see all kinds of shit in the river, don't want to take out my prop."

The brews were starting to take effect on the two partners. T.C. expertly handled the Mako and docked as if he were as sober as a Baptist Preacher. With the boat secure, the two men headed to the galley.

"How 'bout a coldie Mac?" T.C. still wasn't ready to call it a night.

"Not for me; this is more beer than I've had in a while. I think I'll just turn in; let's just say it's been a long and interesting day. See ya in the a.m." MacShane headed down the companion way, opened his cabin door, and collapsed on the soft mattress, falling more into unconsciousness than sleep.

Chapter 6

General Kane and Sergeant Crawford were in the General's office. It was 7:30 p.m., and the buzz of the hallways was starting to simmer down. As the two men further looked over the recon photos, they started to brainstorm about getting a closer look at the Cuban facility.

"General, what about getting that Cuban laborer to go back in and do some up-close recon for us?" said Crawford, throwing out an idea.

"Already had intel people speak with him, no go, he's too afraid of what would happen when they discovered him back on the island, seems like everyone knows when the rafts are leaving and who's on them. He would be picked up and interrogated, probably killed as a spy and just disappear. No Crawf, we need to get one of our own in there and get the lay of the land," General Kane said as he sat back in his large black leather chair, blowing smoke rings into the air.

"Andy we just can't send in the 101st to have a look around," said Sergeant Crawford, calling the general by his abbreviated first name, something only his best of friends could get away with.

"God, don't you think I know that, and the Seal teams won't work either. No, we need a total covert operation, maybe a freelance?" speculated the General.

"No too risky," said Crawford. "How about someone on active reserve, an older man fluent in Spanish and...." Crawford stopped and thought for a moment, "Andy, where the hell is Morgan MacShane? Didn't he say something about going to Florida to buy into some kind of salvage business with one of his old unit buddies?"

"Hell yes! MacShane stopped by right after his discharge to shoot the shit for a while before he left Washington." Kane was starting to smile, he had fond memories of that soldier, having served with MacShane on a few different occasions.

"Sergeant, see if you can come up with MacShane's whereabouts. I think it's time to reactivate him." The General put his feet up on his desk and proceeded to finish his Monte Cristo. "Oh, and Sergeant," Crawford stopped as he was almost out the door, "when you find him, give him this." With that, the General tossed a hand-rolled Opis x cigar in a ceder-lined tube to Crawford. "He'll get the message."

Chapter 7

Morgan opens his eyes and looks around the beautifully appointed stateroom, realizing that this isn't some weird dream and he really did sign up to go treasure hunting. Now more awake, he sits up; his head feels like it is the size of a beach ball. He thinks to himself that he's got to remember that he's not twenty-five anymore, and feeling like this is not a good way to start the day. He climbed out of bed and crawled into a hot shower to try to revive himself. His aching muscles and fuzzy head started to respond to the steaming water. As he steps out of the shower, he still can't believe the fixtures and appointments in the lavish head. Walking back to his stateroom, he stops and gets a whiff of breakfast... bacon, eggs, and coffee!!! Hot and black, now are talking. Morgan checks his Seiko dive watch, a birthday present his brother gave him over twenty-five years ago. He and that watch had been through a lot of shit together, but it always brings a smile to his face every time he checks it, because if that watch could talk, he'd have to shoot it.

"9:30! Damn!" Morgan can't recall the last time he had slept that late. He dressed in a pair of khaki cargo shorts and a black Baltimore Orioles T-shirt, barefooted, he headed towards the beckoning aroma, his mouth already starting to salivate at the thought of a hot cup of coffee.

"Good morning, Mac, how'd ya sleep?" There at the stove stood a bright and cheery-eyed T.C. whipping up an omelet. "Help yourself to a coffee."

"Thanks, I slept great, didn't hear a thing, just feeling a little rough around the edges," replied Mac as he pours himself a cup of black, liquid life. "Where's the princess, still sleeping?"

"Yea she had to pull an extra shift, optometrist's convention in town, the place got hammered. Chicks dancing on almost every table," said T.C. as he expertly flipped the omelet in the pan with a flick of the wrist. "Those guys really throw their money around when their wives aren't with them."

"Doesn't that crap bother you? Having your woman prancing around naked in front of other men?" asked an inquisitive MacShane.

"Used to, in the beginning, but she's safe there, nobody touches the girls or if they do, the bouncers do their own dance on the asshole's face, then the cops come and throw them in the Broward County lock-up. The owner doesn't put up with any bullshit, he runs a straight place. She always comes home to me, and the money's damn good, plus, it's only for a short time longer." With the omelet finished, T.C. flipped it onto a plate and placed it before MacShane. "Denver Omelet, well-done, extra onion, right?" smiles T.C.

"You remembered that?" said MacShane, impressed with T.C.'s memory.

"How many late-night joints did we end up in after a night out? Who could forget!" laughs T.C.

"Yea you laugh now, how about the time I had to get you out of that dive in New Orleans at 3:00 in the morning when you were starting to mouth off to the cop at the counter telling him, 'This ain't no doughnut shop what ya doing here!!'" reminisces MacShane smiling.

"Well yea you pushed me out the door into the street; I stumbled down three steps and hit the sidewalk," said T.C. with a pout on his face, rubbing his elbow as if in pain.

MacShane then added, "I turned around to unlock the car and you're standing in the middle of the street with one hand over your eye trying to read the street sign looking for "Your dream girl's address."

"Man, she was a hottie, wonder what ever happened to her?" They both started to laugh.

"What's so funny?" Holly asked as she walks into the galley.

"Mornin' princess," announced MacShane as he take another bite of omelet. Giving her a mock salute with the fork.

"Mornin' baby, we wake you up?" asked T.C. starting another omelet.

"No, I couldn't sleep anymore, breakfast just smelled so good I thought I'd get up and join you," answered Holly.

"Have a seat my dear, and let the kitchen magician whip up a special something for you," said T.C. as he pulled out a chair and pushing it back in after Holly sat down.

"Well, what do you two have going on today?" asked Holly, more as an inquisitive mother than a concerned mate.

"Mac and I are going to drive around and do some errands, pick up supplies, drink some beers, and then probably take a nap. How about you?" explained T.C.

After that breakfast a nap sounds good to Mac.

"A fine productive day I see." Holly knew T.C. well enough to know when he was telling tales and when he was serious. She knew this was the latter. "Me? I need to give my notice today, fill out some paperwork, start packing and sorting, you know, the stuff I've been asking you to do for the past month. We still plan on leaving the twenty-first?" she asked.

"The twenty-first it is! The longest day of the year, perfect, don't you think?" responded T.C.

MacShane now started to get a strange perplexed look on his face, "Don't you think? the twenty-first? Einstein do you realize that's only a week and a half from now!! Have you ever left the dock with this tub yet? Who else is going to crew? What the Hell...?? Jesus, T.C.!!!" This aggravation is not really helping MacShane's headache.

"Mac, I appreciate you being concerned. I understand you losing your composure, but everything is going to fall into place, you'll see," said T.C., as calm as a cucumber.

Then after a short pause came, "A week and a half! Plenty of time. We just have to get busy," proclaimed T.C. acting as if the timeline finally sunk in.

Holly and Mac just looked at each other, shaking their heads in disbelief.

"Mac I've got to check my e-mail before we leave, com'on down and check out the computer we got on board. Holly could you finish up here, please!?" Mock pleaded T.C.

"Go, get out of here and quit that whine ass begging, it's too early to listen to your nonsense," said Holly.

He gave her a kiss on the cheek, and he and MacShane headed to the converted stateroom that was now doing duty as a makeshift office. MacShane noticed that the office was of the same quality workmanship as the rest of the interior, light paneled walls and bright colorful Haitian art. MacShane was admiring one of the pictures of two Black panthers in a forest of bright green trees filled with what appeared to be bright glowing oranges hanging from the branches. The yellow eyes of the panthers gave them an almost real appearance.

"Com'on in buddy grab a chair. This won't take a minute, looking for a few more items for the trip, and I have to check the closing Ebay auctions," told T.C. pulling up a teak chair to the matching teak roll-top desk as he proceeds to turn on the Dell computer. As the screen came to life, he quickly entered his account name: One Drunkin' Monkee.

MacShane couldn't help but comment on that one. "That's you? One Drunkin' Monkee? Man! You're a piece of work."

"Like that do you? You believe someone else had that before me; that's why I had to spell monkey with two es," explained T.C.

"Where did you ever think that one up?" Mac asked.

"Honestly? You can thank Holly for that one. Right after I bought the Sequoia, Holly and I went out to celebrate and when we returned to the ship, I was so excited that I climbed up the old cargo rigging and started to swing around making all sorts of sounds. Holly yelled up at me to, 'Get down from there before you fall, you're acting like some kinda drunken monkey.' I liked it and took it as my handle. Catchy huh."

"Now let's see, this auction is right about ready to end," said T.C. as he brings up an auction for three new Scuba Pro 3000 dive tanks. "Here it comes... BOOM!" yelled T.C. as he gets the last bid in seconds before the final cutoff. "Got them!"

"Got what? Used dive gear... what's the old saying? There's no such thing as a bargain on parachutes and dive equipment?" told Morgan portraying to be the wise old man.

"You're right Confucius, but in this case the tanks are brand new, coming from a dive shop in Tampa that's going out of business," replied T.C.

Morgan just rolls his eyes and said, "What other deals have you procured for our upcoming adventure?"

"Let's see... one magnetometer with a 1000'-foot reel of cable, a real steal. Can you believe no one else put in a bid on that?" answered T.C., actually believing there would have been a heated bidding war over something like that rivaling an autographed Beatles album. "An underwater sea sled, the engine needed a little work but now it runs like new," continued on T.C. "Some fishing tackle and a few other odds and ends that might come in handy." T.C. could tell from Morgan's looks that he really didn't want to hear anymore.

T.C. browses around a few other auctions and almost put in a bid for an autographed picture of Jimmy Buffet on an auction site run by poolside girl but Morgan is there to talk him out of it.

"But Morgan, Jimmy's my man! His songs have got me through some tough times!" protests T.C.

"When we get back, and if there is as much gold as you say there is, you can buy the house next door to him and you two can hang out in the pool together. Now let's quit fartin' around and get some of these so-called 'errands' done. That nap this afternoon is closer than I thought," said Morgan trying to get T.C. motivated.

T.C. was ready to click off when his AOL signaled that he had mail. "Let me just check this and we'll be off," insists T.C. MacShane sits back on the matching teak chair, crossing his arms on his chest and puts his feet up on the rungs of T.C. chair. 'No telling how long this will take,' thought MacShane.

"Dude! It's from Drake! He's flying in tomorrow! Said he will be on Jet Blue landing at 1:45. Man that's great, he's two days early," exclaimed a jubilant T.C.

"Who's Drake?" questioned Morgan.

"Best diesel mechanic I know. He's also part of the crew, can't leave without a good engineer," replied T.C.

"Where he comes from? Rehab?" inquired Morgan.

"He's been around town for a while, gave the Sequoia's engines the once over after I bought her. Really knows his stuff, used to work for a local repair company but they sold the property and he opened his own thing. Works on just his special customers' boats, hell, those people fly him all over the place if their boats need any sort of repair. His customers won't let anyone else work on their engines." Then T.C. added, "He's a local celebrity around the marina circuit, but he's a bit strange."

"Like how strange?" asked Morgan.

"Well, his real name is Santiago Korkonakis. His father was a Greek merchant marine sailor who met his mother when his ship made port in Havana, Cuba. His dad jumped ship and opted to stay on the island nation, buying the dream of pina colodas beneath the palm trees, but ten years was enough for the older Korkonakis. Island fever started to set in, and he had to get back to sea. He left his wife and little Santiago, promising to return and take them to Greece. It was a long five years but his dad returned and smuggled them out. They ended up in the Greek islands, where Santiago learned to fix engines and was taught about sailing by his dad. Santiago was a Caribbean baby, and the sand in his shoes was making his feet itchy. When he turned twenty, he headed to Florida and the tropical sun." T.C. ending his story as if it were a fairy tale.

"So where does the name 'Drake' come from?" Morgan queried again, feeling that he was being set-up.

His nose. Being a baby of two different cultures, some of the features transcend to the next generation," T.C. explained never being one for a simple answer.

"Yea, yea, I know this, just get to the point." MacShane getting antsy from sitting around.

"Well genetics played a dirty trick on him, with his dad's big Greek nose and his mom's pug nose, ya see, it resulted in Santiago getting a big pug nose that resembles a duck's bill, hence the nickname 'Drake,'" said T.C.

"Bull!" comes Morgan's reply

"He'll be here tomorrow, you'll see. Now come on, you wasted enough time here," laughs T.C. as he logs off the computer, shutting it down.

T.C. and MacShane emerged from the cool confines of the Sequoia's interior, stepping out on deck and into the sweltering tropical humidity. The heat smacking MacShane directly in the face was reminiscent of the jungles of Vietnam. Even the soft breeze coming up the river had little effect on the overwhelming temperature. "Damn! It's barely eleven o'clock and this heat's a killer!" commented MacShane. The men hadn't gone twenty feet, yet MacShane was sweating profusely while walking down the gangplank.

"I'll admit it's a bit unseasonably warm, but on the other hand, Mac, maybe you've been working in an air-conditioned office for too long," said T.C., half joking. "Wait until August' that's when this place really heats up, but you'll get used to it. Besides those beers you had last night aren't helping much," grins T.C.

"Yeah, I know, I got used to this shit over thirty years ago, remember? Seems like every time I got near you, I'd find myself in some tropical hellhole mixed up in something that gave me crotch rot," MacShane refers to the last assignment they worked on together in Panama. "Remind me to thank you later. Now where exactly are we going?" asked MacShane as the men crossed the street, heading for the palm-lined parking area. T.C. was getting a flashback of their last mission and began to laugh. Answering MacShane with a statement.

"Panama City will never be the same," quipped T.C.

"Forget Panama City! How about the R&R we took in Costa Rica? Man, that's the place for me. Up in the cool mountain air, next to a stream, shacked up with one of those Tica chicks. If this thing pans out the way you say, then that's exactly where I'm going. Tell the rest of the world to Kiss My Black Ass!" MacShane's jolly mood takes down a notch when T.C. walks up to a ratty old Ford Ranger that at one time might have been a shiny bright blue. However, that was in another lifetime, the faded chalky paint rubbed off on Macshane's black t-shirt as he brushed by the fender.

"Great! Don't you own anything that doesn't resemble a bad dream?" askedMacShane.

"No can-do Mac, how would it look if I was tooling around town in a new ride and then came home to the Sequoia. People would start to talk, ask questions and be general pains in the butt. Trust me on this one," answered T.C. in his own logical way.

"Christ, I hope the air works at least," muttered MacShane. As he opened the door, watching two empty cans of Miller Light and a Diet Coke fall to the ground and roll under the truck.

"Sorry, left over from the beach. Dude quiet your grippin' and open the window, enjoy the fresh air; we don't have far to go. Sit back and take in the sights," instructed T.C.

MacShane brushes off the threadbare seat of all the loose sand and candy wrappers. Easing himself into the vehicle, MacShane's nose started to cringe. He was now getting ready to experience a smell called the South Florida Funk. It's a smell that manifests itself in a vehicle that's been wet, either from leaving the windows down during a heavy rain storm or coming back from the beach with wet bathing suits and towels. Add to the formula the fact that the vehicle is left to sit closed up in the hot sun, and you get a smell that one must experience firsthand to believe.

"DAMN! What the hell is that smell?" Morgan was ready to jump out of the truck and look for an oxygen mask.

"She's a bit funky, but she sure runs well. Hurry and get your window down Mac, it'll clear out in no time," infroms T.C. unaffected by the challenging aroma.

"Why do you keep fuckin' with me? I've only been here a day and a half and yet it seems like a week. I have to take a cab from the airport, now I see why, I'm dropped off in front of a scow that would be better off as an Air Force bombing target. A naked woman tries to kick my ass, you break out some bogus treasure map that came from who knows where, I have to pay your past due bills and today you tell me some duck boy is flying in tomorrow and we have to go and pick up a few odds and ends... you're the only thing that's odd around here..did I leave anything out??" MacShane's on a roll. The hangover and now the smell mobile pushes him over the edge.

"Well, you did leave out the wonderful accommodations and the gourmet breakfast you had this morning." T.C. wasn't about to be rattled. He started up the truck and told Mac to put on his seat belt saying, "In for a penny, in for a pound."

"What do you mean by that remark?" MacShane was still fuming.

"You've come this far let's go ride it out, come on Mac, you'll get used to this lifestyle," replied T.C.

"Stop saying 'I'll get used to it! How do you know I'll get used to it, maybe I don't want to get used to it. Did you ever think about that?" shot back MacShane, not backing down from T.C.'s comment.

T.C. put the keys into the ignition, but before he turned on the Ranger, he faces MacShane and said in his most serious voice, "Mac, you've got to relax. We really can't attract any attention to ourselves. We're going to be out of here soon, heading to the Bahamas before we set sail to Jamaica. There are too many people that frequently travel between here and the Bahamas and we don't want to draw any attention to ourselves. We need to act like a burned-out freighter crew that doesn't give a shit about anything or we're going to get screwed. Now let's get going to pick up these parts."

Mac cools off and is beginning to understand T.C.'s approach to things. Not a word was exchanged between the two men. Morgan MacShane watched out the window as T.C. navigated through the narrow streets of downtown Fort Lauderdale. Following the detour signs as some of the roads were being dug up to add new water and sewer pipes for the expanding hi-rises being built on the river. Morgan thought about the condos on the river next to a working marina and beside a busy railroad track and couldn't imagine the 600,000-dollar price tag the developer was advertising. Not until the truck pulled into a place called "Sailors Market", a kind of junkyard for boats, did T.C. open his mouth.

"Well, we're here," he announced, the white rocks making a crunching sound as the tires rolled over them, headed for a parking spot next to the building.

"Nice! What goodies are in store for us here?" asked MacShane sarcastically.

"We need some spare rope, an EPIRB, a flare gun and some parts Drake ordered," answered T.C. as the men exited the truck. Morgan couldn't help but notice the amount of rust that fell out from under the truck as he closed the door. Approaching the of the business MacShane was looking at all the fiberglass center consoles from various size boats. Next to them were row upon row of stainless-steel handrails and windshields.

Then MacShane commented, "A boneyard for boats. Look at all this stuff. There must be an acre of boat parts and pieces."

"Two acres to be exact," corrects T.C. "Follow me."

T.C. opened the heavy wooden door with a port-hole window and headed towards the parts counter. MacShane was just glad to be out of the stink mobile, but the smell of old, salty, greasy boat parts wasn't much better.

"Hey T.C., what's up?" comes the greeting from behind the counter.

"Hey, Pete, got my parts?" said T.C. MacShane started to look around and was amazed at the number of cleats in every type of fashion he sees down one aisle. Small ones, big ones: brass and aluminum ones, stainless ones, and even plastic cleats. Towards the back were rows upon row of outboard engines on stands. Next to them were old outboards stacked like cordwood with a handmade cardboard sign that read: you want it, you pull it. Bring your own tools!

"So T-Bone who's the Fed?" queried Pete referring to MacShane.

"No Fed, ex-military, just retired. Mac meet Pete, owner of this fine establishment," introduces T.C.

Mac was now taking a good look at himself next to T.C. Here's Mac freshly shaved, new beige cargo shorts, a t-shirt that's been pressed and has creases on the sleeves, white crew socks, and new Topsider boat shoes. And on the other end of the spectrum was T.C., two-day-old beard growth, sweat-stained black and white Mercury Marine baseball cap, old blue cargo shorts with assorted colors of paint splattered on them, an old gray Billabong t-shirt with grease stains and a pair of Reef Runner flip flops that smell so bad Holly won't let him wear them inside the Sequoia. MacShane was now beginning to fully understand T.C.'s philosophy, and he started to smile outside even though he laughs at himself inside.

"Glad to meet you Pete," greets MacShane with a big, broad smile.

"You o.k.?" asked T.C. to MacShane.

"Let's say that this place really made me think about how all the pieces fit together," responded MacShane, shaking hands with Pete.

"Glad we could be of service Mac," said Pete not fully understanding what had just happened.

"Got any clothing, you know, shorts or shirts?" questioned MacShane.

"Yeah, sure over on the close-out rack." Pete points to a table next to some used electronics. "I also carry some used stuff if you're interested, keep that under the table in those blue bins, help your self." Pete looks at T.C., not knowing what to make of this.

"He alright?" Pete asked T.C. as Mac walks away.

"Yeah, Pete he's going to be just fine."

Chapter 8

At noon the next day, T.C. and MacShane got into the toxic taxi and headed to Fort Lauderdale airport to pick up Drake. Now both men were dressed as if they had just walked away from the local soup line. MacShane was getting with the program and was starting to feel more comfortable in his grubbies.

"Did you call Jet Blue to see if the plane is on time?" asked Mac.

"Yea, they said it's on time, but you know how that goes," answered T.C.

"Drake must rate having you actually going to pick him up," said Mac referring to the cab ride he was stuck taking.

"Drake already knows about my truck; he doesn't have a problem with it. Unlike you, who would have gotten on the next plane back to where you came from," replied T.C.

MacShane started to laugh at that last remark and was somewhat amazed at how easily he was fitting into his new role of a burned-out freighter crewman.

The two men pulled up to the 'arrivals' area of the terminal and pulled the Ranger over to the curb. As they were getting out a Broward Sheriff's Officer called out, "Hey, T.C."

"Hope you know him," commented Morgan.

"No problem," T.C. said under his breath and then yelled back, "Hey, Jim how's it going?"

"Man, you know I can't let you park here," Officer Jim told him. Mac was getting ready to re-enter the vehicle when T.C. put his hand on his shoulder shaking his head.

"Com'on Jim I've got to pick up Drake, this parking lot is a major pain in the ass. Can't you let me slide? I'll tell Tasha you were asking about her." T.C. was playing on the fact that Tasha was a dancer who worked with Holly and he had seen Jim talking to her one night while he was working the door on his day off.

"Drake's back! That's great! Have him call me. I need him to look at my Yanmar, I can't get the damn thing to run right," Officer Jim stated totally disregarding T.C.'s remark about Tasha. If a man's boat isn't running right, all else is secondary. After all, a man's got his priorities.

"Yeah, he's about to land, so how about it, can I leave it here?" asked T.C.

"Sure, for Drake anything, I'll just tell the Sergeant that the thing crapped out and the guy that owns it went to call for a tow; who's going to question that!" answered Officer Jim referring to the dilapidated condition of the Ford.

"Cool, thanks dude," responded T.C. "Let's go Mac, we're in good hands."

"You best tell Drake to call me!" reiterated Jim as the two men walked towards the sliding doors of the terminal, T.C. just turned and waved an acknowledgment.

"I can't believe what I just saw. This guy must be the grand wizard of all mechanics," remarked MacShane in awe.

"Told ya. Having a low-key approach has its advantages. And as for Drake, he's the best in the stated or any other developed country. Arriving at Gate 22, let's go!" Directs T.C.

Morgan and T.C. were standing at the check point when Mac said, "That must be Drake."

An average size man, about 5'10", weighing 170 to 180, with jet black hair and a nose that sloped down from the middle of his brow out to an almost perfect point a good 3" from his face.

"Drake! Over hear!" yelled T.C.

"Hola' my friend!" comes his reply as he rushed over and gave T.C. a bear hug, picking him up off his feet.

"Drake this is Morgan MacShane, my friend and partner I wrote you about," introduces T.C.

"Heard lots about you, Drake. Nice to meet you," greets MacShane extending his hand. Drake looked at the hand and with lightning reflexes, grabbed MacShane and gave him a big hug also.

"This is how we greet old friends MacShane, and anyone who's got the balls to get into this crazy business T.C. put together is a good friend of mine." His accent was hard to place, part Greek, part Spanish, and something that sounded like south side Bronx. It was going to be an interesting trip.

At the baggage claim Drake grabbed one large duffle bag and a red Snap-On tool box. Passing through the security checkpoint, the men walked over to the old Ranger. Stowing the gear in the bed, Drake was ready to hop in with it when MacShane said, "That's ok Drake, I'll ride in the back."

"Oh, I see this thing, no smells better," Drake answered laughing.

"No, I would like to take in the sights unobstructed by the roof. Besides I could sit here and enjoy a cigar," replied Morgan.

"That cigar might help out the inside," told Drake still laughing.

"That's right rag on my ride, make your jokes. Do I see any hands for walking back to the boat?" asked T.C.

"Not us. Were getting into the slumming role, right Drake?" jokes Morgan.

"Yes, my friend, I see I have a new ally for giving T.C. what you call the 'business.'" answered Drake.

As Drake and T.C. entered the cab, Morgan hopped in the back and made himself comfortable on Drake's duffle. Pulling away from their parking space, Morgan was lighting his H.Upman robusto when Officer Jim came running out of the building, calling after them. Morgan rapped on the window and T.C. opened the little center window. "Your buddy seems pissed," commented MacShane.

"Yeah, he'll get over it, Jim's really a nice guy. Drake, think you have time to look at his Yanmar before we leave," asked T.C.

"Yeah, I'll look at it but I ain't no miracle worker; he needed a new engine long time ago. That thing is going to leave him stuck somewhere in the Gulf Stream one day. Maybe he send us a post card from England," said Drake laughing.

"Maybe," replied T.C. while driving out of the terminal.

The faded blue truck handled the extra load of Drake and his baggage effortlessly. Morgan was relaxing in the bed of the truck as T.C. drove away from down town. After about fifteen minutes, the beat-up old red truck pulled off the highway and into Captain Ed's Fish Market. Morgan was only half finished with his cigar and asked T.C. what was going on.

"Drake wants to make everyone dinner tonight. Said he's got a new Snapper recipe he'd like to try out on us. Who am I to turn down such a nice gesture? Let's go Mac, have a look around," said T.C.

MacShane got out of the truck and looked for a place to stow the unused portion of his H.Upmann. T.C. noticed the questioning look on Morgan's face, motioning for Morgan to follow his lead. T.C. dropped the tailgate of the truck and instructed Morgan to place his cigar into the rusted-out opening along the rail of the tailgate frame. "Will that suffice as your cigar holder?" asked T.C.

Morgan placed his cigar into the rusted opening so it gently rested there and he would be able to retrieve it when they came back out and told to T.C., "Man, I can't believe how you pull this stuff out of your ass."

"Yeah, I'm a real Houdini, let's go. Drake's buying, let's not keep him waiting," insists T.C. Drake, Morgan, and T.C. waited for their turn at the counter. Inside the display cases were all different types of seafood. Clams, scallops, king crab legs and of course, the local species such as Mahi-Mahi, tuna, tilefish, and snapper. As seafood markets go, this one was primo. It had the typical decor of nets, mounted fish, and other seafaring artifacts; there was even an old diver's suit standing in the corner. But the fish, the fish was the showpiece and it was always very fresh. The cases were extra clean and behind the counter, the help wore white bib aprons and latex gloves. In spite of dealing with so much seafood the smell was very faint, a sure sign of a high-end establishment. When Drake's turn came, he asked for five pounds of yellow tail filet and three pounds of titi shrimp.

"This is going to be a great dinner tonight, you see. I'm going to make Snapper Nueces. We have a big feast. Now we buy wine." Drake was going all out. After the fish was wrapped, the package was placed in a plastic bag and two frozen gel packs were added to help keep the fish cold for the ride home. The liquor store was on the way, but this time Morgan stayed in the truck and finished his cigar. T.C. and Drake ran in and were out again in record time, with the wine held securely under Drake's arm, wrapped in a brown paper bag. Morgan thought to himself that he was beginning to like this Drake fellow. He knew what he wanted and didn't waste time getting it; Morgan's kind of man—someone who could be a real friend. It's no wonder these people liked and respected Drake. Morgan was starting to do the same.

Arriving at the parking lot, the men grabbed Drake's gear and headed to the Sequoia. As they approached the vessel Holly, who had been sunning herself on the bridge deck trying to get in some quiet time, heard the unmistakable sound of T.C.'s truck and was so excited to see Drake that she stood up, not caring that she was naked and starting waving and calling out a welcome. Her perky naked breasts were exposed for all to see above the railing, swaying in the breeze with every wave of her arm.

"T.C., I see not much has changed since last time. Holly is still a very spirited girl," remarked Drake laughing.

"Yea a real barrel of fun, I thought that she usually greets company by throwing a shoe at them," replied Morgan, referring to his first time on board.

Drake not fully understanding the comment, shrugged his shoulders and headed up the gangplank with his packages. Holly was now on the deck of the boat wearing an extra long t-shirt. She ran up to Drake and gave him a big hug.

"Drake, it's so good to see you again. I can't wait to hear about your trip," said Holly.

"At dinner I will tell you all about my trip and then we will all talk about our new adventure!," said informed Drake as the four of them went into the cool air conditioning of the Sequoia, escaping the South Florida afternoon heat.

Drake was an old hand at finding his way around, first he went to the galley and dropped off his dinner supplies, then to his stateroom which was located next to MacShane's. Then he had to pay a visit to his baby.

"MacShane," Drake calls out. "Please, would you like to visit my family?"

MacShane had at that moment, popped the top on a Diet Coke and was getting ready to sit down when Drake called to him. Expecting that Drake was going to break out a family album, and Morgan, with not much else to do, said, "Drake I'd love to see your family."

"Then come with me, my friend and we will give them a visit. Please help me with my toolbox, okay?" asked Drake

"Yeah, sure, where're we taking it," questioned MacShane.

"To my family, where else," replied Drake.

Now Mac didn't know what to make of this, so he grabbed an end of the toolbox and followed Drake down another flight of stairs leading to the bilge of the ship. At this point, MacShane had visions of Drake's family living in the steerage hold hiding from the authorities. MacShane was getting his temper up and was preparing his thoughts for T.C. for not informing him of this blatant disregard for human life and authority when Drake came up to a hatch. Undogging the latches, Drake yelled out, "Hello, my family... Did you miss your daddy?"

Morgan's face was one of utter disgust as he expected to hear the cries of little children, but as the door to the engine room opened, there was the cleanest, brightest, most organized room he'd seen since his service days.

"MacShane Say hello to my family, this is the Mom and Dad, twin Detroit - Diesels that needed some real tender TLC to get her back together, but now they will push this tub to damn near thirty-five knots. Many of the parts for the turbocharger had to be made by hand because they were so old. And this is my little baby, the 135,000-watt Onan generator. We could almost run a small town on that thing. Many nights I had to sit and hold her hand, trying to piece her back together. My friend meet my family," said Drake as proud as any father in the land. This was without question HIS family, each part was handled with the most extreme care during the teardown and re-assembly, and every part was cleaned and painted to better than new condition. Drake was the proud pappa and was always anxious to show them off.

Morgan was now grinning, his displayed teeth as bright and white as the engine room. As Mac looked around, there wasn't even a hint of dust or grease. "Man, Drake, this place is outstanding! When you kept saying your family, I thought... that... well, you know, you had a wife and child living down here. I was all set to raise hell with T.C. for not telling me about them."

Now it was Drake who was laughing. "You actually thought I had a family living in the bilge of a boat? What kind of guy d'ya think I am anyhow?"

MacShane was listening to Drake's speech and the crazy foreign accent was missing, causing Mac to wonder. "Okay Drake, what gives? Where is the stylish accent *my friend*?" MacShane was starting to smell a rat; then he heard T.C. laughing in the passageway.

"MacShane, my friend, you like Drake's family?" chipped in T.C., mimicking Drake's fake accent.

"What the hell is with you? You're always fuckin' with me," exclaimed MacShane, his voice getting a few octaves higher.

"Well actually it was Drake's idea, he wanted to feel you out, you know, get to know you. I thought it would be fun, something to break up the day," stated T.C. laughing.

"Yea a real blast!" MacShane felt that he was becoming the butt of all the jokes and he was going to do something about it. Maybe not today or tomorrow, but the crew of the Sequoia was fair game and when Morgan MacShane put his mind to something, nothing will stop him. "Well, what about the wonderful dinner Drake's going to make for us, is that all bullshit too?" inquired MacShane.

"No dude, Drake's a great cook, almost as good as me. That's the truth," claimed T.C.

"I'd say slightly better if I do say so myself," added Drake in self-defense.

"Well you kitchen magicians fight it out; as for me I'm going to leave the court jester and the long-lost family man and go take myself a nap. Let's say dinner at seven, ok? And no more pranks today. Now *gentleman* if you will excuse me." Morgan exaggerating the term gentleman as he headed to his stateroom. However, T.C. and Drake got in one more chuckle as Morgan ascended the stairway.

At 6:45, T.C. opened MacShane's cabin door and rang a dinner bell.

"Half hour till dinner masseur, thought you might want to freshen up before we eat," spoke T.C. mocking an old house servant.

"Thank you, Friday, it's good to see you on top of things," answered MacShane laying on top of his bunk in his boxers, now in an obviously better mood since his nap. "I'll clean up, dress, and be ready for cocktails on the Veranda deck in fifteen minutes."

"Very well, I'll inform the others," told T.C. taking a deep bow before he backed out closing the door as he departed.

"The guy is nuts," thought MacShane as he stood up and walked off to the head.

Up on deck Holly and T.C. were already enjoying a cocktail of Bacardi Select and coke with a Key Lime wedge over ice. Morgan joined them, and Holly handed him a Tervis Tumbler with a "crew" emblem between the insulated pieces of clear plastic filled with the same tasty mixture. As Morgan looked closer at the other glasses, he saw that T.C.'s said Captain and Holly's read 1st mate.

"Well at least I know where I stand around here; what does Drake say, Emperor or just King?" questioned Morgan busting T.C. balls.

"Naw, his cup said engineer. Sorry about the lowly crew rating, but they were out of the "fool hearty investor" glasses," replied T.C., causing the three of them to laugh.

"Where's Drake?" asked MacShane.

"Making dinner, believe that? Dude kicked me out of my own galley. Said it was his treat," informed T.C.

"Guy must know what he's doing if you let him work in your shop unattended," responded Morgan.

"Don't worry Mac, Drake can fix a gourmet dinner just as well as he can rebuild a Diesel engine," reassures Holly. "We sure won't starve on this trip. If anything, we might gain a few pounds," she said, patting MacShane's flat, hard stomach. Her last comment brought the three to a slight chuckle.

At exactly 7:00, Drake popped open the hatch to the aft deck and announced that dinner was ready. The three friends entered the air-conditioned comfort and made their way to the dining room.

Flavorful aromas filled the air, light nuances of garlic, brandy and sauteed yellowtail snapper. The table was set for four, with serving bowls of steamed zucchini and baby carrots and for the starch, there was a bowl of a beautiful wild rice blend.

"Sit, everyone sit!" suggested Drake above Tchaikowskij's Klavierkonzerte No. 1, playing as background music, waving his friends to the large cherry wood table as he starting bringing out soup bowls. "You guys start with the lobster bisque, I have a few last-minute things to do."

Morgan just looked at T.C. and Holly in what best be described as sheer amazement.

"Might want to buy some of those bigger pants Morgan," remarked Holly, making a bloated motion as she puffed out her cheeks and pushed out her belly.

"Don't worry dude there is plenty of work to keep us nice and trim," said T.C. with a smile.

Morgan, T.C., and Holly took their seats at the table and started to enjoy their bisque. Drake came out of the galley with a large platter of sauteed snapper covered in an exquisite sauce of titi shrimp and crab meat. Everybody's eyes grew wide with anticipation at what awaited them in this gastronomic delight. After Drake placed the platter in the middle of the table he unveiled the wine, a perfectly chilled Pouligny Montrachet, a perfect accompaniment to the delicate fish.

"Where did this dish come from?" asked Holly, always interested in hearing about Drake's stories and adventures.

"I strong-armed this one out of a chef on the last yacht I had to work on," answered Drake. The yacht was based out of Corpus Christi, a hundred fifty five foot motor yacht named *Big Zeus*. It was the owner's first time in the southern Caribbean, and the ship's engineer had to be airlifted to Puerto Rico for an appendicitis operation, leaving the yacht stuck in St. Thomas with a broken injector system. The captain was a friend of a friend and sent an e-mail to my buddy asking if he knew anyone in the area that he could hire to fix the injectors. Well my friend got a hold of me. I was just finishing up a job in St. Maartin and was on my way to Nassau, but my friend vouched for this guy and told me what a bad spot he was in, so I told him to send me a ticket and I'll be on my way," orated Drake.

"But how did you get this recipe?" inquired T.C., now getting sucked up into the story.

"Well, the captain sends me a ticket and I land in St. Thomas, get a ride to the yacht and find the captain. As the captain is greeting me on the dock a rude little Frenchman pushes his way past us carrying a bundle of groceries without even saying 'excuse me'. Now, T.C. you know nothing gets me madder than rude people and this guy thought he was the best thing since canned soup. So I ask the captain what's his story and he said that he doesn't bother with him much and just stays out of his way, said the owner likes his cooking so he tolerates him," explained Drake with a disgusted look on his face. Drake had his dinner guest's attention and went on to say, "I then ask the captain if the owner was on board, he told me that the owner and his kids took the little boat, a thirty-six-foot Intrepid, out for a day of diving and fishing. I keep this information in the back of my head and ask the captain to take me to the engine room. On our way to the engine room, we had to pass through the galley, and there is little Pierre peeling garlic, well I couldn't help myself and give the guy a slight body check as I pass. The captain smiles, the chef grunts and I shrug my shoulders as if to say sorry and keep on going.

"After I get the injector system working, I start to play around with the circuit breakers and shut down his stove while I'm cleaning up. It took a few minutes for Frenchie to realize his stove wasn't working and then I hear him yelling in French and broken English at the captain. Then I hear the captain coming down the companionway, he enters the engine room and half laughing, asked if I did something to the asshole's stove. The captain is a cool guy so I told him I flipped the circuit breaker off. I thought he was going to wet himself; he was laughing so hard. We sat there for a few minutes and I told the captain to tell the cook that it was necessary for me to do that so that I could run a few diagnostics on the engine. I figured what the hell did Frenchy know? The captain hangs for a few minutes and composes himself enough to go back up to the galley and tell the cook what was going on. I could hear the cook yelling at the captain telling him that I don't know what I was doing and the stove has nothing to do with the engine."

Starting to laugh himself now Drake goes on to say, "Well at that point the owner comes back on board and hears the commotion in the galley and comes down to see what was going on. The cook started to yell and carry on like a spoiled little bitch. By now I finished and was making my way back to the galley, but not before I turned the stove back on. Now that the little prick had an audience, he really started to go off, saying I can't fix anything, where did I come from etc., etc. His timing was perfect, I look at the owner telling him everything is repaired and that I wasn't used to being talked to like this from the pot washer. Now Frenchy's really going off the deep end. The owner of the yacht, caught in the middle, was kind of taken aback for a moment. Think about it, you're out for a nice day in a boat, expect dinner is being prepared and when you get back aboard you walk into this." T.C., Holly, and Mac were all grinning and starting to laugh as they each formed a mental picture.

"The owner not really knowing what had just transpired, looked at me and I say, "Frenchy doesn't think I can fix anything does he?" Well I bet I can fix a dinner either just as good or better than his. The owner, as it turned out was a neat guy and was intrigued by this bet and asked me what would happen if I lost. I told him I wouldn't charge him for the service call, except just for the plane fare. He then asked what I wanted if I did win. I told him that on top of being paid, I wanted a copy of Frenchie's best recipe. The owner was now up for the challenge; however, Frenchie didn't want any part of it and started yelling that nobody works in his kitchen."

"Dude this is intense," interjectedT.C.

"Intense? I thought Frenchie was going to stroke out when the owner reminded him that it was HIS kitchen and he'll let anyone he wants work in it, unless of course Frenchie wanted to pay for the service call and repairs. Well that put a muzzle on the big mouth and quick."

"So how it end up?" asked MacShane.

"Well Mac let's say I'm still undefeated in the kitchen stadium. I got this wonderful recipe, a job offer from the owner of the yacht who happened to be one of those '.com' kind of guys and the satisfaction of knowing that Frenchie is flipping burgers on the beach in St. Thomas,," said added Drake laughing with the rest of the crew.

MacShane enjoyed the story even though he wasn't sure he believed it, but with an outcome this good on his plate, he wasn't going to question.

Drake was halfway through his meal with civility re-establishing itself when he asked T.C. a question. "So, T.C. when is the rest of the crew coming aboard?" T.C. shot him a look as if to say, 'Keep it quiet,' but Morgan picked up on it and dragged the question.

"Yea, T.C. when do we meet the rest of the crew?"

T.C. knew he was cornered and tried to change the subject but MacShane changed it back. Asking again, "How many more crew members are going to join us for this adventure?"

T.C. had to come clean and confess that two other people were invited to partake in this noble adventure. "Dude it was going to be a surprise," spoke T.C. looking towards Drake.

Morgan smiles and said, "Thanks Drake, I for one have had quite enough surprises for this trip. I owe you one."

T.C. realizing that he was up against the wall on this issue, answered only, "Soon dude, very soon."

Drake proved that he was as meticulous in the galley as he was in the engine room. The plates were cleaned and stacked, the equipment wiped down and everything was as it should be. T.C. would let Drake work in his shop any day, and that was a great honor. Holly, Morgan, T.C., and Drake moved the party to the open deck off the bridge. T.C. had set this area up as his observation area with an 8" Mead starfinder telescope. This is where he would come to think, relax and to check out the heavenly bodies. Morgan took out his Calibre wind-resistant lighter and lit up an Aturo Fente, the perfect after dinner cigar, he offered one to Drake who politely declined saying, "Thanks some other time, I need to go out and re-establish some local contacts."

"Translated that means that he's just going out to try and get laid," interjected T.C.

"My old friend, in the words of the great Master Yoda, you either do or you do not, there is no such thing as try. And in my case, there is no such thing as you do not. This is a big city with lots of lovely woman, all I'm going to say is don't wait up. Now if you will excuse me, I need to change and be on my way."

"Sure, sure you go and do what you need to, but be here in the morning we have a lot to go over," said T.C.

"Oh, by the way Dad, can I borrow the car tonight?" questioned Drake on his way below deck.

Morgan was starting to chuckle as he thought of Drake pulling up to a club in the beat-up old truck. "Drake that truck is a real chick magnet you should do well," he remarked.

"It's not the vehicle that's important Morgan, but what's behind the wheel that counts. Hey why don't you come along? I'll show you how it's done," declares Drake.

Holly was sitting back taking in all this male bonding, thinking what extreme measures guys go to for a piece of tail. She didn't understand it but watching it was sure interesting. It kind of reminded her of listening to her brothers talk to each other when they all lived at home.

"No thanks, I'm going to enjoy my cigar, drink my brandy and relax in the cool night air," responded MacShane sitting back with his feet up in a wooden chase lounge, taking a puff on the Aturo Fente; he was smoking. Morgan was very content and wasn't going anywhere. "No, I'm in for the night."

"Take the keys, but be careful with the truck; you know it's almost a classic," jokes T.C.

"Thanks bro, see ya in the morning," said Drake leaving the area.

Ten minutes go by and Holly calls Morgan and T.C. over to the rail to see Drake leaving.

There he is wearing a red Hawaiian shirt with blue, yellow, and white parrots on it, jeans and flip-flops. Drake's attire makes T.C. offer up this comment, "What a ladies' man, with a wardrobe like that he can't miss."

Morgan looked at T.C. not knowing if he was joking or not, but judging by the smile on his face he could guess, adding, "And that ride completes the picture!" Causing the three of them to burst out laughing, wondering what kind of adventures they were going to here about at breakfast.

Chapter 9

No need to set an alarm clock this morning, the local garbage truck was making its every third day pick up of the condominium's dumpster that the Sequoia's slip was located in front of. There's no sleeping through the sounds of a big diesel engine revving up the power take-off to lift the six-yard dumpster and bang it a few times to shake out all the trash. Not the most eloquent way to be awakened but it got the job done.

Morgan was laying in his bunk thinking that the noise was going away but the truck was just repositioning itself for the second dumpster and an encore event of the first.

"Shit! It's 8:00; might as well get up and get the paper," MacShane said to himself.

Morgan got dressed in his paint-splattered navy blue shorts, and a Guy Harvey tee-shirt with a picture of a yellowfin tuna on it, donned a pair of flip-flops and walked towards the head. After relieving his bladder and brushing his teeth, he looked in the mirror. Rubbing his stubble, he decides to forego shaving. "Always wanted to grow a beard. Guess now's the time," he mumbled to himself.

MacShane traversed his way towards the hatch and steps out to another blistery day. Not seeming to mind the heat as much today, Morgan deactivates the annoying boarding alarm and walks off the boat, ambling to the corner store down the tree-lined street, weaving his way around the numerous potholes in the road.

Inside the old, run-down store, he pours himself a cup of coffee and grabs a newspaper at the counter.

"So, you the new man on that old boat?" asked the East Indian attendant.

"Why you asking?" answered Morgan with a question in return, not liking the fact that strangers know his business.

"I see you arrive; you not looked too happy," stated the clerk.

"Yeah, she's a real Queen Mary," replied Morgan trying not to get drawn into a conversation about the Sequoia.

"You work for T.C.? He's nice man, he take good care of you," offered up the merchant.

"I hope you're right, I could use a break," said Mac now playing the role. Wondering if the clerk would be so fast to offer up a conversation if he was dressed differently.

"He good man, you tell him Raja said hello," told the clerk.

"Sure will, as soon as he wakes up. See-ya," responded MacShane, walking out of the store and back to the ship.

While heading back to the ship, Morgan glances over the headlines and notices that the Marlins won another game, *'Could it be two years in a row?'* said the subtitle, referring to the World Series win of last year; South Florida was ailing for a championship team. As he approached the birth, he hears the familiar sound of the smell mobile coming down the street. Turning, he sees Drake pulling into the parking spot. The truck comes to a stop and Drake gets out looking kind of rough. He sees Morgan and a big smile comes across his face. "Morgan, you should have come along; there's a travel agents convention in town, something called a 'PowWow,' and all I can say is WowWow!"

MacShane listens to Drake as he reports on last night's exploits as they ascend the gangplank.

"Did you at least get any sleep?" asked MacShane, getting tired from just hearing about everything.

"I did manage to grab some between four and six this morning; there's more important things than sleep, you know Morgan. All I need is a shower and a hot breakfast, don't fret 'bout me," answered Drake.

'Ah the wonders of youth,' thought Morgan remembering a portion of his youth, being awake for two days during an offensive back in Nam. Without the luxury of a shower or a hot breakfast. Oh for the good old days.

Morgan sat at the galley table, drinking his coffee and reading the paper. Drake went below deck to the head and fired up the rain locker, but not before he started up a pot of coffee. A hot shower and some black coffee will have him back on track in no time. By the time the coffee was finished, Drake was showered and dressed and was starting to look like a new person.

"Want a heater Morgan?" asked Drake as he filled his cup with the hot black liquid.

"Sure, I could use another, thanks," replied MacShane.

"Let me ask you Mac, do you mind If I call you Mac?" asked Drake.

"Not at all, been called that most of my life," answered MacShane.

"Well Mac you seem like a smart guy, how the hell did T.C. con you into this treasure-hunting crap?" queried Drake in all sincerity.

Mac started to grin, "Yeah it was a con job alright. He sends me a picture of a real beautiful yacht and said that we can go into the charter business, you know, really laying on the bullshit."

"Man do I!" said Drake.

"I was getting out of the service on retirement, not having any real plans for the immediate future. I started to think about hanging around on a yacht; it sounded kinda like the rich and famous lifestyles, so I bit and sent him some cash. I get my discharge papers, get on a plane in Washington D.C. headed for Fort Lauderdale, grab a cab, get left off at this address and just about beat the ever-loving shit out of T.C. right on the dock. Then I walked inside and shall we say, I started to become attached to this old girl. It made me a real believer."

"Yeah I know the feeling. This old tub has some kind of comfortable serenity built into her, since the first day T.C. brought me aboard to check her out, I felt like I belonged here, at least for now," answered Drake.

"At least till we get that gold!" added T.C. as he entered the galley and joined the two men.

"Coffee Capt?" asked Drake.

"Good morning crew; nice to see you so bright and early Drake, didn't work out as you planned, I guess? How'd everyone sleep?" inquired T.C., acting as cruise director. Morgan would have to wait to finish his conversation with Drake, which is too bad, he was starting to enjoy it.

"Like a baby," said Morgan.

"Sleep? I'll have plenty of time for that when I die," said Drake.

"You still plan on getting this road trip started on the 21st? You only have a few days to get this tub ready to put to sea," said Morgan, interrogating T.C.

"Dude, how many times do I have to tell you, things are going to fall into place! See Drake's here and his babies are all ready to do their thing. Right Drake?" asked T.C., sipping the coffee Drake had poured for him.

"My engines are like me; we're ready for anything," responded Drake proudly.

"See Morgan, just because you don't see things happening doesn't mean that nothing's getting done," quipped T.C.

"I'll believe it when I see it," was all that MacShane said continuing to read the paper.

"Well, if that's how you feel, I'll just make myself busy and check my e-mail," said T.C., walking away in a mock huff. As he headed below, he passed Holly in the passageway and said loud enough for Mac and Drake to hear, "Watch out for Morgan today he seems a bit grumpy."

Holly waved him off, ignoring him as she entered the galley. "Mornin' all, any coffee left?"

Drake was quick to answer, "For you anything."

"Mornin princess," offered up MacShane, not looking up form his paper.

Holly opened the Hobart reach-in and was preparing to grab the gallon of milk when all three shipmates heard T.C. hollering down below breaking the morning quiet... The sudden noise startled Holly causing her to drop the milk onto the galley floor.

"Damn-it! What the hell is he yelling about now? He should realize by now that he's not the only one on board this tub!" vented Holly.

"This is great! This is just friggin' great!" yelled T.C. as he bounded up the passageway stairs and jumped into the galley.

"What the Hell man! You always go around hooting and hollering like that?" asked MacShane.

Now it was Drake's turn, "You win the Lottery or something, Jesus dude!"

"No, much better! Mac, you know the rest of the crew you're worried about, well I just opened an e-mail from them and they're coming early. This is great we can leave a few days ahead of schedule," said an ecstatic T.C.

"Now you going to tell me who else you bullshitted into coming along?" inquired Drake.

"Yea, I guess it's alright now," muttered T.C. "It's Bonbon and Captain Spider." T.C. was beaming now with the news of the rest of the crew's arrival. "Man, this is great!" he repeated.

"Bonbon? I thought he was deported for arriving into the U.S. illegally," said Drake.

"No man, that was his brother, big mix up, Bonbon's a citizen now," shot back T.C.

"You know these guys, Drake?" asked Morgan. He looked at Holly and she just threw up her hands in a gesture that said, 'Go with it Mac.'

"Sure, I know these cats. They're quite a team, been working together on yachts for years, damn good sailors. But I heard Spider got a job as a paramedic?" explained Drake, looking inquisitively at T.C.

"Yeah he did, now we can go to sea with a paramedic on board. Never know when you'll need a doctor," said T.C. wisely.

"So we have an engineer, a paramedic, an exotic dancer, you and me. Now how does this Bonbon guy fit into the equation?" Morgan was trying to put a lineup together in his head.

"Bonbon can do it all dude! Fiberglass work, welding, operate the crane, fill scuba tanks, you name it. The guys a real find," boasts T.C.

Holly tired of the mutual admiration society said if the trip was going to leave ahead of schedule, then she had things to see to and headed off to get dressed and run her errands.

"And Spider is a technical diver, as well as a boat captain and dive master, rumor has it he can also fly a plane if the need arises." T.C. was now getting Mac's attention and hoped he was believing it.

"Drake, he for real?" asked Morgan, pointing his thumb in T.C. direction, not believing T.C.'s slant of things.

"This one's on the money Mac. Spider and Bonbon are going to be a real asset on this adventure. And with your background we won't have to worry about the pirates," stated Drake with a wink.

"I guess that this is what is referred to as a real motley crew," laughed Morgan, finishing his coffee.

Drake and T.C. headed towards the engine room to inventory the spare parts while Morgan got his laundry together to do some personal house keeping. During the middle of the spin cycle Drake and T.C. call out to Morgan that they have to go and get a few more spare parts for the voyage. Asking MacShane if he wanted to come along and MacShane said, "No thanks, think I'll hang around and get acclimated to my new surroundings. Besides I'm not up for a ride in the toxic taxi," referring to the nefarious stench.

"Suit yourself, there's plenty to eat if you get hungry. We should be back in a couple of hours. I'll set the alarm when we leave so no one bothers you," said T.C. on his way out with Drake in tow.

Morgan was starting to get a feel for the old ship. He walked to the end of the passageway on the stateroom deck and opened a door revealing a library and an elaborate entertainment center with a 76" television screen and a copious supply of DVDs and VHS tapes and dish network. Morgan was truly amazed at the way this old girl just kept surprising him. In front of the large TV, a blue leather Natuzzi sofa, a couple of matching overstuffed leather chairs and a beautiful teak coffee table which made for an inviting scene. The only thing missing was a bowl of hot buttered popcorn. Over in the library section of the room, built-in teak wall shelves were filled with both hardcover and paperback books. As Morgan examined the titles, he found Hemmingway, Twain, Clancey, Asimov, Cussler and the complete works of Robert Ferrigno. Books from all across the spectrum, he guessed that the Daniel Steel books were Holly's but with T.C., there's no telling. A reading chair and lamp were accompanied by a side table in such a way as to set this area off from the rest of the room providing a sort of sanctum from the rest of the ship. Morgan saw a copy of Mark Twain's 'Following the Equator.' Thinking this an appropriate title he sat down in the overstuffed chair to catch up on his reading.

Morgan was only ten pages into Twain's exploits when the boarding alarm sounded. Startled he put the book down and hi-tailed it up to the open deck to see the cause of the interruption. Morgan unlatched the hatch swinging the heavy door outwards, as he was about to step out on deck, he heard a thud and a voice yelling, "Dammit!"

Now it was Morgan's turn to shout back, "Who the hell are you and what are you doing on my ship?"

"Your ship? The Sequoia? T.C. told me it was his ship! Where is that asshole?" said the man holding the side of his bald head.

"Let me guess, Spider or Bonbon? Let's see, with your eloquent use of the English language, you must be Spider? Correct?" suggested MacShane.

"Yeah, I'm Spider and that's Bonbon bringing up some of the gear," said Spider, pointing to a medium-sized black man stepping onto the deck. "You T.C.'s partner? Mac... MacDougle?"

"MacShane, Morgan MacShane, sorry about the hatch. T.C. told us you wouldn't be here for a few days yet," spoke MacShane sincerely.

"Yea I know. I was able to switch some of my days off; I couldn't wait any longer. I can't wait to get this party started! Don't worry about the knock; not the first time won't be the last, MacShane? Eh, you don't look like any Scots man I've ever met," said Spider still rubbing his head trying to make a joke. To Morgan, Spider's bald head looked like a cue ball with a beard sitting on top of his sunburned shoulders. That comment had MacShane rolling his eyes, like he never heard that one before.

Bonbon now noticed what was going on and ran over to his friend, "You okay boss?"

"Fine Bonbon, just fabulous, com'on let's get the rest of the gear out of the car," replied Spider.

"I'll give you a hand, you want some ice for that bump?" asked Morgan in earnest.

"No, I'll just pound down a few coldies after we get this gear stowed. But thanks anyway. Bonbon, this is MacShane, the "partner" T.C. told us about," said Spider now laughing.

"Hello big Macut," calling Morgan a Creole name for soldier— more or less, "T.C. tell me you big military hero or something?" inquired Bonbon.

"Yeah, or something!" answered Morgan as he walked down the gangway with the two men, not knowing exactly what T.C. had told them.

Morgan was impressed with the equipment they were carrying on board: two sets of Ocean Management Systems dual C85 scuba tanks, a double tank set up with 170 cubic feet of air, enabling the wearer to stay down for quite a while. Two Phantom Dive lights, a rebreather, four Scuba Pro buoyancy compensators, some luggage and a long, thin aluminum case.

"Here, I'll take that bag Morgan; it's got my regulators in there. These babies never leave my sight," told Spider.

"Mac. Call me Mac," responded Morgan as he handed Spider the bag.

"Okay Mac. Bonbon, we've got everything? How 'bout moving the car into the lot? And lock up the steering wheel; this neighborhood is kinda shaky," commanded Spider to his, what appeared to Morgan to be Spider's manservant.

"Bonbon have another name or is it just Bonbon?" questioned MacShane trying to get to know these guys better as Bonbon drove the car into the parking lot.

"Want some friendly advice, Mac?" said Spider.

"Sure."

"In the tropics it's not good to ask last names nor too many questions," offered Spider as he hefted the duffle over his shoulder and headed up the gangway.

MacShane slowed in his pacing of Spider as the last comment he made mulled around in MacShane's head. He wasn't too sure if he was going to like this tall, blond, bearded, baldy-headed, bossy individual. Or was this some kind of act also?

Spider stowed his and Bonbon's gear in an empty stateroom and caught up with MacShane as he was sitting at the galley table making a sandwich. "Sure, could use that cold one now," he said to MacShane.

Morgan knew by the way Spider found his way around that he had been on board before and was quite aware of where the beer was kept. Morgan wasn't about to cow tow to this F.N.G. (what they used to call in the service 'fucking new guy') and told to Spider, "Beers in the ice box, help yourself."

Spider looked at MacShane and a slight grin appeared on his tight, sun-burned face. Then he told MacShane, "T.C. was right about you, you can be a hard ass if you want to." Spider then opened the reach-in and grabbed two beers and a Diet Coke for Bonbon.

"Here you go Mac, by the way whadya makin' there?" Spider had taken the edge off his demeanor and was trying to make some small talk.

"Ham sandwich." But Mac wasn't ready to buy into it yet.

Morgan finished making his sandwich and took it and his beer out on deck to clear his head. 'Where in the hell was T.C. when he could have used him?' thought Morgan as he chomped away at the sandwich.

Chapter 10

Drake and T.C. were finishing up at Sailors Mart, getting a few more essentials for the trip.

"Drake grab a couple more Raycor water separators; the last time I fueled up in the Bahamas, they were pumping more water than fuel into the tanks," said T.C. to his engineer.

"Yea, you see that a lot over there. Some of those old single-walled tanks are just about rusted through; that shit will foul up a fuel system in a heartbeat. But hey! It keeps me in business," replied Drake.

T.C. and Drake push there cart up to the checkout counter and Pete sparks up a conversation. "T.C. where's the fed? You lose him already."

Drake started to laugh at the reference to MacShane and said, "Man leaves an impression everywhere he goes. Doesn't he?"

T.C. answered Pete's question, "Naw we left him back at the ranch to keep an eye on things. You know, who better to watch your stuff than an ex-fed."

"Oh, I see." Pete's been in the business long enough to know a brush-off when he hears one so he changes the subject. "When ya leavin'? Must be soon, now that you got your engineer in tow."

"Pretty soon, you know go out for a shake-down cruise and find out how she handles. What's the total Pete?" queried T.C., now in a hurry to get out of there. Pete has a reputation for being an old washwoman when it comes to discussing other people's business. T.C. wanted to keep everything on the QT, so the quicker they leave, the better.

Pulling out of the parking lot, Drake told T.C. to head over to Rio Vista Blvd. So he could take a look at Officer Jim's Yanmar.

"How long is **that** going to take? Just stop at the florist, pick up some flowers, and leave them on the engine cover with a sympathy card, better yet we can leave two cards: one for the engine and the other for all of Jimbo's money that he's going to spend on a new engine," directs T.C. ever the wise guy.

"Dude, you told him I would look at the engine and that's what I'm going to do, now give me a piece of paper so I can write my prognosis." Drake wrote some words on a yellow legal pad and tore off the sheet, folded it, and stuffed it into his shirt pocket.

T.C. drove into Officer Jim's driveway, parked under the tall Ficus tree, and the two men walked into the backyard to the dock and climbed on board the old boat.

"Just as I thought," said Drake as he lifted up the engine hatch. "Hand me that fish hook in the gunwale," Drake told T.C.

Drake fiddled around in the bilge for a few minutes and took the fish hook, and tied the leader to the latch on the overhead radio box. Next Drake took the note out of his pocket and hung the note on the fish hook and then said to T.C., "Okay we can leave."

"But you didn't do anything," replied T.C.

"Read the note," was all Drake said.

T.C. leaned over, read the note and started laughing. "Man, you got a big set of balls! Let's go."

T.C. was still chuckling to himself over the note. It read, "Boat Broke, buy a new engine you cheap bastard!" And on the bottom of the yellow paper was this:

1 Dockside service call............................ $50.00

1 Mechanic (one-hour min).......................$75.00

1 Mechanic's Helper (one-hour min)........$45.00

1 mobile shop charge.................................$25.00

Total:...$195.00

Less good customer discount 15%......................<27.00>

Total due..$168.00

Make check payable to cash!!!! And mail it to my P.O. Box number.

"Think Ol' Jimbo's going to pay ya?" T.C. asked Drake as they got into the truck and started to pull away.

"That dude bought that house over twenty years ago. It's gone up over six times in value; let him take out a home equity line of credit. Besides he's the one that asked me to look at it," replied Drake.

"Good thing we are leaving soon is all I gots to say! Other wise I don't know if I could afford you!" was T.C.'s comeback. Adding, "Let's get back to the ship, Im starvin'."

The 'toxic taxi' using MacShane's terminology, pulled up to the dock next to the Sequoia and the two men started unloading the extra parts and supplies. As they got on deck, they saw MacShane sitting on a lounge chair under a green and white striped umbrella, eating his lunch.

"What? You couldn't wait for us?" asked T.C., joking with his old buddy.

"Nope, needed to sit outside and chill for a while," replied MacShane.

T.C. knew this was not a normal trait for Morgan and asked him what was up.

"Had some visitors right after you left. Said they were looking for some asshole named T.C., the owner of this tub." Now it was MacShanes turn to screw with T.C., and he started to lay it on thick. "had a couple of papers they wanted you to sign, something about causing an environmental hazard by dumping untreated waste overboard, I don't know, said they had a court order to search the vessel. Something about the EPA or DNR, I told them to go ahead that I was just the mechanic." Morgan was trying to keep a straight face, T.C. was getting tense, and the color was starting to drain from his face.

"You let them go inside? By themselves?" T.C. was almost speechless at the thought of his trusted buddy letting total strangers wander around the inside compartments of the Sequoia.

"Hey, they had a court order. What was I supposed to do, throw them over the side, get arrested and go to jail? We're leaving in a few days anyway or is there something you're not telling us about this arrangement?" inquired Morgan still sitting in the lounge chair sipping on his beer to keep from cracking up.

T.C. wasn't going to debate with Mac any longer and sprinted to the hatch and flung it open, yelling inside for the inspectors to show themselves. Morgan was now laughing out loud and Drake was looking at him with curiosity.

"Not really inspectors, are they?" Drake quipped.

"Nope!" answered MacShane, taking another sip of the gold fluid.

"No one in there at all, is there?" asked Drake.

"Oh, there's someone in there alright. Just not what he's expecting," answered MacShane.

"You going to tell me?" questioned Drake.

"Spider and Bonbon," was all Mac said, wiping his mouth with a napkin.

"That's cool! Good one Mac!" Drake told him approvingly as he ran into the ship after T.C. to greet his new shipmates.

A bright yellow and green water bus pulled up to the seawall just astern of the Sequoia, and Holly got off carrying her bundles from a day of shopping. "Thanks Captain Finch. I really appreciate you bringing me to my front door," Holly calls back to the captain as she exited the vessel.

"Miss Holly, we couldn't let you walk with all those bundles now, could we?" Captain Finch was an old, familiar face along the New River. He and T.C. worked together at the Water Bus for a while and still kept in close contact. So when Finch saw Holly walking down the city dock he pulled up and offered her a ride home. "Tell that boyfriend of yours I said 'hi' and to call me sometime."

"Will do Captain, thanks again." Holly was now walking up the gangplank as she heard all sorts of noise coming from inside the ship. The hatch was left wide open, letting all the a/c out. 'Great now what are they up to?' thought Holly as she walked into the galley and saw the four men sitting around with empty beer bottles piling up on the table.

"Spider! Bonbon! T.C. told me you wouldn't be here for a few days yet! How are you?" said Holly, glad to finally see the rest of the crew.

"We're great darling! Bonbon and I wanted to get this thing going so I moved my vacation up a few days. Want a beer?" asked Spider, holding out a cold Becks.

"Isn't this perfect!" exclaimed T.C. "Now we can get underway. Day after tomorrow whatdya think hon?"

"I think that if we're leaving that soon, those beers better get put away, and some finish-up work needs to be done. For instance, now that everyone's here, I need to do the final food shopping. Come on boys, pool together about $1000.00 bucks. Second, if we are leaving in two days, you're taking me for a nice night out, tonight! Someplace where you can't wear any of those stupid-looking flowered shirts of yours. Now do what you have to, but be ready to go out by 7:30," instructed Holly, sounding more like a den mother than T.C.'s true love.

"But babe, we're just getting to know each other, you know for Mac's sake," pleads T.C.

"Don't get me involved on this one!" replied MacShane, acting much more at ease with his new crew. He and Spider were actually starting to get along or at least tolerate each other. Amazing the effects a few cold beers can have.

Drake, Bonbon, and Spider were just sitting back, taking it all in.

"Two days huh? Well, I know what I need to get done. T.C. plan accordingly, 7:30 dinner at Jackson's 54," said Holly as she left the room.

"Dude, guess you better get your ass in gear. You're going to have to take a shower and everything. That place is *expensive!*" remarked Spider shaking his hand and exaggerating the expensive part.

"That little furry thing got some big power, eh T.C.," chipped in in Bonbon.

"Or lack thereof," answered MacShane, referring to Holly's shaving preference.

"Yeah you guys laugh, but she's a partner too," was all T.C. could come back with.

The rest of the men started to make fun of T.C.'s situation. It was a well-needed joke fest that brought the men closer together, getting them on the path to being a cohesive unit.

Chapter 11

Morning came early on the Sequoia. The coffee was made and finished; no time for a big breakfast today. Spider and Bonbon were double-checking the dive equipment. Drake was instituting a few minor repairs on the winch motor. T.C. and Holly were still under the sheets from their big night out and MacShane was looking at what was going on and felt totally out of place for the first time since he'd been on board the ship. MacShane walked over to Drake and asked if he could use a hand. Drake spoke, "No thanks Mac, I'm almost finished here. How about Spider, does he need any help?"

"No. He sent me up here to check on you." Mac was feeling useless.

"I know what you can do Mac," said Drake.

"Yeah, what's that? Go and make everyone sandwiches?" he replied sarcastically.

"No. For real, the magnetometer is still in its crate, noone's had a chance to check it out yet. If you read up on it, that would give us a good jump for when it came time to use it," commented Drake.

Morgan now thought he was being ushered off to do busy work and keep out of the way. Imagine someone with his background and confirmed kill record being sent off to read a book. "Great, where is this trolling magnet?"

Drake could tell by the sound of Mac's voice that he wasn't too enthralled about this particular task and could use a pep talk. "Mac this piece of equipment is the key to our mission being a success. This little doll will pinpoint the location of what were all after, and then it's just picking up the loot off the ocean floor."

"Nice sales job! Now where is this hot rod?" repeated MacShane.

Drake took MacShane to the stern of the vessel and flipped over an old tarp, raveling a large cardboard box with the words J.W. Fisher Pulse 12 printed in large black letters. MacShane opened the box, studied the long yellow tub. The stabilizer fins reminding MacShane of a scaled-down version of a Sidewinder missile. Pulling out the instruction booklet, Morgan found a comfortable spot in the shade to study while Jimmy Buffets' 'Down to the Banana Republic' played over the on-deck speakers. Morgan sat and listened to the words for a second, thinking how apropos most of the words were... *leaving no forward address... hustling the senoritas as they danced beneath the stars.*

Morgan had started reading the fifth page of the instruction booklet when T.C. surfaced with a cup of coffee in hand. MacShane looked up and said, "Nice you could join us Captain Chaos, if we're leaving tomorrow you best call everyone together and have a plan ready."

"And nice to see you Mr. Christian!" answered T.C., looking like he was no doubt hung over. "Crew muster in the dining room in ten," said T.C. as he goes back inside to seek out some a/c.

Morgan spread the word to the crew, and within ten minutes, Drake, Spider, Bonbon and Morgan were all assembled sitting around the large polished dining room table. T.C. walked in still looking a wreck, but by now his hair was at least combed.

"Gentleman. We are still planning to leave by first light tomorrow morning." T.C. stopped and took a sip of an ice-cold bottle of Zypher Hills spring water. Then he went on unfolding a navigation chart as he spoke. "From here," pointing to Port Everglades In Fort Lauderdale, "we head to Nassau, Bahamas. There we will clear customs, take on fuel, and I'll firm up some arrangements with my old friend Barry, who owns the 'Gems of the Caribbean' jewelry shop in downtown Nassau." T.C. was getting some strange looks from the guys at the mention of his visiting a jewelry shop and then the questions started.

"Hey you mean you're finally going to ask Holly to marry you?" spoke Drake.

Then it was Bonbon's turn. "She makes you good wife. I'm happy for you."

T.C. couldn't believe these guys were getting the wrong message so he went into an explanation. "No man, we're not getting married! Barry, besides owning the jewelry store, is also a dealer in antique silver and gold artifacts. We just can't bring them back into the Stated; the feds will take at least eighty percent of our find. Barry has outlets for this kind of stuff, collectors that will pay big bucks. Married? Please!" T.C. shook his head and swigged some more water. It was at that point that Holly poked her head into the 'board room' catching the last bit of T.C.'s speech Holly spoke directly to the self-proclaimed chairman.

"And what do you mean by that remark, 'Married please!'" Holly's presence taking everyone off guard. T.C. trying to be smooth with a recovery, gave her a confused look.

He answered, looking directly at Holly, "What? I mean he will be able to sell some of the stuff, I didn't say married please. I said market with ease. What's wrong with your ears, you need more coffee." T.C. was playing it to the hilt.

But Holly wasn't backing down, "I know what I heard and I know what you said; don't try to bullshit me Tommy Chaddon." with that Holly left the room and headed back to her bunk, slamming the door to her stateroom behind her.

"Dude, she's pissed!" commented Drake. "Better let her cool off."

"That's what you get, confined living makes for confounded situations, no room for gossip," added MacShane with his infinite wisdom.

"Good woman, but bad temper," remarked Bonbon.

"Yeah, I know all about her temper. She'll be alright, I'll check on her after the briefing. Now let's get this schedule down," said T.C., directing everyone's attention back to the chart. "After Nassau we'll head east past Eleuthera and south to Great Inagua, taking on fuel and supplies in Matthew Town. My old buddy Nine Fingers has a marina there, way off the tourist route, no questions, everyone keeps to themselves. A lesson they learned from the old drugger days. From there we head through the Windward Passage on towards Kingston, Jamaica. We go through customs, obtain a cruising permit and proceed to get rich. Simple!" proclaimed T.C.

Parroting T.C. Morgan said, "Simple! My Black ass! In fact, it's so simple it's moronic! Morgan being used to operating military operations, couldn't believe that he was the only one questioning this hollow plan."

"What about checking out all the equipment, becoming proficient with this stuff. What do you expect us to do learn on the job?" Morgan was getting upset. Here they were getting ready to leave in a matter of hours, and there are still lots of unanswered questioned.

"Relax Mac, this isn't some high financed, special forces extravaganza. We all know our jobs," replied T.C.

"Well then what about my job. Maybe if I had some more understanding of what everyone is doing, I would feel better about this whole affair," ranted MacShane.

"You, you're in charge of the electronic sensor program. Didn't you start reading the instruction manual for it?" offered T.C.

"That's only because I had nothing else to do!" shot back Morgan.

T.C. was quick to point out, "Mac with all your experience you gained at the taxpayers' expense, operating this little bit of equipment should be a breeze. What about all those listening posts we set up back in Panama? Who was the one that had to take it apart and replace some of the microchipped in that broke during that god-awful parachute drop? And, put it back together in the dark while it was raining? That's right it was you, or did they erase that from your memory banks before you were discharged?" The mission T.C. was referring to was a black op that took place weeks before the United Stated invaded Panama. Morgan's team was low leveled, dropped into the jungles of Panama and had to make their way to Noriega's resident where they were to install parabolic listening laser devices surrounding the compound. With some being placed as far as one mile, but as long as the units were in the line of sight of the glass, they would still work by picking up conversations inside the building. Operating on the principle of sound waves vibrating the window glass, the laser would then pick up the vibrations and turn them into sound, in this case, human conversation. This was some very high-tech stuff at the time and would work rain or shine.

Mac's face tightened, he didn't like to talk about those missions and responded by saying, "That mission is still classified and as far as everyone here is concerned, that mission never took place."

"Lighten up Mac, nobody's calling the papers with a hot scoop," said Spider, looking at MacShane in a new light.

"My point is Mac, that when it comes to the electronics end of the operation, you're not a rookie. Just like the rest of the crew everyone knows their duties and are experts in their particular fields. And me? I'm coming along to keep everyone in complete harmony, you know like a band leader. Besides it was my idea," said T.C., trying to get some levity back working for him.

"Yeah, your woman going to give you some real harmony. I think she going to use your head as a bass drum, maestro," said Bonbon, mocking T.C.'s ability to keep the piece in his own household.

Drake who had been sitting back taking all this in, said, "My families in perfect harmony and I'm going to keep it like that. My babies won't let us down. Just say the word and we'll get this party started!" spoken as a truly proud engineer.

T.C. stood up and proceeded to close his briefing. "Tomorrow morning, at first light, we set sail for Port Royale, Jamaica. And for riches, we can only dream about!" Little did he know how true those words would be.

Chapter 12

9:00 a.m. Sergeant Crawford pulls open the single glass door to the convenience store and a man of mid-Eastern descent approaches him wearing the name tag 'RAJA.' "Good morning sir. Can I help you today?"

"Maybe, I'm looking for a friend of mine named MacShane, Morgan MacShane. Supposed to have a boat tied up around here someplace," said Crawford trying to feel out some information.

"Many boats around here sir," replied Raja.

"This boat is special; it's like a salvage vessel or freighter. My friends a big black guy. Maybe you see him around?" inquired Crawford.

"Oh, you must mean the new man on T.C.'s boat. Not real friendly man. Old boat, very rusty. New man been in a few times to buy paper and coffee. He never said much. He your friend?" responded Raja.

"Could be, know where they tie up?" Crawford questioned.

"They tie up at the end of the street. But they leave this morning. I see them leave about 6 o'clock when I come over the bridge to open the store. Lots of smoke for such a boat," offered Raja.

"Know if they'll be back today?" asked Crawford, picking up the morning paper.

"No, no. T.C.'s girlfriend, Miss Holly, came by yesterday to buy one month's worth of Lotto tickets; no come back soon," said Raja, not giving the Sergeant the answer he wanted to hear. "Can I get you something?"

"Shit!" was all Crawford said as he left the counter and walked out the door.

Chapter 13

Eleven hours out of Fort Lauderdale, the Sequoia is located at 26*14'n., 78*11'w. Drake was at the helm pulling wheelhouse duty, monitoring the autopilot's heading, which should be just about ready to make a course adjustment, turning the old girl south into the Tongue of the Ocean. An area of ocean so deep the navy uses it for testing their submarines. At any second the preset course adjustment will swing the bow of the Sequoia in a southernly direction headed for Nassau, the capital city of the Bahamas.

In the dining room the crew was sitting down for their first full meal on the open sea, a true T.C. gastronomic experience. Gracing the solid cherry wood table was a beautifully roasted standing rib roast with garlic mashed potatoes and a lightly sautéed blend of zucchini and yellow squash with rosemary sprigs. The aroma of the cooked herbs was filling the air, tempting everyone's appetite. Wine glasses were filled with a beautiful Fife .98 Kenwood Cabernet Jack London Wolfs head vintage, and the mood was festive. T.C. picked up his Hinkle-slicing knife to make the first cut of the rib when over the intercom came an alert from the bridge.

"T.C., you better get up here... we're getting hailed from a Coast Guard chopper ordering us to a halt. They want to speak to the master of the vessel," shouted Drake into the ship's intercom.

"Drake, respond and tell them we'll comply," commanded T.C. with a blank look on his face.

Drake radioed back, telling the helo-pilot to stand by for the vessel's captain while he was complying with their request to take the ship out of gear. As Drake brought the binnacle controls to the neutral position, the forward progress of the Sequoia started to slow, the huge wake from the displacement hull started to subside until it was hardly a ripple. Now the ship lay motionless in the middle of the dark blue sea.

"All right," said MacShane. "NOW WHAT!" The rest of the crew, which were poised for a threat, put down their glasses, focusing their attention on T.C. and MacShane. "Did you file all the correct paperwork? Did you forget to pay someone? Why the hell are they stopping us? For leaving the country?! Which one of you is illegal, is that it!" exclaimed MacSahne, looking at Bonbon. The little Haitian immediately pulled out his wallet to show MacShane his Green card. Mac took the napkin from his lap and slammed it onto the table. He was not enjoying his first ocean voyage as a civilian, now starting to feel certain that some bad shit was about to come down.

"Calm down Mac, this kind of stuff happens all the time, probably got a look at the Sequoia and decided to do a safety check. Let's get to the bridge and find out what they want," T.C. spoke. Then he and Mac left the dining room and doubled timed it down the panel-lined passageway and up the stairwell until they reached the bridge. Once their T.C. picked up the Icom VHF handpiece and keyed the mike.

"This is T.C. Allen, captain of the Sequoia to the Coast Guard copter. What can we do for you sir?" T.C. was now acting in his official capacity as master of the vessel.

"Captain, this is Lt. Commander Miles Holiday U.S.C.G. Please bring your vessel to a stop and prepare to be boarded," was the reply over the radio.

Tension on the bridge was at a peak. T.C., Drake, and MacShane were looking out the bridge window, watching the bright orange Aerospatiale HH-65a Dolphin helicopter hanging in the air motionless, hovering about fifty feet above the flat cargo deck of the Sequoia. T.C. picked up a pair of binoculars, but all he could see was the pilot and co-pilot, their eyes obscured by the dark sun visors of their helmets.

The VHF radio barks, "Are you prepared to accept boarders captain?"

T.C. keyed the mike and replied in a deep bass tone, almost as if he had grown a pair of balls twice his size. "What is this in regards to Commander? We are in International Waters; please state your intentions."

"My intentions are to lower a boarding party! As you should be aware of, captain, a ship of the United Stated registry can be boarded by the United Stated Coast Guard anywhere in the world. Now make ready to receive a boarding party." The copter was now at about thirty-five feet above the deck, with the nose of the copter facing directly at the ship's bridge, which was now crowded with the rest of the crew trying to find out what was going on.

"Well, we best get ready to meet our guests. Drake keep everyone up here and hold the Sequoia stationary; Mac and I will go see what in the hell these dicks want," T.C. ordered. "Let's go Mac."

As the men were descending the passageway, making their way to the open deck, the sliding side door of the hovering bright orange machine opened, and a man in a harness was being attached to the hoist and lowered to the deck. The crew of the HH-65A Dolphin were well trained and the man on the end of the tether touched down with hardly a thump. T.C. and Mac opened the watertight hatch and stepped onto the deck amidst the swirling hurricane-force wind and water spray created by the spinning thirty-nine-foot blades of the Lycoming LTYS-101-750B gas turbines. The new arrival was releasing the winch line from his harness, waving a thumbs up to the flight mechanic on board the copter. As the hoist line was being retrieved, the HH-65A Dolphin was gaining altitude and seemed to be flying away.

"Alright, what is this all about? And where is that chopper going?" demands T.C. with MacSahne on his heels.

The new arrival turned to face the two men, unfastened the chin strap of his flight helmet, and with a well-practiced move, pulled it over his head, placed it under his arm and raised a snappy salute to the stern of the ship. "Permission to come aboard Sir?"

"Holy Shit!!! Crawford!! Sergeant Thomas Crawford! What the hell are you doing out here? When did you join Hooligan's Navy?" (an old slang term for the Coast Guard) MacShane was a professional and not the type of person to be surprised but this was something he never would have expected.

"You can run but you can never hide. The General sends his regards Morgan." With that remark, Crawford reached into his blue flight suit and handed Morgan the cigar Kane had given him, along with a high-resolution satellite picture of the Sequoia passing the sea buoys off Port Everglades.

"Shit! The Opis X," MacShane froze in mid-reach.

"Who's this Mac? What's going on?" T.C. was totally in the dark.

Mac made the introductions. "T.C. Allen, meet Sergeant Thomas Crawford. Confidant, man Friday, personal henchman and right-hand man of General Andrew Kane."

"You mean 'Insane Andy Kane?'" said T.C., referring to the General's nickname.

"I see you heard of my fearless leader, T.C.," said Crawford.

"Jesus! Who hasn't. I heard that back in 'Nam he single-handedly took out a Cong supply dump when everyone else said we couldn't get near it. Heard he crawled on his stomach wearing a Gilly suit for two days to get near enough to blow it up," said T.C. with true admiration.

"That's a fact, got him a promotion and put his career on the fast track," answered Crawford.

The rest of the crew was now coming through the watertight hatch to see what this boarding was all about. Crawford saw the crowd coming and asked if he could speak to MacShane in private.

"Captain will you please excuse us… I have important business with Colonel MacShane," told Crawford.

"Retired, you need to put the word retired in front of that Colonel, Sergeant." Mac didn't like the sound of Crawford using his old rank title and threw that correction in before Crawford could get any further.

Crawford undaunted by MacShane's interruption, continued on, "Explain to the crew that we had to go over some questionable paperwork with regards to transporting certain equipment out of the country, some Homeland Security stuff. Roger that?"

"Understood sarge. I'll do my best," replied T.C.

"Com-on Crawf, we can use my stateroom," offered Morgan.

Crawford was now getting a good look around at the clutter and rusting hulk of metal he had landed on and wasn't sure if MacShane had lost his mind or not. Crawford was told to follow MacShane through the rust-covered watertight hatch, and he started to laugh at the incongruity of the term. "What's so funny?" asked MacShane.

"Just your use of the term watertight. If that thing is watertight, I'll kiss your ass in Macy's window." Mac smiled knowing how he felt on his first visit. Mac undid the latch dogs and swung open the hatch. The blast of cold air caught Crawford by surprise. Now MacShane rapped on the steel door, indicating the strength and integrity of the unit. Crawford's eyes widened as he inspected the condition of the hatch. "Please apply chapstick before you kiss my ass. The skin in that area of my body is very sensitive," said Morgan, unable to hold back his laughter.

"What kind of tub is this? The documents have her listed as a salvage rig," spoke Crawford, not believing the ice-cold air conditioning and the immaculate appointments inside the vessel. "What gives?"

"Only a lowly salvage rig like your papers say," quipped MacShane.

On their way through the passageways, Crawford had to reach out and touch the beautiful paneled walls because he could not believe his eyes. Nothing this fine could ever be concealed beneath the ugliest vessel he had ever been on.

Crawford was dumbstruck as MacShane opened the door to his stateroom. The teak dresser, with matching night tables, the queen-sized bed, the royal blue wool carpet and the colorful Haitian oil paintings adorning the walls made for a very comfortable way to while away the hours on long ocean voyages. At the base of the bed were two matching teak chairs with light blue upholstery, adding a nice contrast to the carpet.

"Have a seat Crawf. Tell me what's so important that the general had to send you 1300 miles, drop you on a string like some venomous spider and personally present me with one of his 50.00 cigars. The last time he gave me one of those, he was sending me to Somalia for an advanced recon mission."

Crawford was still having trouble accepting what he was seeing. "Damn Morgan! What the hell is this ship?"

Morgan knew he would have to settle Crawford's curiosity before he would get anything out of him, so Morgan gave Sergeant Crawford a very brief sinopias of how he ended up on the Sequoia.

"Now that that's out of the way, tell me what the General wants this time... but you best remember that I'm retired!" said Morgan

"Well Morgan, retirement is what you make of it," started Crawford. Morgan had stood up and was looking for a cigar cutter on his dresser when Crawford laid the big bomb on him. "I wouldn't light that just yet, Mac," said Crawford, bracing himself for the dreaded response he knew was coming as Morgan turned to face him.

"And what do you mean by that remark?" asked MacShane, turning towards Crawford and leaning his elbow on the top of the dresser.

"You've been ordered to Washington. The General's calling you in Mac; here are your orders," replied Crawford as he handed MacShane the sealed envelope.

"BULLSHIT!! Do you hear me!! BULLSHIT!! I'm friggin' retired. Let me spell that out for you, enlisted man. R-E-T-I-R-E-D!!! I did my time, let someone else step up to the plate!" MacShane knew that the enlisted man crack was out of line, he knew about Crawford's past and that he could have been an officer except for

140

his problem. MacShane didn't care, he was pissed off and was lashing out at the closest whipping boy he could find.

"I understand how you must feel, Mac. But just calm down and give me a minute." Crawford expected this behavior and had gone over a few different scenarios in his head so he would be ready with a reply.

"Then understand this, NO! I'm a partner in this salvage business, and we're underway to a sight now. Noway, scram Crawf!" Macshane was starting to cool down and feeling legitimately sorry about the disrespectful remark he lambasted Crawford with. "Sorry about the enlisted man crack Crawf, but you took me totally off balance with this crap."

"No apology needed my friend. If it was me getting this news, I think I would have taken a swing at you. We've been through too much for me to take offence. However, the General is exercising a little-used clause in your retirement paperwork that was added somewhere in the Patriot Act and is re-activating you for a special project he needs help with. Mac, you know he wouldn't be calling you back if it wasn't really necessary." Crawford was making headway with Morgan and knew he was set up for the closing.

"God Crawf, what kind of problem could be so important that he needs a retired old man like me?" stated MacShane, who wasn't really old and now wasn't retired either.

Got him, thought Crawford and preceded to spring the closing line. "You'll find out soon enough. The General is expecting you for breakfast tomorrow."

MacShane knew he had been duped, the look in his eyes said it all, but the professional soldier in him knew that arguing and putting up resistance to an order from the general wouldn't be in anyone's best interest either so he asked Crawford, "Is this an overnight bag or should I break out the duffle?"

"One night, maybe two, and you'll be back in the tropic sun working on your tan before you knew it. Now Colonel, if you will excuse me, I need to get back to the bridge and notify the Coasties to return and pick us up," said Crawford, already referring to MacShane as a superior officer. As Sergeant Crawford opened the stateroom door, he heard these words muttering from Morgan MacShanes lips as he started to organize his clothes.

"One, maybe two, fly to Washington, have breakfast, back in two days... Bullshit!"

MacShane slung his tan leather weekender bag over his shoulder and headed to the deck of the Sequoia. Crawford was already there waiting for him along with the rest of the crew.

T.C. was the first to speak. "Mac, Sergeant Crawford explained you're needed in D.C. for a day or two. We'll be docked at the East Bay Street Docks next to Brown's Boat Basin in downtown Nassau.

Here's the number of the dock master. He should be able to get ahold of us if you need to. But remember, don't even bother to call after five. Those dudes are out the door like union workers."

T.C. was taking this interruption in his usual stride, keeping a positive attitude, knowing everything works out in the end.

Holly was a little more concerned, "How can they do this? Just drop out of the sky and cart you off, it doesn't seem… American."

Mac smiled at her sentiment and assured her he will be back as the Sergeant had promised; he'd been down this bumpy road before. As the HH-65A copter set up for the retrieval, the crew watched as first Crawford and then MacShane made the journey up the line to the bright Orange beast. As MacShane was about ten feet into the air, he yelled to T.C., "Hey! You best save me one of those famous Cannolis of yours." With that MacShane gave them a hearty salute as he entered the side of the copter. The crew of the Sequoia watched from the deck as the sliding door shut and the bird flew away, headed towards Miami.

"Well, that was fun. Might as well go back and finish dinner, hate to see a beautiful rib roast get flushed down the tubes." T.C. always had a way with words.

MacShane was sitting on the jump seat next to Crawford; the conversation was general and light. MacShane knew better than to try and pry any information out of him. General Kane sent Crawford on a mission to bring him in, not to discuss or drop hints about what the General wanted.

"I've got to ask, how'd you find me Crawf?" asked MacShane.

"Paper trail... the General knew you were headed to South Florida to hook up with an old buddy. Ran a search through MYFLORIDA.com and got a new business listed with Morgan MacShane. And the rest, as they say, is history. I only missed you by three hours this morning. I spoke to a good friend of yours, the corner store guy. He said you were not a friendly man." It was now Crawford's turn to smile.

Macshane was now starting to sport a friendly smile. "When da man wants ya, he gonna git ya! Is that it?"

"Something like that, yes," said Crawford.

" It's really good to see you Crawf, despite the current situation." There was a genuine feeling of kinship in MacShane's remark and Morgan slapped his old friend on the shoulder. "I would have thought that you would have been put out to pasture by now," said Morgan.

"They keep trying but I keep putting another quarter into the machine and end up coming back for more. What the hell would I do in civilian life, sit inside a condo staring at the walls, worrying about if someone is parked in my spot when I come home? Get a nine to fiver? That would be a great interview, wouldn't it Mac?

Sitting in front of some little wise-assed prick, who probably never left the state, asking me such in-depth questioned as 'Where do you see yourself in five years?' and you know me, I'd just have to say something profound in a weak and timid voice such as, 'Well sir if I haven't killed one of my co-workers for pissing me off over something inconsequential, then I think I will be sitting in your seat asking stupid questioned to people on the other side of the desk from me.' Man, I love that answer." Crawford always had a way of cracking himself up, and this was no exception. He was having a full belly laugh and MacShane was joining in, getting a visual of Sergeant Thomas Crawford sitting in an interview wearing his civies, giving the interviewer the cold hard stare only a man with years of military service could muster, a look that has seen more death and destruction then should be allowed in one lifetime.

"You got this all figured out, do you? Really Crawf... what do you plan on doing when you get out?" MacShane really wanted to know. The airlift to the copter from the deck of the Sequoia, seeing his old friend again, the rush he got when he was being sent on special ops projects, MacShane was now starting to second guess his retirement. He was actually starting to miss the action.

"Me? I've got my money saved, going to buy a ranch and raise live stock. Making a living letting animals screw. Man, what a country! Got the place all picked out: 155 acres on the Colorado-Wyoming border. Beautiful place Mac, you'll have to come out and visit," said Crawford earnestly. Despite the fact that the two men hardly kept in contact with each other, it seemed like that whenever they got together, they picked up where they had left off. This was a sign of true friendship.

Before Morgan could comment on Crawford's plans, Lt. Commander Holiday got on the intercom and announced that they were about to land at the Coast Guard air station in Opa-Locka. The HH-65 Dolphin touched down with only the slightest bump, the sliding side door opened, and Holiday announced over the intercom headset.

"Colonel, when you exit the aircraft, please make your way to that HU-25 on the tarmac. They have instruction to depart immediately for Washington."

"Thank you, commander. Sergeant Crawford, our chariot awaits," acknowledges MacShane.

"Not ours pal, yours. I have other ordered; we'll catch up sometime, knock back some cold ones and do in a few neurons. Good luck, my regards to the General." The two men shook hands and MacShane was off on the second leg of his adventure.

The only outward variation between a millionaire's executive jet and the HU-25 was the paint job. The bright orange stripe and black block U.S. COAST GUARD lettering didn't leave any doubt as to the mission of said aircraft. Inside the fuselage, there wasn't very much headroom. Morgan slouched down the short aisle and slumped into the black leather seat. With his seat belt buckled, he tilted his head back and closed his eyes as the White and Orange Falcon jet taxied out for take off. The pilot ran through the routine safety announcements and informed MacSahne that they were cleared for immediate takeoff. As the small jet sat at the beginning of runway 53, the twin Garrett ATF3-6-2C Turbofan engines were winding up for launch. Screaming for release, the turbofans were like caged animals waiting to be set free. The pilot, now satisfied with the engine's readings, unleashed the aircraft and sent it hurtling down the runway at max speed, indicating a performance takeoff. This guy was in a hurry. With the fifty-four-foot wing span digging for air, the 30,000-pound jet was aimed almost straight up into the sky, nose pointed for the heavens. "Next stop, Washington D.C., we should arrive in approximately one hour forty minutes. Tonight's in-flight movie is 'Airport,' so sit back and enjoy the ride Colonel, compliments of your friendly neighborhood Coast Guard.

"Great, another wise ass," muttered MacShane as he reclined in his seat and tried to catch some shut-eye.

Two short dings of a bell and the fasten seatbelt light popped on. "Please put your seats in the upright position as we prepare for landing. And if you enjoyed your flight with us this fine evening, kindly remember that since the federal cutbacks, we are now accepting gratuities. Enjoy your stay in the Washington D.C. area.

The small jet bounced around as the pilot made his descent through the cloud layer. Morgan noticed water vapor on the window, a typical summer evening in the nation's Capitol, wet, humid and sticky. Wonderful!" thought Morgan. The HU-25 broke through and touched down at Andrews Air Force Base.

Taxing to a pre-designated area of the tarmac, the jet came to a halt, and the ground crew rolled out the boarding ladder so the passenger and crew could disembark. "What no red carpet?" MacShane said to one of the ground crew, a young man of about nineteen.

"No sir, sorry sir," came the reply. The young man could not help but notice the loud Hawaiian shirt and paint-splattered shorts, a far cry from the standard uniform of the day on the passenger. However; he was quite sure it must have been someone of major importance to be flying on a government aircraft alone in the middle of the night, and the young recruit wasn't taking any chances on upsetting anyone.

MacShane, noticing the uneasiness of the young recruit, gave him a snappy salute, saying, "I'll let it slide this time Private, but the next time you see the President's cousin, you better have one available."

"Yes sir, sorry sir, I'll put in a requisition for one immediately," said the Private as he returned Morgan's salute questioning in his head of what he had just heard.

"This way, Colonel," said a staff Sergeant, directing MacShane towards a dark blue Ford Crown Victoria. "I'm your driver while you're in D.C., Colonel. Sergeant Moss at your service."

"Thank you, Sergeant. What hotel did our illustrious leader make my reservations for?" asked MacShane, thinking he was going to take a hot shower and order some room service.

"My ordered are to take you to the Bachelor Officer Quarters, sir," answered the Sergeant.

"Cheap Bastard! In that case, Sergeant can we stop by the Mess Hall, I haven't eaten since lunch. Or is there a peanut butter sandwich on my bunk?" MacShane was getting sarcastic now.

"Yes sir, the Mess Hall it is, the General thought you might be hungry."

"Well how considerate of the General." MacShane sat back and waited for the car to reach the Mess Hall. After a quick dinner with numerous stares at his casual attire, MacShane was taken to the Barracks where Sergeant Moss instructed Morgan that he will be out front at 06:30 to take him to the General.

"Thank you Sergeant, I'll see you in the morning. "Said MacShane offering up a half-assed salute to the Sergeant's well-practiced meticulous one. MacShane entered his room and got ready for bed. He peeled back the green wool blanket with the 150 thread count sheets. He ran his hands over the course sheets, and they felt like sandpaper to his touch, compared to the ultra-smooth 600 thread count he had grown accustomed to during his brief time on the Sequoia. Damn, he was missing that old tub right about now.

After a fitful night's sleep, MacShane was awakened at 05:30 by the O.D., giving him an hour to get ready. By 06:20, MacShane was out front in his beige cargo shorts, a red Florida Panthers t-shirt under an open tropical printed shirt with surfboards and old cars on it, a beat-up pair of deck shoes and a battered Shirttail Charlie's baseball hat that he borrowed from T.C. The full beard just added to the overall character. MacShane thought about wearing his Reef Runner flip-flops but didn't want to appear too impertinent. If the General wanted him then this is what he was going to get. Sergeant Moss pulled up exactly at 06:30. Stepped out of the car, and walked around to open the door for MacShane. "I did tell you that you were to meet the General for breakfast this morning?" the Sergeant asked.

"Yes Sergeant, you told me. I was asked to leave at short notice and this is what you get." answered Mac.

"Yes sir, but it's not me you're meeting for breakfast." was all the Sergeant said. He couldn't believe that this man was going to have a meeting with one of the Army's most important Generals at the Pentagon dressed like a beach bum. But it wasn't his business.

The car pulled up to the front door of the Watergate Hotel, and a doorman opened the rear passenger door and let MacShane out. The look on his face was priceless, and MacShane was playing it to the hilt. "Ya Mon! Do tell me where the breakfast buffet is, don' cha know!" said MacShane in a Caribbean accent he was working on with Bonbon.

The doorman, having worked in Washington for many years just pointed to the front door, not letting this crazy person get to him. Once he was inside the front door, he would be someone else's problem. Don't worry, be happy!

MacShane found his way to the dining room and immediately spotted General Kane sitting with Major Anthony Chandler and approached the table. "Good God Morgan! What the Hell you dressed up for?" said Kane as he stands to greet MacShane.

"I'm retired, remember? This is how retired people are supposed to dress. Nowhere to go, nothing to do, you know every day's a Saturday," answered MacShane as he shook the men's hands and sat down. Chandler was still having a problem with Morgan's attire judging by the look on his face.

"Morgan, I know this is a bit out of the ordinary but Tony and I have a plan, and we need you. I really want to have you, shall we say, volunteer, but if need be, I can re-activate your status under the heading of national security, and you'll be forced back into active duty without any say-so. It's up to you." The general wasn't pulling any punches and laid it right out on the table. He knew Morgan well enough to know that a meeting in a public place such as this one would keep MacShane from blowing his lid. No matter how MacShane felt internally, he would keep it sequestered until they were alone. MacShane had too much respect for General Andrew Kane to cause a scene in public and the General was counting on that.

MacShane sat there, not saying a word. His eyes were telling the whole story, shooting daggers hell. MacShane's eyes were launching nuclear warheads. A waitress came up with a cheery smile and asked if he would care for breakfast; MacShane just barks, "Coffee!"

"Relax Mac, have something to eat, make ya feel better," threw in Chandler.

"Only thing goin' make me feel better is getting on a plane and climbing back aboard my ship." MacShane surprised even himself with that remark.

"And that's exactly where you're going to go. Back on board your ship," said Kane.

Morgan wasn't sure how to take this bullshit he was hearing. "You sent Crawford out to drag me up here to have breakfast and then you tell me you're going to put me back on board my ship. But only after I 'volunteer' for one of your missions," said MacShane drinking his coffee.

"More or less, can't talk too much about it here. How about we head over to the General's office and give you the full layout?" asked Chandler, with Kane sitting next to him nodding his head, indicating to MacShane that a no answer wasn't in the equation.

Chapter 14

At the Pentagon, the three men walked up to the security gate where General Kane vouched for MacShane and were issued I.D. tags. But not before MacShane drew some heavy-duty stares from the M.P., Kane opened his office door and flipped on the lights, closing and locking the door behind him. "Sit down Mac; you're going to have to see this one for yourself."

Mac did as instructed and Chandler and Kane laid out the recon photos that were recently taken with the U-2 flyover. There on the makeshift docks were freighters from all different nations, loading and unloading cargo. "That Mac is what we need you for. We need you and your vessel to transport a special forces outfit into Cuban waters and get them close enough to see exactly what is going on. Your vessel is the perfect cover for this operation. The size, configuration and condition of the Sequoia will make it a breeze to slide in under their radar and to let the Special Ops guys do their thing."

Kane and Chandler let Morgan study the photos for a few minutes and then broached the question again. "So Mac, do you volunteer, or do we have to draft you and commandeer your vessel?" asked Kane.

General Kane could see that the mention of commandeering the Sequoia really grabbed Morgan's attention. "You What? How can you do that? That's private property," protests MacShane.

"Simple Mac. Your partner T.C. Allen? When he registered your ship, he filled out documentation papers, which gave him a reduction on his insurance. However, there is a clause that if for a national emergency or in time of war the United Stated Government can commandeer a documented vessel and use it as the Government sees fit. And in this case, I'm the Government and I see fit to use your vessel."

MacShane knew his back was up against the wall and was being given very little choice. It was either sign-on for whatever these two had planned, or Kane was going to take the Sequoia anyway.

"All I wanted to do was retire, relax, hunt for buried treasure, goof off for once in my life. Just when I get a taste of what it's like on the outside you come along with a plan that has to have me involved. Not somebody else, ME! Well General, this flat-out Sucks! And what of the rest of the crew? We push them overboard so no one's left to tell the tale? God Damn!" Mac was letting it out now, everything that was holding back in the hotel dining room.

"So? You in?" asked Kane.

"So? I have a choice? Yes, I'm in. How long will this take?" MacShane was coming to grips with the ordeal and was starting to gather up his composure.

"We start the briefing now," said General Kane unrolling a navigation chart on top of the recon photos. Not wanting to delay this any longer than needed, Kane reached into his inside jacket pocket and retrieved a silver collapsible pointer. He extended the shiny instrument and started by smacking the tip of the pointer down on the island of New Providence, Bahamas. "You catch a plane to Nassau and get the Sequoia to Fort Jefferson, in the Dry Tortugas ASAP." Kane moves the pointer across the chart as if following a preset course. "Fort Jefferson will be closed to all visitors; we have a press release going out saying the Fort is in dire need of repair from all the boat and tourist traffic through the National Park. And while closed, the Fish and Game Division is going to use that time to do a survey of the reefs surrounding the facility. You know some environmental bullshit to keep the public out of the way. At Fort Jefferson you meet up with the U.S. Coast Guard cutter Thetis. Our Special Ops team will transfer form the Thetis to the Sequoia at Fort Jefferson. The Thetis will act as your support vessel on this mission, she's stationed out of Key West and is usually seen in this area on normal patrol, so her presence won't be out of the ordinary. After the crew and supplies are transported onboard, your vessel will leave the area and take a course out of Fort Jefferson heading West South

West towards the Yucatan Channel staying as far from the regular shipping lanes as possible, having no contact with any other vessels in that area, including cruise ships." This area is heavily traveled by most of the cruise ships going to Cancun and Grand Cayman. This was going to be a tough chore.

The General moved his pointer to the island of Grand Cayman and continued on. "You will no doubt be needing fuel at this point. Head to George Town, Grand Cayman and take on fuel at the local dock. Tell them you just came through the Panama Canal and are running on fumes, which will probably be the truth. If they ask where your headed be vague, if they push for an answer drop the line that you're a freelance freighter crew and go where the money is. See if any one approaches you about moving any cargo. We have reason to believe that the Cuban government has a few spies working the docks in George Town, since most ships use those docks after coming out of Panama. The South American ports are too unstable and corrupt for most Gringos to use, so most captains push the limits and head to Grand Cayman, much safer."

MacShane was taking this all in and was starting to formulate some questioned. "Excuse me General, but how did the Coast Guard get involved with all this and what kind of support can they provide? Rescuing overboard weekend warriors and looking for missing fishing boats isn't my idea of support."

Answering the question Kane cut his eyes at MacShane saying, "The Coast Guard was requested to assist in this operation under the Homeland Security Bill. And as far as providing support, the Thetis is a 270-foot cutter with twin 3650 horsepower ALCO 18-cylinder turbocharged diesel engines that can probably go twice as fast as that tub you'll be cruising in."

MacShane impressed with the general's knowledge still wasn't feeling sure this was the best support Kane could come up with and continued to initiate questioned. "That's great, what are they going to do when they find us, give everyone mouth to mouth? Where's the Navy in all this?"

Kane was starting to lose his patience with MacShane but he continued on with the briefing, after all a man has a right to know the facts if his ass is on the line. "The Navy's out. You know we can't deploy a warship in Cuban waters, it would start an international incident that this administration doesn't want nor need at this time. The Coast Guard on the other hand is seen internationally as a search and rescue operation, helping people in life and death situations."

MacShane immediately shot back, "Yeah, hopefully helping people like us."

Kane continued ignoring the comment, "What you and most of the world isn't aware of is that the Thetis is equipped with a computer aimed and operated MK-75, 76-millimeter gun battery used for surface and air targets, and two mounted .50 caliber Browning machine guns. Also, in the armory are two SRBOC launchers. The Super Rapid Blooming Offboard Chaff is effective for deflecting incoming missiles by creating a false return on the missile's radar, and the usual small arms for the crew. And that's just the ship without the helo."

MacShane started to relax a bit and said, "Thanks General I'm sleeping better already." As the General went on to explain the finishing touches to his speech.

"As I was about to say. The helo is the main part of your support because what you also don't know is that this helo belongs to the newly formed unit called the Helicopter Interdiction Tactical Squadron which was commissioned just last May. These boys are equipped with .50 caliber precision rifles and M-240 machine guns, and are the only airborne law enforcement unit trained and authorized to fire at targets from their helo. This will be your life raft if anything goes wrong."

MacShane's respect for the Coasties had just jumped quite a few notches and was letting this new admiration sink in.

Kane continued on, "After fueling in Grand Cayman continue on to the Zapata Peninsula and motor into Cayo Matahmbre, this is where our intel has the dock facility you will be investigating. And that's an order, investigating ONLY! No hero stuff, no demolition, investigate and report, and get back to the Cutter, nothing else. Is that clear Colonel?"

"Yes sir! Crystal sir. How about the Special Ops people? They getting the same lecture?" asked MacShane referring to the wonderful rep that Special Ops have.

"You leave that to me; your job is to get them there and return them to the Thetis with the intel. And maybe cut a deal while you're there to transport some arms to a terrorist cell somewhere," added Kane with a wink and the closest thing the General could come to a smile.

MacShane sat there studying the chart and asked, "You want us to try to make a deal we're going to need some serious cash. Can you afford to bank role a project like that?"

Kane looks at Mac and said, "You get that tub there and leave the finances to me. Whatever you need will be loaded onboard your vessel from the Thetis. Now Colonel is there any further questions?" asked Kane as he proceeded to roll up the nav chart and stow it in a cardboard tube.

"Just one more General," said MacShane, "once at the docks and if by some freak chance things start to go south, how much assistance can we expect to get from Gitmo?" Really knowing the answer even before he asked it, but had to ask anyway.

General Kane's answer came in the form of a Bahamas Airplane ticket that he took out of his top desk draw. Handing it to MacShane his only words were, "Here's your ticket to Nassau, Chandler will drop you off in front of the Peabody Hotel, grab a cab to Dulles airport, your plane leaves at 1:40, good luck Mac." With that said Kane stood up shook MacShane's hand and gave him a salute, then handed Mac the photos and the navigation chart. Mac followed Major Chandler out the door for the long walk to the parking area.

Chapter 15

As MacShane left the Pentagon a light rain started to fall, ah, summer in the south. The warm rain was just hard enough to get his overshirt wet before reaching Chandler's car. "This is great! I love flying in wet clothes," complains Morgan as he took off his Ray-Ban sunglasses and looked around the car for something dry to clean them with.

"In the glove box," said Chandler. "There's some paper napkins inside."

"Thanks Major. So, what do you think our chances are?" asked Morgan.

"I'm not paid to think and I like it that way," answered Chandler. Morgan started to wipe off his lenses and after a minute rephrased his question to Chandler.

"You a betting man Major?" probes MacShane.

"Been known to lay down a wager here and there, what d'ya have in mind?" questioned Chandler.

"Odds on the mission," stated MacShane.

"With the crew, you've got going... 20 to 1. No offence," replied Chandler.

"Non taken, 20 to 1... I'll take some action on that Major. Got a crisp new Ben Franklin in my wallet doing a whole lot of nothin'. Think it's time to put that sucker to work."

The car was pulling up in front of the Peabody and MacShane was digging for his wallet. "Well Major you in? I'll even let you hold the money till we get back. You know, just in case," he said with a grimace. MacShane opened his wallet and held the new bill out for Chandler to see.

"That's two grand if you get back." Chandler was hesitant.

"Yea but it's a real nice dinner if I don't," responded MacShane.

"I hate to jinx your mission... but I'm in." Chandler took the hundred and stuffed it into his shirt pocket. "Good luck Mac, I mean it."

"With a two thousand buck bonus waiting for me when I get back, now that's an incentive. See if you can get the General to back you, I would really love to take his money over yours," said MacShane grabbing his gear. He was out the door before Chandler could answer. As Chandler drove away, he looked in his rearview mirror and saw MacShane entering a cab, the mission was under way.

MacShane entered the taxi and gave the cabbie directions. As Mac's taxi pulled out into the street a traffic jam was starting. "How long to the airport, I've got a plane to catch?" asked MacShane.

"Sit back and relax pal, we have to get around this crash up ahead," answered the driver in an unmistakable New York accent.

This guy was a real traffic jockey, wildly spinning the necker knob on the steering wheel he had the cab out and around the accident in no time, pushing his way into places the car didn't look like it would fit. As he wheeled the cab past the accident MacShane failed to notice that the car sandwiched up against the utility pole and a delivery van was the one he had just climbed out of. There sat Major Anthony Chandler slouched over the steering wheel, airbag draped in his lap. Concerned about the tight flight schedule, MacShane averted his eyes from the wreck as he adjusted and organized his belongings making sure that all the paperwork the General had just given him was secure. Weaving in and out of the Gawd awful traffic MacShane hoped his mission had a safer rating then surviving a Washington D.C. commute.

He arrived at the airport with no time to spare. Walking at a trot to the Bahamas Air counter MacShane flashed a large toothy smile at the cute Bahamian girl behind the workstation as he passed her his ticket. "No time for the grinnin' boy, de plane jus bout t'ru boardin'! Hirry up now and git yur bottom down de concourse to gate tree!" Her sing-song voice seemed annoyed yet humorous to MacShane as he hot-stepped it by the posters showing all the beautiful people on the beaches, and he thought 'Welcome to the Bahamas, give us all your money, now leave.'

MacShane made it on board right before the flight crew was closing the 737's door. Inside the plane, Morgan in his elegant attire, was getting some of the usual stares that he now was becoming accustomed to. Stowing his carry-on in the overhead and ignoring the harsh looks of his fellow passengers he proceeded to an empty row and stretched out on all three seats. Sitting there in the half-full plane, filling out the Bahamian Immigration card MacShane came to the question of occupation and hesitated, at first thought he wanted to write in 'Shanghaied, sorry assed Mother Fucker' but he didn't think the Immigration Officials would appreciate the humor, so he just answered 'retired' and left it at that if they only knew the truth he thought. Finished with the card MacShane closed his eyes and pretended to fall asleep, not wanting to have to make any small talk with the civilians.

The flight was smooth and arrived on schedule. As soon as the plane came to a stop Morgan was up grabbing his bag and started towards the door, stepping and ducking around all the happy tourists. Off the jet MacShane headed to Bahamian Immigrations, he handed the uniformed young man his paperwork and waited to be waved through. Unfortunately for MacShane this young man felt like chatting. "Welcome to our home mistah Mac Shane 'ow long will you be stayin' with us?"

"A few days maybe a week. Depends if the fishing is good," answered MacShane as he gives the young officer the once over.

The man's light blue shirt and dark blue pants were perfectly pressed and despite the heat and humidity, the creases in the shirt sleeves were still crisp. His white hat was flawless not a speck of dirt nor a smudge on the shiny black brim of the officer's topper.

"Fishin' good this time of year, I see you retired maybe you can stay longer? By the way Mistah MacShane where are you stayin' I noticed that you left that question blank," said Spiffy.

"Haven't decided yet Simon, figured it's the middle of June shouldn't be too busy, I'll look around and find something, I'm sure," answered MacShane, using the young man's name listed on his I.D. Badge, trying to hide his frustration.

"Not so, mistah. Dis is Goombay Festival, big party every night, de 'otels mostly full," added the officer.

"I'm sure I'll find something; they usually always have a cancellation or two," said

MacShane, not trying to make a big deal out of it.

"Well, if you can't find some-ting you come back and find me. Me sister works in a 'otel we try to get you set up. Ok. Mistah," said the young man trying extra hard to please the tourists.

"Very well Simon, I'll do that." MacShane was about to say anything just to get the hell out of there.

"Enjoy 'ur stay Mistah MacShane," voices the officer in the same sing-song tone as the counter girl in D.C.

MacShane put his papers back in his carry on as he was under full steam headed outside looking for a cab. As he stepped out of the terminal a large old white Cadillac was parked in front, the black overweight fifty-something driver was arguing with a group of men about some soccer game. "You for hire?" interrupted Macshane still looking for an alternate ride.

"Yes sir! Names Washington where to capt'n?" answered the driver.

"East Bay Street Docks down by Brown's Boat Basin," replied Morgan.

"Not much going on down dere capt'n, how about I let you out at de Straw Market? Lots o' pretty tings dere," suggested Washington trying to be helpful.

"No thanks, just take me where I asked for," shot back Morgan. His tolerance for native hospitality was getting extremely low.

"Climb in capt'n. You buyin' I'm drivin'," quipped Washington waving to his buddies as the old car left the terminal and started down John F. Kennedy Drive headed towards old town Nassau.

Morgan was taking in the four-lane palm tree-lined road and was noticing what a far cry it was from the super highways he had just left.

"Stayin' long capt'n?" inquired Washington, trying to make small talk.

"Maybe a week or so." Never knowing who's related to whom on these islands MacShane decided to stick to his story.

"Here by yourself capt'n?" Washington keeps it up.

"Yeap, all by myself. Going fishing and I couldn't get anyone to come with me." MacShane was growing weary of all this small talk. He was now in a mission mode and all he wanted to do was get it started. The car finally was going through the old section of Nassau. Passing a Butler and Sands liquor store Washington pointed out. "Capt'n dats de place for all your rums. Cheaper then anywhere's else. You let them know dat Washington sent you .Ok." this guy was working every angle.

"Almost dere capt'n remember if you need anyting, you know a good boat to fish on or some woman to go to dinner with you remember to call Washington. Dis is my Island and every one know Washington." MacShane sat back, elated that his ride was almost over.

The old Cadillac turned onto East Bay Street stopping in front of a chained link fence with a hand-painted wooden sign stating 'Browns Boat Basin.' "Dis it capt'n, you sure you want out here, not much going on, just like I tolds you," said Washington pointing out the obvious.

"Thanks Washington this is fine, I'm just going to walk around for a while, take in some sights and get some air. How much I owe you?" MacShane was trying to blow him off as soon as possible. He couldn't help but flashback to the cab ride that started this whole boondoggle. Note to self, stay away from cab rides.

"Twenty-five dollars capt'n. You wants me to come back and pick you up. Not much to see 'round here, 'cept for that old freighter." MacShane having a deja vu moment of a cab ride that started this whole mess. "You wants to see some nice yachts let me know. Here's my card you call any time" Once you rode with Washington, he considered you a customer for life and would do whatever it takes to keep you. And God help the rookie driver who tried to steal his fare.

"Yea, thanks Washington, here's thirty I'll give you a call if I need you. See you later."

MacShane was attempting to keep up appearances and not piss off the locals. Don't need them standing around talking about the asshole tourist that was dropped off downtown. Everything ends up becoming big news on small Islands.

MacShane slung his tan leather bag over his shoulder and started walking down the street as Washington drove away. As soon as the Cadillac turned the corner MacShane waited a few minutes to make sure his new best friend had really left and just wasn't circling the block. Feeling confident Washington was out of the picture MacSahne turned around and headed for Brown's dock master's shack out on the pier. The boat yard was perfect for the Sequoia, old boats of all sizes were up on blocks in all different stages of repair littering the yard. MacShane entered the small shack and was overwhelmed by the noisy window air conditioning unit and the loud radio.

"Excuse me," MacShane addresses the old black man behind the counter. He was filling out some paperwork and put his greasy index finger up in the air as if to say one minute. MacShane looked around the inside of the dirty office and rested his elbow on the counter. About 150 feet separated him from the Sequoia. 'So close but yet so far,' MacShane told himself, feeling a strong desire to get back on board his ship. "Excuse me, sir," MacShane reiterated after a few more minutes.

The old man looked up and replied, "What kin I do for you boy?"

"I'm due back on board the Sequoia and need to check in," stated MacShane.

"Check in? Boy dis ain't the Ritz Carlton ya kno'. Walk on down and climb aboard, we 'ave no bellman here so ya 'ave to carry your own bag." The old man waved MacShane off and went back to filing out his papers.

"Nice security you have here. Thanks." MacShane turned and walked out of the office and down to the ship. She was a sight for sore eyes, and the closer he got the faster he walked. His gait was at its maximum as he bounded up the gangplank. "Damn! That friggin' alarm," thought Morgan as he heard it going off. Stepping onto the deck Morgan saw Drake come pouncing out of the hatch wielding a Remington1100 semi-automatic 12-gauge riot gun. The nickel finish reflecting the bright daylight. "Holy shit, Mac! Damn! It's good to see you! What the hell happened? What's going on?" Drake's friendly big smile was a welcomed relief for Morgan. "Nice shotgun Drake," commented Morgan. "Where the hell is everyone?"

"In town, it's my watch. You got nice timing Mac, I go below for a few minutes to take a leak and you try to commandeer the vessel," said Drake laughing.

"You're righter than you know," Morgan said under his breath. "Drake this is extremely important. I need you to go into town and find the crew. Do you know where they went?"

Drake sensing the urgency of Morgan's questioning and spoke, "Yea, T.C. and Holly went to the Green Shutters Pub for a burger and Spider went to gamble somewhere an' I don't have a clue where Bonbon got off to."

"You know where this pub is?" asked Morgan.

"Sure!" answered Drake.

"Good, hand me that shotgun and get your ass over there as fast as you can. I'll explain when everyone gets back. By the way, did you take on fuel yet?"

"Yea we're slammed full; I always make sure we fill up when we arrive," Drake told MacShane as he handed him the shotgun. "Safety's on and you're loaded with five rounds of triple ought buck, no sense fuckin' around when it comes to security."

"I agree wholeheartedly my friend. Now find them and get back here as soon as you can."

MacShane reset the boarding alarm and went inside to the same beautiful dining room table that started the treasure-hunting adventure and prepared to make a sales job of his own. Laying out the charts and photos the General gave him, MacShane began working on his speech to the crew.

Thirty minutes later the alarm blares its obnoxious sound. Morgan grabs the shotgun and looks out the porthole, he sees T.C., Holly, and Drake walking across the deck and shuts down the alarm. "Up here, in the dining room," MacShane yelled out the open port. The three crew members entered the wood-paneled dining room and gathered around the table gazing at the display laid out in front of them with puzzled demeanor. T.C. was the first to speak, "What the hell is so important that I couldn't finish my burger and pint of Guinness."

"Nice to see all of you too," started Morgan sarcastically. "I've got these papers laid out on the table and we need to go over them, come on," announced Morgan.

The group ambled about for a moment and started pushing the papers around the table not knowing what they were looking at, until Morgan had enough and took control of his meeting. "Sit down and I'll start the briefing." Morgan was already into his role as mission commander.

"Briefing! You're joking!" remarked Holly.

"What gives Mac? What the hell is going on?" stated T.C.

"I'm going to give it to you down and dirty, you know General Kane had me picked up and flown to Washington. There he showed me recon photos of some sort of a suspected free trade zone Castro has set up on the south side of Cuba for terrorists to sell and trade all kinds of weapons." MacShane paused for this information to set in, and then went on. "The only problem is that the tropical foliage makes it hard to determine exactly what is taking place, as you can see from these pictures."

"Man, they have a lot of nerve!" injects Holly.

"Damn Mac! You're retired what the hell does he want you to do about this?" asked T.C.

MacShane looked at each of them as he continued his briefing. "Me? You should rephrase that as US!" MacShane wished he had had a camera to capture the looks on his shipmates' faces as the bomb dropped. A turd in the punch bowl would have been a more welcomed guest. Mac continued, "He wants us to go to Cuba, get into the dock and give it a look-see, and even try to pick up some weapons for transport if possible."

"Us! What the fuck! Us! He can't mean that. We're private citizens BULLSHIT!" T.C. was the most upset Morgan had ever seen him. The king of low-key was now blowing a gasket.

MacShane proceeds on, "You can thank yourself for this one T-bone. Whose idea was it to get this vessel documented anyway?"

T.C.'s face was a shade of fuscia that Morgan had never seen before. If it wasn't for such an important mission Morgan would have enjoyed this response. "My insurance agent! It was his bright idea. Said we would save *'all kinds'* of money on the coverage and the government *'never'* calls the vessel into service. He said everyone with a large boat does this."

"Well, you can drop him a line when we get back and tell him he's full of shit," said Morgan.

"T.C. what the hell is going on here? What does all this mean?" asked Holly sitting next to Drake who was just hanging his head and shaking it back and forth.

Morgan answered Holly's question by saying, "Miss Holly we've been drafted!" the look on Holly's face let Morgan know she couldn't believe what was going on, so he continued. "Once Captain Chaos over here filled out the papers to document this vessel it meant that the government could exercise a clause in the documentation, commandeering the vessel and putting it to work for them whenever they see fit. And with the new Patriot Act, they can reactivate T.C. and myself. Which just so happens to be the case we have here. T.C. more so under the Homeland Defense Bill, his captain's license is issued by the Coast Guard which is now directly under Homeland Security and printed right on the front of his happy little paper it reads 'issued to Merchant Marine Officer Thomas Chaddon Allen..." MacShane paused for effect and then dryly added, "As I said we've been drafted."

"BULLSHIT!" yelled Holly.

"Must be the word of the day around here," spoke Drake commenting on Holly's continued use of the colorful metaphor. "So where does that leave us Mac?"

"The General gave us ordered to get underway as soon as possible, and leave whoever couldn't be reached immediately, sucks to be Spider, however; we will desperately need an engineer, you don't know any that might want to volunteer do you Drake?" queried Morgan.

"Volunteer, you couldn't get me off this ship. Where ever the Sequoia goes so does Drake. NOBODY touches my engines. Nobody!"

MacShane looked at Holly who was still sitting there in disbelief. "Sorry darling but the treasure hunting will have to wait until we get back. Now get your things and we'll get a cab to take you to the airport."

"Don't think so Mac, my names on that paperwork also, and if this ship goes anywhere, I'm going with it!" said Holly quite sternly.

"No way man, T.C. get her off of here. We can't afford to have her around to fuck up the mission. Start getting her packed." Mac was commencing to lay down the law.

"Sorry Mac, she stays. The Feds want the Sequoia then they get the whole package or we don't move." T.C. was pushing his hand.

Mac knew he couldn't beat both of them so instead of starting a screaming match he silently coincided. MacShane wanted to do the rest of the briefing once they got underway but he decided that since everyone was here, he would continue and lay out the whole enchilada. "I wanted to wait on this part but since we're all here and all going, we might as well get it over with. We are meeting up with a special ops group in the Dry Tortugas. From there we travel to Grand Cayman and then to Cuba. Holly, this could become extremely dangerous and you would be better off back in the Stated."

Mac tries one more time to reason with Holly but to no avail, when the redhead has her mind made up there's no turning back. Mac would have had an easier time trying to have a period than getting Holly off the ship.

"Tough Mac, I'm not leaving. How hard can this be, cruise into Cuba take a look around, and split, right? Besides having a woman on board might throw off any suspicion as to our legitimacy." Holly was making her stance known. But for insurance added, "And besides you never know who in the press I just might happen to run into and share a bizarre story with."

MacShane was feeling the tension of not having full control and he wasn't liking it. "We'll take you as far as the Dry Tortugas. From there it's up to the Special ops people."

"Good call Mac," said Holly, giving him a shit-eating grin.

MacShane finished his briefing without further incident, and afterwards the crew went to their designated stations.

Chapter 16

Drake had the big twin diesel engines fired up and running strong, "Make ready to cast off the lines." ordered T.C. from the bridge. In the ship's log he entered 17:34, the time the engines were started along with the names of all crew members making this trip, weather conditions, and any other interesting facts T.C. could muster, if for nothing else then to make for some interesting reading for when he gets old and gray.

Drake was now on the stern and MacShane was on the bow, each man ready to handle the mooring lines at the captain's command. The Sequoia was tied up starboard side with an intense six-knot current running under her keel. MacShane and Drake already had the spring lines hauled in and were awaiting further instruction from T.C.

"We have a strong stern to current so we're going to release the bow line first." T.C. was barking ordered from the bridge window. "Ready Mac, release the bow."

MacShane motioned to the dock hand to release the line from the mooring bollard. As the heavy rope dangled from the bow of the ship MacShane started hoisting up the line hand over hand, yelling up to the bridge, "Bow clear!"

T.C. then gave a prolong and then three short blasts of the signaling horn indicating he was backing the ship down. Slipping the throttles into reverse T.C. gave the Sequoia slight astern propulsion to release some of the tension on the taught stern line, then barked an order to Drake in the aft "Drake, release the stern line."

The stern line was released and the Sequoia was free of her constrains. T.C. positioned the starboard engine in forward gear, the port engine in reverse, gave a single prolonged blast of the horn, and headed the old tub gently away from the dilapidated cement dock, moving out into the channel. Once totally clear of the dock T.C. smoothly engaged the port engine in forward and the Sequoia was on her way.

Mac was almost finished pulling in the last of the bow line when he turned so he was looking aft of the ship. There he noticed a Twin-engine Grumman Otter seaplane flying in for a water landing under the Paradise Island Bridge in route to the seaplane heliport terminal just to the east of Casuarina Beach. The plane's amphibious bottom smoothly cut into the calm blue water, spray, and foam shot away from the plane's hull as it slowed and gently lowered its full weight into the warm Bahamian water. At that particular moment, Mac's mind drifted, and he promised himself that when he gets through with this mission and if they did find any treasure, he was going to take flying lessons so he could set his own schedule and come and go as he pleased.

After fresh water washing the lines and stowing them on the deck to dry Mac and Drake came up to the bridge.

"Hope Spider and Bonbon get that letter you left for them. Man are they going to be pissed!" said Drake referring to the letter MacShane left at the dockmaster's office for the two missing crew members. The letter, explaining the situation without going into too much detail was the least they could do for the stranded pair.

"Pissed? Spider said he had a month off. Who would get pissed at being left abandoned in the Bahamas, I can sure think of a lot worse places," said MacShane.

"Yeah! Like where we're going!" shot back T.C. brusquely.

"Don't start!" said Mac as he cuts his eyes towards T.C.

"Spider's not going to be mad about being stuck in Nassau, he's going to be pissed beyond belief that we have all his dive gear," added Drake half ass smiling.

"Better here than with that pirate in the dockmaster's office, at least with us he's got a chance of seeing it again," remarked MacShane." Is the course laid in?" changing the subject.

"Yeah, we're all set. Autopilot is set to engage as soon as were pass the sea buoys. Autopilot is nice but we still need someone to keep watch in the wheelhouse," stated T.C.

"I'll take the first watch," offered MacShane. "Why don't you two get something to eat and grab some sleep? What's our ETA?"

"24-30 hours depending on sea conditions. From the last report, NOAA issued we should have some smooth sailing. I got the VFH standing by on channel 16 and the radar is on so you're all set," said T.C. giving Morgan a quick tour of the operating equipment. "Holly was making some sandwiches; I'll have her bring you one. See ya in six hours." Morgan was getting situated into his watch, giving the instruments and dials the once over every few minutes, checking the radar every so often and making sure the auto-pilot was on course.

Standing a watch at sea is one of the loneliest, seemingly unproductive ways to spend one's time. For a person like Morgan who normally doesn't like to sit still for too long, the passing of time feels like an eternity. Morgan looked around the wheelhouse and found an empty black-and-white composition notebook and then he started to jot down some notes. Mac was on page three when Holly came up to the bridge with two roast beef sandwiches and a hot mug of coffee. Morgan put the notebook down and reached for the plate and mug.

"Thanks Holly I sure can use this, but maybe I should have someone taste it for me first," said MacShane with a chuckle. Alluding to their last encounter.

"Yea you go and find someone, Drake and T.C. already turned in. Left me with the dishes again. Whad'ya writtin'?" asked Holly referring to MacShane's notebook.

"Keeping a journal of this whole thing, call it my stress management class. You know how on watch some guys stare out the windows and dream, while others listen to music and still others keep asking themselves, how by some small insignificant turn they made one day, and each man will be able to tell you exactly when it occurred, they might not remember the exact date but they will know the time of day and the situation that we're involved in, that if they made a left turn instead of taking a right, what might have happened. Thinking about the smallest of things that lead them to be on a ship in the middle of a huge unforgiving ocean, wondering how they got into a position to be one of the only crew members awake, responsible for the entire safety of the ship and all aboard her. And how this is going to be their last voyage away from home, that when it's over they are *really* going to take that 9-5er job where everyone dresses the same, doing the company shuffle, going through the paces until one day the front office sends for you and told you they're going to give you that gold watch you were looking forward to for so long. But now you realize the only thing that watch is good for is to remind you it's time to take your blood pressure pill or your hypertension pill or god knows whatever type of pill some Doctor could come up with. Damn Holly by the time your done working so is your pecker." Mac's philosophical views were getting way too deep into waters Holly didn't want to tread so she thought she would try to lighten the atmosphere.

"You know Mac they even have pills for that problem," acknowledges Holly.

"WHAT! HELL NO! I don't have a problem like THAT!" said MacShane indignantly. "I'm just taking a view of how people sometimes don't really know what they want, usually not until they had it and lost it. I'm saying I could never be one of those clock punchers going to the same place seeing the same faces every day for thirty years. I don't know how people do it?"

"It's called working for a living Mac. 90% of the population does it," answered Holly.

MacShane was pounding down a sandwich and chasing it with the hot coffee between his philosophical ranted. Holly continued. "Ya know Mac, not everyone could say they accomplished as much as you have in your life. Nam, Dominican Republic, Panama, and who knows where or what else you've done. A life of unforgettable experiences, I'm sure some were great and others that must come back and haunt you. Many a night I've been awakened by T.C. yelling and thrashing about in bed, waking up in a cold sweat, screaming for the ghosts in his head to take cover from incoming enemy rounds. He won't talk about that stuff much and I don't push it."

Holly was doing some soul-searching of her own. Mac listened and shook his head, gesturing that he understood what she must go through on those dreadful nights. Now it was MacShane's turn to lighten the conversation. "And that's what the journal is for. I figured as long as I have all this alone time I might as well document what I can remember of my life's history, especially now with this new crazy shit thrown into the mix, there's got to be a book or movie deal in here somewhere," said MacShane pointing to the temple of his bald head with his index finger, twisting it back and forth.

"Well, novelist MacShane if there is, you make sure you get someone beautiful to play my part," teased Holly.

"Wouldn't have it any other way, my dear," answered MacShane as he handed Holly the empty plate and mug. "Thanks that was great! Why don't you get some rest yourself it's going to be an interesting few days."

"No thanks Mac. Think I might stay up a bit longer, go up forward and read awhile. See you in the morning. Good night."

"Night Holly." Mac felt that he gained a whole lot of ground with Holly tonight and got a new insight into what made her tick.

Alone again Mac light up a Davidoff vintage 2000 panetela. After a few draws on the stogie Mac was enjoying the woody, wheat nuances of the big stick, managing to write a few more pages in his journal while keeping an eye on the business at hand.

At one point an old small coastal oiler tanker came within a quarter of a mile of the Sequoia.

MacShane using the binoculars, managed to get the name of the vessel from the lighted stern of the ship and logged it in, as well as the time, position, and estimated course of said vessel into the Sequoia's log book. "Hey, ya never know," thought MacShane to himself.

The rest of the watch was pretty uneventful, logging in the GPS way points, entering the estimated speed and fuel consumption, sea conditions, and weather. All basic seamanship paperwork, however, even the smallest of duties are a welcomed relief when there's not much else to do.

At 23:15 Drake walked into the wheelhouse eating a sandwich and drinking a Diet Coke. Mumbling a "How's going?" through a mouth full of sandwich.

"Glad to see you're on time. Man, I could use a break," said MacShane as he rubs the back of his neck, rolling his head from side to side. MacShane started to give Drake the rundown of his shift and what he should expect. "Everything status quo, all gauges within safety margins, weather clouding up a bit, may get some rain before your watch is through. You check the engine room yet?"

Drake still with a mouth full of sandwich nodded his head and swallowed. "Checked it just before I made this sandwich. Everything appears to be in order. No leaks, no fuel smell, everything down there was jake."

"Glad to hear that, I can't wait to turn in," said Mac obviously fatigued."

"Night Drake see you in the a.m. I stand relieved." MacShane exited the wheelhouse and headed towards his bunk.

Chapter 17

Drake was making himself comfortable as he adjusted the captain's chair, putting his feet up on the bridge console, stretching out his legs, and listening to a favorite collection of classical music. His thoughts were bouncing back and forth from how much he loved being on the sea to when or if he was ever going to settle down. Meet that one special girl, the one you'll change your whole life for. So far Drake didn't have any prospects, only a vision of who she was and that was an image he held inside his mind's eye, unable to share it with anyone, one day.

"I'll turn a corner and there she'll be," said Drake out loud to the empty wheelhouse. Drake turned his head and was looking out the window as the ebony sea laid before him. The moon gives the water a kind of surreal effect, with shiny slivers of light resembling shaved silver flecks, undulating on top of the pitch-black water, giving the appearance of a million eyes winking open and shut. "The gods are watching over us," commented Drake as he lifts up his diet coke in a sort of celebratory toast to those ever-watching eyes. "Guard us well, heaven knows we're going to need it."

An hour later Drake got up to peruse the instruments and stretch his legs. He stepped out onto the bridge wing to take in the weather change. The steamy tropical night was a vast difference from the air-conditioned comfort of the wheelhouse. Drake took a deep breath of the ozone-charged air that usually precedes a storm, giving him an invigorating feeling deep inside his body.

Cloud cover had moved in blocking the Moon and it's Devine guiding light. Now everything was the same drab dark gray; the horizon vanished, the ocean undistinguishable from the sky. The tepid light mist that was falling was now giving way to a steadier stream of water. Drake felt the warm liquid envelope his body and it felt good. He was actually becoming a living part of the whole environment. The feeling of wind, rain, and sea lead Drake to a revelation, to experience a sense of being he had never felt before. Drake was now feeling complete inner peace, totally accepted into the bosom of Mother Earth.

Drake's enlightenment trance ended when he felt the sea beneath him start to rise. In the distance, he heard the faint clap of thunder and the sky filled with the streaks of lighting. Covering the heavens reminiscent of the veins on the back of an old woman's hand. The wind was now picking up to a steady force of about twenty-five miles per hour, with stronger gusts thrown in for fun. The Sequoia was starting to heave with the rising swells. Drake was back in the wheelhouse drying himself with a roll of paper towels he found stuffed between the windshield and the dash.

The waves were now starting to increase, the autopilot would have to be taken off, and Drake would have to handle the vessel himself. In the diminished ambient light, trying to read the waves was extremely difficult indeed, it was more of an attempt to establish the rhythm of the waves and stick with it. By quartering the large waves, Drake was able to gently guide the ship up the front face of the wave, push her over the top and effortlessly glide down the back side. The Sequoia was now getting into some heavy seas. Drake reached for the intercom and made an announcement, "T.C! Holly! We are getting into some big water; make sure all loose items are secure and check on Morgan; he was pretty beat when he left here." there was no response, so Drake yelled again. "T.C. wake up!"

A groggy reply came from below deck. "OK! We're up, feels like Mister Toad's wild ride. What the hell you doing up there?"

"We had some weather move in on us, waves picking up some, need you to double-check the equipment in—" As Drake was about to finish his instructions to T.C., the moon broke through the overcast, giving off just enough light for Drake to see a huge rouge wave coming straight for them. "Holy Shit! Hang on!" were the last words heard over the intercom before the bow of the Sequoia took a drastic nose dive, feeling as if the ocean had been pulled right out from underneath her. And just as quickly as the bow was lifted up thirty feet into a near vertical position, Drake was expending every bit of strength to hold on to the wheel and keep the Sequoia from succumbing to the force of the violent behemoth wave.

The hull was now shaking from the stress of Drake pouring on maximum power, trying to get the vessel to muscle its way through the monstrous wave as the angry foaming water was doing its best to try and send her to the bottom. Drake, on the bridge was as busy as a one-armed paper hanger, putting a death grip on the wheel with one hand, trying to hold the rudder on a course to steer through this giant and the other on the throttles, adjusting the power as needed.

Green water was blasting its way over the bow, causing the fore deck to become awash from the huge wave. As the old ship poked her bow through the first wave, a surprise second set was there waiting for her. This time, the bow went under, and the wave came up to the windows in the wheelhouse. Drake was too busy to be scared. He was trying to keep the old bucket from turning turtle. With what appeared to be superhuman strength, Drake held the wheel, bracing his body with his shoulder jammed under one of the spokes, trying to keep his bare, wet feet from slipping on the teak deck. Silently praying that he could get the vessel to bust through the huge wall of water. As Drake finished his prayer, he heard the CD playing. Wagner's flight of the Valkyries' da da da dum dum! He told himself to make a note to toss it overboard the first chance he got, knowing that if he ever heard that song again, it wouldn't remind him of his favorite scene in Apocalypse Now but would give him flashbacks of this nightmare he was presently living.

Slowly the pressure on the rudder was commencing to decrease. Drake could feel the ship starting to begrudgingly respond but, the controls were still feeling extremely heavy. Looking ahead, he saw the reason for the slow response in the controls: the gun whales of the Sequoia were sitting almost dead even with the ocean's surface. As the ship slowly started to rise, he saw thousands of gallons of green sea water rolling off the deck and back into the ocean. Saltwater was draining out the scuppers as fast as the laws of physics would allow. Thank god the hatches held shut or it would have been an express trip to Davie Jones Locker; the Sequoia wouldn't have had a chance. Drake would make a mental note to find out what prison the members of the Cartel were in that overhauled the Sequoia and send them a thank you note for spending the extra money to reinforce those hatches, even though they did it to keep their cargo dry it was the deciding factor in keeping the ship and crew safe and sound. The old girl had held together and with Drake's new revelations, he felt so alive that nothing could stop them now.

Drake gathered himself together and got back on the intercom. "T.C., Holly, Mac! You guys alright?" Again there was a long delay before an answer came back to the bridge.

"Yea, Holly and I are all right we're trying to get the stateroom door open, but it seems to have jammed during the ordeal. Have you heard from Mac?"

"Not yet, can you get out?" Drake asked.

"Stand by… we're giving it another try," came the reply. "Yeah that got it, we got it open. I'll check on Mac and be right up," replied T.C.

Holly and T.C. had the same trouble with Mac's door as with their own. "Mac you alright? Mac?" inquired Holly as she pounded on the beautifully finished door. T.C. grasped the doorknob and shoved his shoulder into it, forcing the door open. There was MacShane, lying face down on the blue carpeted floor, unconscious. Holly and T.C. raced to turn him over and check his pulse.

"Still breathing, that's a good sign," said T.C., not trying to be funny but it came out that way.

"Don't be an asshole! You Asshole!" Holly was still shaken after that ordeal. It was her first time ever experiencing weather like this, and she was beside herself. Holly noticed a large bump on Mac's forehead.

"Must have been pitched out of bed and hit his head on the wall," suggested T.C. "Holly run up to the galley and get a bag of ice." T.C. was trying to get Mac into a sitting position when he began to regain consciousness.

"What the hell happened? One minute I'm lying in my bunk sound asleep, and the next you're squatting next to me in your boxer shorts, picking me up off the floor."

"Dude, we just came blasting out of a double set of rouge waves," informed T.C.

"He alright?" Holly was standing there in front of MacShane with a bag of ice in her hand wearing her pink terry cloth robe.

Mac saw the ice in Holly's hand and made a comment that everything looked fine from where he was sitting. It was at that point that Holly noticed she was standing there with the bottom portion of her robe open with nothing on underneath. Staring at his forehead, Holly took the bag of ice and roughly placed it on the knot on Morgan's head.

"Ough! How the hell did that happen?" asked Mac reaching up to adjust the ice and feel his bruised forehead. Holly said nothing as she snapped her robe closed, giving him a look of disbelief.

"Best as we can figure, you were tossed out of your bunk and hit your head during the melee," replied T.C.

"Hey what's going on down there? Everyone alright?" the voice came over the intercom.

"Yeah Drake, Morgan hit his noggin and has a large egg in the middle of his forehead. Other than that, we're fine. I'm getting ready to do a complete inspection now."

"I'll go with you," said Morgan and then falls back down as soon as he tries to stand.

"You go sit in your bunk, Mister Peepers!" commanded Holly. "I'll go with T.C."

The ship was still pitching and yawing, making for a very unstable deck. Morgan wanted to go but thought the better of it and capitulated to staying in his bunk.

"I just need a few minutes' rest. You guys go ahead, and I'll catch up," said Morgan as T.C. and Holly helped him back into his bunk.

Chapter 18

T.C. and Holly quickly dressed in a pair of work overalls and were off to inspect the Sequoia. Grasping the handrails in the passageway made for easier walking, but the ship was far from steady. An occasional bounce of the hull would have them bumping into the wall as they tried to walk the hallway. "Easy Holly, make sure you use the handrail," T.C. instructed. "Will start in the bilge and work our way up."

The pair made their way to the engine room and opened the hatch. Water was slouching around the compartment and was up to the bottom of the oil pans of the big diesel engines. "Damn! That's too close." T.C. stood for a minute to make sure the pumps were working.

"What's wrong?" asked Holly.

"Listen... the pump's running, but it doesn't sound right. I've got to check it out." T.C. stepped between the loud running engines and into the bilge water. The engine room's bilge pump was located in front of the engines, about two and a half feet below the oil pans. T.C., not looking too happy, got down on his knees and reached for the pump, trying to feel if there was anything stuck in the strainer which would restrict the flow. His face inches from the diesel fuel-polluted water, his eyes were starting to burn from the fumes. As he felt around in the bilge water, he felt something wrapped around the pump's strainer. Peeling it off, he lifted it above the water and gave Holly a furious look. "This!" he exclaimed. "This could have gotten us fucking killed!!!" In T.C.'s grimy, wet hand was a bath towel. "How the hell did this get here???!!!"

Holly knew she was in deep shit; it was her fault the engine room was flooded. She didn't know what to say. "I'm sorry. T.C. I'm sorry! I took a shower after you went to bed, and I went up forward to read. I used all the towels and knew you would be up in a few hours and would want a dry towel for your shower, so I hung it in the engine room to dry out and then I forgot about it and went to bed. I can't believe I was so stupid." Holly started to cry, more from the total stress of the past day than anything else.

T.C. was still furious and jumped on her again. "If that water was any deeper, it would have caused one or both of the engines to stall, and we would have been dead men. Morgan was right when he said you should have been put on a plane to the Stated. You're banned from the engine compartment; you are NOT to come in here again, understood!"

"Yes" was all the normally mouthy Holly could mutter.

"Go check on Morgan while I finish the inspection," commanded T.C., now acting as captain more than as her lover.

Holly knew that there was no point in arguing and begrudgingly left T.C. to finish his inspection. She proceeded back through the ship to the stateroom level to see how Morgan was doing. On her way down the passageway, Holly started to notice that the waves weren't as rough as they had been. She reached Morgan's room, and it was empty. Holly immediately got on the intercom and called up Drake. "Morgan up there with you?" she yelled into the intercom.

"Yeah, he's here, holding a leaking bag of ice on his head, not looking too good but he's here," answered Drake.

"He's supposed to be in bed resting. That's a bad knot on his head," insists Holly.

"Look princess, I've done worse to myself by slipping on a bar of soap in the shower. This is an emergency and all hands are needed on deck," fires back Morgan.

"Cut the chatter," interrupted T.C. "Mac if you're up to it, I could use some help re-securing some equipment down here in the hold."

"On my way Capt," replied Morgan, tossing the ice overboard and putting the plastic bag in the trash.

Holly stood in the passageway listening to the dialog between the men and just shook her head as she went back to her own cabin and laid down; the testosterone was too overwhelming. She tried to sleep, hoping that when she woke up in the morning this would have been only a bad dream.

Chapter 19

Morning met the Sequoia with calm seas and a beautiful sunrise. No evidence of last night's incident remained. Drake was finishing his watch and was being relieved by T.C.

"How you feeling T-bone?" asked Drake.

"Marvelous! Mac and I finished in the hold about 3 a.m. Luckily none of the equipment was damaged. What's our position?" inquired T.C.

"We should have a visual on Fort Jefferson around noon. We're just south of Rebecca Shoal at 24o 33'N 82o36'W," answered Drake, pointing to the navigational chart. "That storm threw us off course a little bit, but I managed to coax my babies into making up some of the lost time," boasts Drake.

T.C. couldn't bear to bring himself to tell Drake what Holly's towel almost did to his "babies." He thought that this would be a good story for another time far from here. "Thanks Drake, you stand relieved. Go below and get some breakfast. I made some French toast, should still be warm. Then grab some sleep. I need to have you awake and alert when we meet up with this Coast Guard tub," commanded T.C.

"Aye, aye skipper," answered Drake, offering up a mock left-handed salute as he left the bridge, tossing his classical CD over the side just before he headed below deck. T.C. noticed the flying disk and inquired why Drake tossed it. "Bad juju boss. Offering it up as a gift to the gods, I'm not superstitious mind you, but it couldn't hurt," laughed Drake, shrugging his shoulders as he disappeared down the stairs.

T.C. returned the salute and gave the instruments the once over. Setting himself up in the wheelhouse, he sat back and thought about Holly. He pondered if he had been too hard on her with his remark about shipping her off to the Stated. She was still part owner of the Sequoia, and he wondered if he would have said the same thing to Drake or Morgan if they screwed up like that. But Morgan and Drake were professionals they wouldn't have done something as dumb as that. Or could they? Holly, being a rookie to the boating scene was an easy target. T.C. would have to speak with her about life at sea and patch things up between them. Right after she wakes up, he thought.

Drake re-engaged the autopilot an hour before his watch was over. T.C. checked the heading to make sure the ship was on course. Satisfied with the way the ship was running, he sat back and contemplated for some time how he was going to approach Holly. He really needed to give her another chance. After all no one else knew about her screw-up, and he sure wasn't going to tell anyone. T.C. looked at his watch when he heard some rousing noises going on below deck,11:15. He knew that the best way to approach Holly was straightforward. He figured that there was no time better than the present. Pressing the transmit button on the intercom mic, T.C. callsfor her, "Holly please come to the bridge." Not happy with her lack of response, he hails her again. "Holly, I need you on the bridge. Will you please come up here." As soon as T.C. put the mic back into its clip, Holly came stomping through the hatchway onto the bridge.

"What? You going to hang me from the yard arm or have the crew keel haul me?" asked Holly indignantly. T.C. could tell she was still upset from last night. So he calmly stated.

"Pull up a chair; we need to talk," said T.C. pointing to a chair by the radar station.

"OK. Let's have it, but I want you to know that I already started to pack," counters Holly.

"About last night... I might have overreacted... no one else knows about it... I guess I was a bit stressed out," started T.C.

"And this is your way of apologizing; call me up here and sputter out some half-thought-out sentences. You—" Holly was silenced by T.C. putting up his hand and covering her lips.

"Let me finish. Yes, I'm apologizing, I don't want you to go. I'm saying you made a mistake and anyone could have done it. Drake could have left a shop rag lying around and that would have done the same thing..." explained T.C.

Holly was starting to smile behind the fingers pressing against her lips. Her eyes were starting to well up, and she began to giggle. She moved T.C.'s hand away from her face and wrapped her arms around his body, giving him a big wet kiss, stopping him in mid-sentence. "Thank you… T.C.," she whispered in his ear.

T.C. pulled away and looked her dead in the eye saying, "Consider this a warning, sailor. I want you to be extra careful from here on out. Remember, this tub belongs to you too. Let's try to take care of her. Alright?"

"You got it captain," remarked Holly as she wraps her arms around him again, thanking him for being so understanding. As the two were engaged in what would have appeared to have been a grope fest to an outsider, MacShane stepped onto the bridge. Grasping a steaming cup of coffee, he voiced his displeasure at catching them like that, "Damn man, you've only been on watch a couple hours. Can't that shit wait till later!" Breaking up their embrace, T.C. and Holly started to laugh. "It's not what you think, Mac. We were just—" said T.C.

"We were just celebrating getting through the storm," continued Holly.

"That's great, but if it's not too much trouble, how about starting the morning off by letting the rest of us deckhands know where the hell we're at?" asked Morgan.

"Glad to see you're feeling better Mac," added Holly, looking back as she made her way off the bridge. "I'll go below and start lunch. Seems like the troops get a little testy around here if they're not fed on a regular schedule."

"We should be in visual contact any time now; Fort Jefferson popped up on the radar screen about an hour ago. Take a look for yourself," offered T.C.

"No thanks, I trust ya. Besides I'm going down to the galley to put some more ice on my head. The bastard's still throbbin'," said Morgan as he heads to the galley.

Chapter 20

Holly, Drake, and Morgan were in the galley getting ready for lunch when T.C. shot them an alert over the intercom. "Better set another plate at the table; looks like we're about to get some company." Hastily the three left the galley and headed towards the bridge. Peering through the salt-encrusted windows, the crew saw a helicopter hovering alongside the Sequoia, keeping pace with her. It was the same type of helo that had picked up MacShane a few days prior, a Dolphin HH-65A.

"Here we go again," expressed Morgan less than exuberantly.

"He contacted you yet?" asked Drake.

"No, just been hovering alongside for the past few minutes," replied T.C.

"Look, the side door is opening!" Pointed out Holly.

From inside the helicopter, an orange-suited crewman was giving them a hand across the throat motion as if to say, cut the engines.

"What do you make of it Mac?" questioned T.C.

"Looks like he wants us to stop, put the throttles in neutral and give him the thumbs-up sign," replied MacShane.

Having done that, T.C. and the crew waited for the momentum of the ship to slow itself down. The large displacement hulls' forward speed finally subsided. The blue, flat sea lay motionless beneath the old freighter as she glided to a slow drift. "He's coming back around. It appears like he's setting up to lower someone or something down. Mac, since you're such good buddies with these guys, why don't you go down to the deck and welcome our new guest aboard," instructed T.C.

MacShane gave T.C. a stare that could have frozen moving water. But being a good soldier, he followed his captains' ordered and made it to the deck as the orange-suited stranger was about twenty-five feet overhead. With the person on the end of the string getting closer, MacShane reached up and grabbed the Coastie's black boot to try to help stabilize him from swinging and spinning in the vortices of the powerful rotor blades. Now with both feet firmly on the nonskid surface of the Sequoia, the coastie released the tether and waved the helo off with a snappy salute.

As the new arrival was removing the dark visor and large white helmet that covered their head, MacShane offered a welcome to the new guest. "Welcome aboard the... holy shit!" Mac's salutations were abruptly interrupted when the Coastie removed her helmet, giving her shoulder-length jet-black tresses a shake to loosen them up. Under the stunning dark hair was the most beautiful face MacShane had ever seen: round dark eyes, natural red lips, and perfect olive skin tone, had MacShane awestruck.

"Thanks for the welcome; it's nice to see you too. Lieutenant Consuelia Lopez United Stated Army, Special Ops reporting in... mister?"

MacShane was still getting over the shock of this beautiful woman popping out of a flight helmet, and totally missed the Special Ops intro, but he got hold of himself and managed an answer. "MacShane... ah... Colonel Morgan MacShane, recently reactivated."

Lieutenant Lopez, upon hearing that she was addressing a full bird colonel, jumped to attention and offered up a hearty salute, muttering, "So you're MacShane," under her breath, giving Mac the once over.

"Consuelia is it? Well Connie, we're a little more... no make that a lot more relaxed aboard this craft. No need for saluting and all that other crap," MacShane said as he half-assed returns her salute, "as you were soldier. Now what brings you aboard our mighty vessel?" inquired MacShane.

As Lopez was about to answer T.C. and Holly exited the hatch and were fast approaching, distracting Lopez and MacShane, causing them to look in their direction.

"Here comes the rest of the happy campers now," commented MacShane as he pointed in T.C.'s direction. "This is Captain T.C.

Allen and his first mate, Holly—" MacShane was cut off in mid-sentence.

"For god's sake, Mac… why don't you bring our guest inside? She must be dying out here, standing around in that flight suit. Really Mac!" stated Holly.

"Yeah, right, let's get you inside, and you can brief us on why you're here," stammered Mac.

Stepping inside the Sequoia, Lt. Lopez was stricken with the same disbelief as everyone else before her. However, Lopez had a job to do and needed to get started on it ASAP! The crew, minus Drake, assembled in the dining/meeting room to be brought up to speed," T.C. said he would fill Drake in later.

"First captain," started Lopez, pulling down the front zipper of her flight suit and removing a handheld communication device. "This radio is equipped with a scrambled satellite communication system and is to be used to establish a com link between this vessel and the Coast Guard Cutter Thetis. Repeat, this device is to be the only com link between the two vessels. There are far too many ears on the open frequencies. That's why the hand signals with the helo today. Were about an hour out of Fort Jefferson, in thirty minutes, we are to establish contact with the Thetis and get docking instructions for taking on fuel and cargo. The Thetis will be referred to as Vatican City, and we are to be the Crusader, any questioned so far?" asked Lopez.

"Did you eat yet?" asked Morgan earnestly.

"Excuse me?" Lopez couldn't believe she was being asked this question in the middle of her briefing.

"Let me ask this another way then: are you hungry Lieutenant Lopez?" reiterated MacShane.

"I'm hungry!" piped up T.C.

"I'm in the middle of a briefing!" exclaimed Lopez still not believing what was going on around her.

"Let her finish, I'll go and make some sandwiches; I heard enough anyway. Do you want turkey or ham?" queried Holly as she stood up, bored with all this military stuff.

"Turkey with some mayo for me please," said Morgan.

"I'll do both, mustard on one side, mayo on the other," added T.C.

Lopez was in noticeable shock, she was sitting there quite literately with her mouth hanging open in astonishment, wondering how she had lost control of her meeting. MacShane noticed her demeanor and offered up these words of advice. "Connie, if your hungry now's the time to speak up."

"Ah, yeah I am," sputtered Lopez.

"The choices are ham or turkey Lt," offered MacShane.

"Ham please," answered Lopez.

"I told you we don't go in for all that regulation crap on board this tub. However, now that lunch is handled, will you please continue with your briefing?" asked MacShane.

"Yes sir! Well, once were rafted off next to the Thetis we are going to take on some small defensive munitions, some spyware and the rest of my team when we will all meet for the complete mission profile," continued Lopez.

"What do you mean your team?" probed MacShane.

"I mean the team I'm leading on this mission. Besides your crew, we will have onboard a spyware systems expert, a munitions expert and a CIA operative. And one backup trained to replace any of the other three in case a problem occurs. As the General told you, we're supposed to be a freelance operation looking to make some quick cash moving some illegal goods," explained Lopez.

"I'll be damned! And just when the hell did Special Ops start to recruit women?" inquired MacShane.

"It's the twenty-first century, Colonel. You must try to keep up with these changing times," kids Lopez. She added, "But outside of the general and his staff, the only other people that know are the ones at the training school; we try to keep it very low key. You know, to catch the enemy off guard," replied Lopez with a sly Latin smile and a wink of her pretty dark eyes. A move that T.C. picked up on right quick. MacShane wasn't sure if she was coming on to him or was just patronizing him. Either way, he didn't seem to mind. MacShane was ready to start a series of questioned to the Lt. When Holly came back in with a platter of sandwiches. "Enough business, lunch is served," she said, handing out the Sourdough creations to their perspective owners.

The crew ate a quiet lunch with some light small talk. T.C. could tell Mac was taking an interest in the Lieutenant as he sat there about mesmerized as Lopez talked about her test scores during basic training, which would eventually lead her to be recruited into the Special Ops division.

After lunch Holly cleared and then offered to show Lieutenant Lopez her stateroom. Leaving T.C. and Mac alone in the galley cleaning up. "Nice, eh Mac?"

"What are you talking about?" responded Mac.

"You know, the lieut? Some hot stuff there buddy," remarked T.C.

"Didn't really notice. I still can't get over that Special Ops hired women," said Morgan.

"Yea sure. You were listening to her tell you her test scores like she was singing your favorite song," teased T.C.

"I was being polite. We're going to have to work together, just being polite, that's all," replied MacShane, not finding this at all humorous.

"Dude don't try to fool the old T-Bone. I saw that wink at the briefing," added T.C.

Mac was getting ready to respond when Connie and Holly walked into the galley.

"Time to contact the Thetis Colonel," spoke Lopez.

"Thanks Connie, comon' T. Let's go to the bridge and see if this hi-tech bullshit works," remarked Morgan.

On the bridge, T.C. turned on the handheld and tried to make contact. "Vatican City, Vatican City, this is Crusader. Copy?" T.C. was adjusting the squelch on the hand-held unit when it barked to life.

"Crusader, Crusader, this is Vatican City we copy. Prepare to receive docking instructions," came the authoritative voice over the small speaker.

As T.C. held the comlink, Drake wrote down the docking instructions and coordinates to meet up with the Thetis. "Roger that Vatican City we copy. Crusader standing by."

"Well, this looks like a fun time," added Drake as he spun the wheel, trying to keep the Sequoia in the designated channel. Fort Jefferson came upon them fast, a stronghold from another time, the brick structure sitting regally out of the water like a castle of old. At any minute, Drake was expecting to see pirates hoisting up the Jolly Roger and firing their cannons from the safety of the parapets at the passing intruders. As the old cargo ship passed by the high bluff of Fort Jefferson, Drake sang out, "Thetis dead ahead, Captain." Anchored off in the gin-clear water of the harbor lay the shiny white Thetis, all 270 feet of her. Its official designation, WMEC-910 plastered on the side in huge black letters just in front of the unmistakable bright orange stripe.

Chapter 21

Drake maneuvered the Sequoia to come along side the larger vessel, noticing that the helicopter that delivered Lieutenant Lopez was already back on the flight deck. As he got the Sequoia closer, Drake could see the deadly Mk-75 cannon on the fore deck. This beauty is capable of sending a 76mm shell through the steel hull of a hostile ship, downing enemy aircraft, or it can be used to defend the Thetis against an incoming missile attack, indeed a most impressive weapon. On either side of the ship, Drake noticed two 50-caliber Browning machine guns, which were manned and ready in case of a problem with uninvited visitors.

The crew of the Thetis, having already dropped huge docking fenders over the side to keep the two ships from rubbing together, were now waiting with mooring lines to secure the old freighter. MacShane and the others were on the deck preparing to handle the lines which will tie the two ships side by side. As the Sequoia was inching her way up along side the Thetis, MacShane heard a voice above his head say, "Damn! You guys must have a huge set of balls to put out to sea in that bucket." Mac looked up at the flight deck, and on the rail amidst the red, yellow and blue colored vests of the Thetis crew were a couple of Coasties wearing purple vests hanging over the side to get a better look, laughing and pointing at the Sequoia.

MacShane immediately shot back, "If anyone should know what the size of my balls are, who better then the grapes in my fruit of the looms!" referring to the similarities of the color. With that comment, the rest of the crew lost it and were all laughing at the two purple-vested crewmen. As their complexion turned a bright shade of red, they embarrassingly sulked away from the front of the line.

Drake was on target and put the ship in neutral, letting the natural momentum float her into the docking fenders. With a slight squish the Sequoia was alongside, and the Coast Guard crew tossed the lines to Mac and T.C., securing the two boats as one. "Good job Drake!" shouted T.C. to the bridge. "Now let's meet the rest of the gang."

Drake shut down the engines and joined his shipmates on deck as the Thetis crew was lowering down a cargo net ladder to compensate for the size difference in the two crafts. Lopez was the first to scurry up the ladder, and MacShane got a real good look at the seat of her pants as she wiggled her tight butt up the netting. "Hardly noticed her, sure, you keep telling yourself that Mac, you might get yourself to believe it some day," said T.C. breaking Mac's concentration.

"Let's go, there's no time for that T.C. I was checking out the super structure of the Thetis; she's some fine vessel. Don't you think?" asked Morgan, trying to change the subject.

"Yeah I think, I think you're full of shit! Let's get up there and find out about loading the supplies."

Holly stayed on board waving up to the sailors as an answer to their cat calls and whistles, while the three men climbed up the netting to the deck of the Thetis. Once on deck, each man saluted the ensign and were met by the captain and his exec. "MacShane, I'm Captain Hathaway, and my exec is Commander Boone. We need to start the transfer of supplies to your vessel. Will you inform your crew to make arrangements... We need to meet in the briefing room where the rest of the Special Ops people are waiting."

"You just told the crew captain, except for that little lady back on the deck over there," said MacShane, pointing to Holly.

"This is it! Four crew members to operate that, that ship! What the Hell was Kane thinking!" Hathaway was alternating a scowling look between his exec and MacShane.

"She ain't pretty but she's home. And as far as General Kane is concerned, we don't like this anymore then you do, but dem's our ordered, and we'd do as we're told, right Captain?" replied Mac, giving Hathaway a big toothy smile. Turning to Drake, Mac spoke, "You best stay and help load the supplies. T.C. and I will fill you in later."

"I'm always being filled in later. Drake drives the ship. Drake loads supplies. For once, I would like to sit in on one of these briefings!" complains Drake.

"It's not all it's cracked up to be buddy. We'll be down as soon as we're finished. Can't take that long," commented T.C. as he tries to smooth Drake's ruffled feathers.

Drake climbed back down the netting as MacShane and T.C. followed Hathaway and Boone to the briefing room. Inside waiting for them was the rest of Lopez's team; the Lieutenant stood up and made the introductions. "Colonel MacShane, Captain T.C. Allen, this is Sergeant Sam Brody munitions, Atwater, CIA, and Sergeant Kim Dixon computers."

MacShane looked the team over, sizing up each person, trying to get an overall impression. Brody was a tall, slender man in his late twenties to early thirties with sandy-colored hair. Atwater was a typical spook, average size, build and plain features, making him indistinguishable in a crowd, a real joe average. And the last member, Sergeant Kim Dixon, a fairly tall woman, being a mixture of European and South American breeding with a Roman style nose, round eyes and mocha-colored skin.

A real cross-section of humanity, thought MacShane as he passed judgement on the rest of his new shipmates. Captain

Hathaway took his place at the head of the table and began the dissimilation of the information.

"Your friend General Kane has a small change of plan for you," started Hathaway as he looks directly at MacShane and T.C. "We procured a nice piece of equipment that's going to make you guys a real popular item in Cuba."

"I can't wait!" exclaimed MacShane as he lets out a deep breath and sits back in his chair.

"If I may continue!" snapped Hathaway, not used to being interrupted while he was talking. "Working jointly with the Navy, we were able to come up with a Tomahawk Missile that we're going to load on board the Sequoia. We believe that this piece of equipment will make you, shall we say irresistible to those vermin and should bring every one of them out of the woodwork to take a look at it. You'll get to see all the players and learn as much as possible about their operations."

MacShane and T.C. sat straight up in their seats and T.C. blurts out, "A Fucking What!"

MacShane couldn't believe his ears either and asked the captain to repeat himself.

"You heard me, we are going to load a real Tomahawk onboard your vessel, only this one has been slightly modified. It's carrying an extra 100 pounds of C-4 in the fuel tank with a remote wireless detonator that can be activated from Langly once the sequence of firing codes has been entered. That's where Dixon comes in," explained the captain, gesturing in the Sergeant's direction.

Mac and T.C. both took a deep breath and leaned back in the black leather chairs, they could start to feel sweat gathering under their pant legs causing them to stick to the smooth leather. A recon mission was one thing but, delivering a live Tomahawk missile was quite another. This shit was getting deep.

"When and if you make it to Cuba," continued the captain, "you work your way into port and find out who the players are, who has the money to take it off your hands. When the transfer is complete, we can track the missile with the integrated homing device, which is also activated when the firing codes are entered. We follow the ship it's loaded on using satellites, and when it reaches its destination, we flip a switch, and whoever was buying it gets a first-hand, up-close look at what a Tomahawk missile can do. No returns, no rain check, no money back. Scratch one terrorist cell. And the best part is no Americans are anywhere near it. The incident gets written off as human error."

"Damn! That's brilliant! A Trojan Horse with a real kick!" said T.C.

Morgan was sitting there taking it all in, but before he swallowed it, he had a few questioned of his own. "Ah Captain, just how in the hell are we supposed to have appropriated a Tomahawk missile? by being the highest bidder on eBay?"

"The missile has been documented as missing since we invaded Afghanistan. All the serial numbers are actual in case there is an intel leak somewhere. One of our Frigates showed it as missing on its manifest from the Nato base in Izmir, Turkey. From there, it was boxed up and shipped to Langley, where it was modified to its present condition. Then it was boxed up again and shipped via commercial truck lines to Key West Naval Air Station as spare parts. It was loaded on the Thetis, and here it is. What story you want to come up with, you can work it out on your way to Cuba. Maybe a drug-dependent dock hand in Turkey had to pay off his local dealer, corrupt Turkish officials. Hell I don't care if you blame the friggin' Mafia," ranted Hathaway. "Figure it out!"

Morgan couldn't hold back any longer and asked, "Afghanistan? How long has this quarterback sneak been planned?"

"Well… Colonel, your original mission is only a few weeks old, the Tomahawk has been around for years. The only thing missing was a delivery system. The General saw this as a perfect opportunity to tie the two together," added Hathaway.

MacShane looked around the table at the Special Ops team and zeroed in on Atwater, the CIA man. "And how does the CIA fit into the equation? Well Atwater?"

Atwater put down his pencil and looked straight at MacShane as if no one else was in the room and spoke, "To save American lives Colonel. That's how the CIA fits in." His voice was soft and flat but not weak. He was not excited nor flustered. His stare went right through Morgan, and for the first time in a long time, MacShane felt uneasy.

Chapter 22

The captain kept the meeting going at a rapid rate, finishing it off with a question-and-answer period. MacShane piped up and asked, "Exactly what is the price range of a low milage Tomahawk missel anyway, Captain? We wouldn't want to ruin the market value or cause a glut."

Captain Hathaway was barely tolerating the wise-ass commented from MacShane, and his blood pressure was on the rise. "Well Colonel, a new one costs approximately $569,000, so judge yourself accordingly. And once you make the sale you are to use the money to purchase some other weapons and bring them back for examination. We need to find out where the majority of these WMDs are coming from and what kind are on the market. Any further questioned?!" Captain Hathaway announced as more of a deterrent than a solicitation for further discussion. "Very well, briefing is adjourned, and the Colonel can supervise the rest of the cargo transfer. Good luck gentlemen and ladies." *You're going to need every bit,* he thought to himself.

Still standing after the captain walked out of the room, the team members were eyeing each other up, and then MacShane spoke, "Well folks grab your gear and get you over to your new home for the next few weeks. T.C. I'm going to finish loading the cargo. Will you show our guests to their quarters?"

"I can't wait to see this, probably has hot and cold running rats from the looks of her," commented Atwater.

"Birds of a feather..." quipped T.C. under his breath.

"Atwater you did say you were with the Central Intelligence Agency, didn't you?" asked MacShane.

"Yeah and?" snapped Atwater.

"Just checking... T.C. make sure you put those rat guards on the ropes holding up Atwater's hammock. Don't want any of those little critters climbing down on our guest while he's sleeping," informed MacShane.

"Roger that Colonel, I might even have some extra mosquito netting to drape over the hammock. Makes it real romantic like," teased T.C.

Lopez was holding back, staring at the floor to keep from busting out in laughter. She never got a chance to tell the rest of her gang about the lavish setup they were getting ready to walk into.

Atwater had enough of the nonsense and headed out the door. Lopez walked up to MacShane, openly laughing now and remarked, "Wait till he gets on board, is he ever going to be surprised."

"The real surprise will come at dinner, T.C. has got something special in the works," answered MacShane. "Come on Connie, let's get over there and see the Intelligence Man's face when he climbs onboard."

Atwater, Brody and Dixion were milling about the deck of the Sequoia as T.C., MacShane and Lopez caught up to them after disembarking from the boarding net of the Thetis. "Nice ship, MacShane. What time is shuffleboard scheduled?" asked Atwater sarcastically, looking around at the rusting hulk.

"Shuffleboard is a little rough on the finish, but we prefer skeet shooting off the Lido deck," responded MacShane. "T.C., why don't you take our guests below and show them the bunks in the forward cargo hold while I finish up with the Coasties."

"Will do Mac. If you would follow me, ladies and gentlemen, I'll show you, your accommodations," announced T.C., playing the role.

T.C. opened the hatch and the ice-cold air escaped and hit everyone right square in the face. "Keep close now, and will the last one in please secure the hatch?"

"You coming Lieutenant?" questioned Brody to Lt. Lopez.

"No, you go ahead; I already saw inside. I'm going to see if the Colonel needs any help on deck," answered Lopez.

"See you in the cargo hold," said Brody as he shut the door behind him.

T.C. took the new crew members down the gangway to the galley without saying a word. The response was what he thought it would be. Everyone, including Atwater, was walking around with their mouths hanging open. Atwater was the first to speak. "What the Hell is this tub? Where did it come from?"

T.C., being the proud papa, responded to his questioned. "Since we're all in this together, I guess I could give you a quick history lesson." T.C. proceeded to tell the team about how he saved the old girl from the scrap yard, the partnership he and MacShane had and how they got scammed by the General into being put back into service. He could tell by the look on Atwaters face that something was amiss. "Feeling alright, Atwater?"

"This ...this is the Sequoia? The cartel ship?" spoke Atwater.

"One and the same, you've heard of her?" asked T.C.

"I thought this vessel was sold off as scrap and cut up," responded Atwater.

"She was headed that way but, I couldn't let that happen. I outbid everyone and saved her. Wait, I should clarify that Mac and I outbid everyone," boasts T.C.

"Try again, hotshot," interjectedHolly as she was coming out of her statcroom fresh off a power nap.

"What I meant to say was that Holly and I, as well as Mac, outbid everyone to save her. This is Holly, my better half and partner," told T.C., trying to make a quick recovery. "Holly, this is Sergeant Brody, Atwater, and Sergeant Dixon. The rest of Connie's team. I'm taking them to their staterooms."

"Hi all! T.C., I could do that; you go help Mac so we can get the Hell out of here," offered Holly.

"Thanks babe, see you in a few," replied T.C. as he started to leave.

"T.C., where did you buy this boat anyway?" questioned Atwater, grabbing T.C. by the shoulder and stopping his progress.

"Fort Lauderdale, why?" shot back T.C.

"Just curious, that's all, nothing else," answered Atwater.

T.C. shrugged his shoulders and headed out onto the deck to help MacShane, not giving Atwater's questioned another thought.

Chapter 23

T.C. caught up with Mac and Lt. Lopez as the Tomahawk missile was being lowered onto the deck of the Sequoia. A makeshift wooden cradle was being assembled by a couple of the Coast Guard crewmen as the large instrument of death swung above them in its harness.

"How's it going?" T.C. asked Mac

"Great, these guys are sure good at what they're doing. Once this thing is secured and covered with some tarps, Hathaway said we can start a fuel transfer. And when that's complete, we're on our way to Grand Cayman," answered Mac.

The three of them watched in silence as the Tomahawk missile with its attached booster was guided into the cradle. The wood giving off a groaning sound as the full 3500 pounds came to rest in its berth.

"Damn! That thing sure is impressive," remarked T.C., staring at the big bird.

"Hurry and get it covered up, pronto! Put some crates up forward by the nose so we can conceal this thing's outline. We also need to do something about these 9-foot wing spans." stated MacShane.

T.C. and Lopez moved some of the smaller crates from the stern of the ship and placed them along the fuselage. "Grab a tarp and get this shit secured," commanded MacShane.

The three tossed and tugged at the tarps to get the missile camouflaged as well as making it secure for the long journey ahead. "Last thing we need is to have this thing drop its britches, and someone gets a look at it before we reach Cuba. Make sure those lines are tight!" ordered T.C., lashing the braided nylon rope to the deck cleats.

As the last knot was secured, a purple-vested coasties shouted over the rail to MacShane.

"Excuse us, Colonel. I'm seaman 1st class Heyworth of the fueling team. We were instructed to assist you in re-fueling your vessel, sir," announced the prior wise-ass coastie, now with a whole new demeanor.

"Thank you, seamen; lower the transfer lines and we'll secure them for taking on fuel," answered MacShane. "Holy shit, I wonder what changed his attitude," chuckled MacShane to Connie.

"I can't imagine," commented Lopez, smiling.

Once the fueling lines were connected, Heyworth and his two-man crew started to transfer the diesel fuel. "Keep it comin', Heyworth and don't forget to check under the hood and clean the windshield," ribbed MacShane. "Damn! It feels good to bust his balls," he told Lopez, who was standing next to him with a fire extinguisher at the ready.

"You miss that, don't you?" she asked.

"What?" replied Mac.

"Being in command," she told him with a sly smile.

"I'm retired, or I was trying to be. Remember," responded MacShane dryly.

"Yea, bullshit Morgan! I see the look on your face when you order people around or when someone challenges your authority," Lopez retorts.

"Well, what the hell you expect? I've been giving ordered my whole life, and that's the regular look on my face, thank you very much," answered MacShane.

"If you say so, but you're not foolin' this Latino Chica, baby," Lopez teased in a Cuban accent, testing the waters and seeing how familiar she could become with MacShane.

"Sir," throws back MacShane with a stern look.

"Ok, chica baby. Sir!" she added with a wink and a smile.

"That's better, lieutenant," replied MacShane. "Now get this fuel line disconnected so little happy Heyworth can get back to watching SpongeBob."

Once the fuel lines were safely back on board the Thetis, T.C. came out on deck to help MacShane and Lt. Lopez make ready to get underway. All the new arrivals were still below deck settling in while Drake was in the wheelhouse warming up the big diesel engines, checking his gauges and laying in a course through the Yucatan Channel for Grand Cayman. At his signal, the acting deckhands made ready to untie the vessel. "Alright get this tub underway!" shouted T.C. from the bridge window.

With that MacShane, T.C. and Connie untied the lines, with one prolonged blast followed by three short ones, the Sequoia started backing away from the large white Coast Guard vessel. Drake took this opportunity to crank up a steel band CD in the ship's sound system playing, "Who Put The Pepper In The Vaseline" reminiscent of a cruise ship leaving port. As the old girl proceeded to back down, the members of the Sequoia's crew looked up at the Thetis amidst the island music. There they witnessed the entire accompaniment of sailors, including little 'happy' Heyworth, all lined up on the rail, at attention, giving them a snappy salute send-off. Morgan and crew returned the salute and added a thumbs-up signal, causing the Coasties to openly cheer and wave. On the bridge of the Thetis, Captain Hathaway muttered under his breath, "Good luck, you crazy bastards. Godspeed."

Chapter 24

Leaving Fort Jefferson and the Thetis in her wake, the Sequoia was steaming westward through the Straits of Florida, where calm seas prevailed. With all the grunt work finished and close to dinnertime. T.C. was in the galley preparing the evening meal when Mac walked in to grab a cold beer.

"Thought we'd never get underway, but now that we are, I'm not so sure that it's a good thing," said Mac after taking a long swig on the cold bottle.

"Nervous?" asked T.C.

"Concerned more than anything. I look at it like this, big mission with little to no backup, some asshole CIA spook on board. Computer geeks, women in the Special Ops." MacShane shook his head as he took another swig of beer and then added, "Something's just not sitting right with all this," confided MacShane to his old buddy.

T.C. was building a deep dish of lasagna as he listened to his friends' thoughts between the ladling on of meat sauce and the delicate placement of the noodles. "Ya know Mac, the world is constantly changing around us. Sometimes we keep up; other times we fall back onto what is comfortable. I think the latter is your problem. You want to operate in a world you know and understand, but that was over a while ago. These new kids coming up can multi task with ease. Carry on four to five different conversations online at one time. They look at us like we looked at our parents, who couldn't change the time on the VCR after a power failure. The 12:00 blinking on and off never seemed to bother them. Now, we are our parents... blink, blink, my brother."

"Thank you, Master Yoda. But I'd still feel better with air support and a fully loaded 50-caliber machine gun. What happens to the new kids when their batteries wear out?" commented Morgan.

T.C. was ready to reply when Connie and Holly entered the galley. "How're our guests getting along babe?" asked T.C. to Holly.

"They're fine except for that Atwater guy, something weird about him, can't figure it out yet," replied Holly.

"Typical spook, weird is what keeps them alive. Where'd he come from anyway?" said Morgan, directing his comment to Connie.

"The General sent him, something about trying to get better intel out of Cuba. The guy is supposed to have been connected with Castro's brother, Raul, in the old days. He was one of the guys to tip off the CIA about the Mariel boatlift weeks before it happened way back in the seventies." Connie answered.

"How soon before the lasagna is ready? I'm starved," interrupted Holly, changing the subject.

"Just finishing up the last layer. Just need some sauce, a little sprinkle of grated Mozzarella and Parmesan with a gentle hint of Romano tossed in, and pop it into the oven. While that's cooking, I'll make up some meatballs and a fresh garden salad. You're looking at about 45 minutes to an hour. Go and let the others know, ok babe?" queried T.C.

"You got it! Sam and Kim were going up forward to check out the movie library, and Atwater was in his cabin with the door closed. Com'on Connie, I'll show you the rest of the ship," responded Holly, overjoyed to have another woman on board that she could hang out with.

"If you don't mind Holly I'd rather stay here and get a cooking lesson from T.C. I never had much time to learn how to cook," said Connie. She further added, "The only thing my mother could ever make was reservations."

Holly was T.C.'s biggest fan when it came to his cooking. "He's the best, and he's also quick. You better get some paper and take a few notes. See you at dinner." And Holly was off in a flash.

"*Do* you mind if I take some notes T.C.?" asked Connie. "I know how temperamental some chefs can be."

Morgan was getting another beer out of the fridge when he saw Connie reach into her bag and pull out some kind of hand-held computer contraption.

"What the hell is that thing?" inquired Morgan as he watched Connie start typing on it with her thumbs.

"My Treo PDA, I keep all my important information in here. This thing is great!" answered Connie.

"Blink, blink, my brother," teased T.C.

"Think I'll go on deck and check our cargo," huffs Morgan as he headed towards the passageway.

"What's up with him?" asked Connie, shrugging her shoulders.

"You know, old dog, new tricks. Now get ready to make the best meatballs you ever had." And with that T.C. proceeded to divulge the formula for his famous meatball recipe.

Dinner was served in the beautifully appointed dining room. A generous pan of lasagna was accompanied by bowls of meatballs and salad. In the middle of the polished cherry table were two bottles of Chianti slightly chilled, the condensation slowly forming droplets down the side of the bottle, making their way to the coaster underneath. Around the table sat the whole crew minus Drake, who was in the wheelhouse.

"Dig in folks, and pass the meatballs," instructed T.C. enthusiastically. He was starving and wasn't standing on formalities.

From the look on Brody and Dixons faces they still couldn't believe what was going on in this rust bucket. Atwater was sitting there, not showing any feelings whatsoever.

"Have some wine T.C.?" suggested Connie, lifting the bottle in his direction.

"No thanks, Connie. I've got the next watch," replied T.C.

"How about you Mac? Want a little?" grins Connie, giving Morgan a quick wink.

"I'm really glad to see everyone so relaxed and enjoying themselves... We're not on a friggin cruise ship here, people!! We need to fine-tune this mission before we get there, or it's going to be one big cluster fuck!" Atwater was openly annoyed at the goings-on and wasn't about to sit still for it much longer.

"Chill out dude!" said T.C. "It's our first night together; let's try to get to know each other. Find out where we're all comin' from before we get all bogged down in the mission. Why don't you try to take it easy tonight and enjoy the lasagna."

"I'll take it easy when this mission is over. DUDE!" Somehow that word didn't seem quite right coming out of Atwater's mouth. He continued to berate Lopez. "Lieutenant, if this is your idea of how you plan to proceed with this assignment, I'm going to have to mention this in my report to my superiors," attacks Atwater.

"Stand down, Atwater! This night off is my idea," MacShane said stepping in to squelch Atwater's barrage on Connie.

"Well colonel, I hope you know what you're doing. There's a lot at stake for you to be hosting dinner parties instead of briefings," shot back Atwater. "Now if you will excuse me, I prefer to have dinner in my cabin, where I can get some work done!"

Atwater grabbed his plate and stormed off towards his cabin. "What an asshole!" remarked Holly. The group hesitated, unsure whether to laugh or try to ignore her comment until T.C. spoke, "Don't hold back Holly, tell us how you really feel about our guest."

With that comment breaking the ice, the rest of the group settled into a relaxing evening getting to know one another. MacShane looked around the table and was assessing each person's personality from the small talk they offered. He learned long ago that the best way to find out about someone's character is when they're lighthearted and not focused on a task.

The dinner proceeded without any more flair-ups. Once Atwater left, it was actually quite civil as the group became better acquainted. After the homemade cannolis and coffee, the crew all pitched in on the K.P. to straighten up the galley. It was close to T.C.'s watch, he put a nice plate of lasagna together for Drake and brought it up to the bridge. "Mind if I go with you?" questioned MacShane.

"What? You don't want to go and watch 'Scarface' with everyone else," quipped T.C.

"Not tonight, we need to talk," replied MacShane.

"Follow me," commanded T.C. as he heads towards the bridge with Drake's dinner.

As they entered the wheelhouse, it was fast approaching sunset. The Sequoia's heading was taking her straight for the setting sun, and the burst of colors was breath taking. The sky from the horizon to the north to the horizon to the south was changing every minute. MacShane took a moment to enjoy the scenery. Pinks, yellows, and blues turned to red and grey as the sun got lower in the sky. The reflected light off the stratus clouds provided a palette a master such as Van Gogh would have been proud of.

"Damn,! I could never get enough of this. There's nothing like a sunset at sea," he stated.

"Yeah, it's beautiful; what'd ya bring me to eat?" inquired Drake. "I'm starved."

"Lasagna and meatballs, you can hit the Chianti when your watch is over," answered T.C. "Now, what's up, Mac?"

"Wanted to get your take on this 'team' of ours. You think you're ready to entrust your life to them?" queried MacShane.

"Man, I just don't know. They seem kind of green to be on this type of mission," stated T.C.

Drake shoveled a forkful of lasagna into his mouth, as the two men exchanged viewpoints. Listening to every word as he chomped his food. "That's my observation too. Did you catch Brody's answer when I asked him why he enlisted?" said Mac.

"Yeah, it almost made me spit out my food. 'It was either this or jail, and since I couldn't blow up anything in jail, I told the judge I would enlist.' What kind of shit is that?" responded T.C. Adding, "I think this dude is going to be a loose cannon."

"I think you're right, we're going to have to keep an eye on that one. And Dixon, what kind of computer geek gets into special ops? Something just ain't right with this group. And that's without throwing Atwater into the mix. What kind of bullshit did Kane set us up in?" MacShane wonders aloud. "After breakfast, we need to get down to business. We need to start to finalize the details and see who has what to bring to the table."

"Yeah, you guys do that, but right now, I'm going for another plate full of lasagna and going forward to watch 'Scarface' with everyone else. They should be at the part where Tony is in Freedom Town under I-95, and he knifes the old man for his green card. 'Revenga!'" shouted Drake mimicking a knife thrust into MacShane's side. "Man, I love that part! See you guys later. By the way T.C., I stand relieved!" Those were Drake's last words as he scampered off the bridge and headed towards the galley.

Chapter 25

Breakfast wasn't a big deal: scrambled eggs, bacon, hash browns and toast. After the mess was cleaned up, MacShane told the crew to meet in the dining room for a mission profile. With the helm on autopilot, Holly was given the wheelhouse duty so everyone could attend. MacShane started by unrolling the navigation charts and giving everyone a position update.

"We're right here," pointing to a place on the map to the northwest of Cuba. "Getting ready to turn into the Yucatan Channel. We only have but a few days to become a cohesive unit and come up with a story that sounds believable to the terrorists. Atwater any input?" questioned MacShane, trying to get the CIA man to open up.

"Well now you're talking, Colonel. We need a rock-solid story about the Tomahawk, or we're all dead. I think that even though Hathaway was throwing out ideas, the Mafia angle might just be the ticket. Think about it; the Mafia is a business operation; if they can turn a few dollars, why not? Why should they give a shit where the money comes from as long as it's green. What are the Cubans going to do? Call them and check on our references?" Atwater almost cracked a smile as he finished presenting his idea.

"How about you Lieutenant? Any ideas?" asked MacShane, acting as master of ceremonies.

"Personally, I think a story about buying it on the Black Market in Turkey might be a better..." Lopez was cut off by Atwater in mid-sentence.

"Hell no! There are only a few guys over there that are able to deal in this type of weapon, and if there are any real terrorist's cell members in Cuba, they would more than likely know the people who'd be selling it. Don't forget they communicate with scrambled satellite phones now, information exchanges happen at the touch of a button. No, bad idea, remember we're supposed to be coming off a passage through the Panama Canal." Atwater continued, "The Mafia ploy is far better for our story, too many branches to keep track of. We can say we picked it up off the coast of Acapulco and made the trip through the canal to Cuba. No, I say the Mafia angle is the only way to go."

"Brody, Dixon? What do you say?" chipped in Morgan.

"Fine with me, one lie is as good as the next," chimes in Brody.

"It's good by me," answered Dixon. "The simpler the better."

"Drake?"

"Dude I don't know—" But before Drake could finish his sentence, Atwater butted in.

"What's to know? This used to be a smuggling ship, right? We say we were in Acapulco sitting in MiMi's burger joint getting ready to put another shipment together when our doper contact introduced us to this Mafia guy who had a real big problem. His crew hijacked this missile, and now he was stuck and had no way to move it. We set up a meeting and cut a deal. Using our drug buy money for the Tomahawk purchase instead. The words out that the big money now is in smuggling arms, not drugs. Leave that shit for the cowboys in South Florida. The real money is with weapons, so we bought this thing from the Mafia and headed to Cuba to do some business." Atwater sat back after his dissertation, crossed his arms on his chest, and waited for his accolades.

"Might work," commented MacShane, looking at the rest of the crew.

"Might my ass! It's perfect!" interjected Atwater.

"Give us some names," stated MacShane.

"What?" asked Atwater.

"Names, ones that will make it believable. This shit came too easy for you. Atwater, how many times did you do business with the Cartel? How many tons of pot did you run to fund your secret missions?" interrogates MacShane.

T.C. jumped up like he was shot in the ass with a bolt of lightning. "That's what all the questioned were about when you found out that this was the Sequoia. No wonder you looked like you'd seen a ghost."

"Well Atwater? You have all of our undivided attention, doesn't he, group?" MacShane was looking at the reactions of the rest of the crew and they sat there, not saying a word.

"Watch it Colonel, you're getting into water that's way over your head," warns Atwater.

"Don't worry about me. I'm an excellent swimmer," replied MacShane. "Give it Atwater! What the hell are you doing on this mission?"

"You don't know the first thing about what we do, Colonel. All you know is what we tell the newspapers to publish. Do you have any idea what it takes to keep your precious freedom around, Colonel? Do you, Lieutenant? Any of you?" Atwater continued on without waiting for an answer. "It takes money folks, lots and lots of money. Keeping foreign Governments in power that are favorable to the U.S., getting rid of governments that aren't. Just where do you think this money comes from? Congressional approval? Yeah sure, I could hear it now ...Mister Speaker, we need 45 million dollars to help overthrow Baby Doc Duvalier in Haiti in order for us to put the Reverend Aristide in power. This way, we will be able to keep his fellow countrymen on the island and stop the flow of Haitians from landing on our shores with 150 people per 36-foot boat. Yeah, C-SPAN would be all over that one. Wise up people. So, we run some pot, so who gives a shit? A few kids get high in the neighbor's garage and eat some Twinkies, big friggin' deal! Starting and stopping revolutions costs big money, and big money leaves a trail when it comes to the Federal Government, so we had to improvise." Atwater was standing now, staring down at everyone at the table.

"How many of these uprisings are you responsible for, Atwater?" questioned MacShane.

"This briefing isn't about me Colonel; I've divulged too much information already. All I've got to say is read the papers, and you figure it out. Now, if everyone isn't in too much shock, I suggest we get back to the mission at hand."

Silenced fell upon the room for what seemed an eternity. After a long pause, Lopez spoke, "We need to operate as a team, and team members cover each other's back. Atwater is here to do a job like the rest of us. Each person's performance could be a vital part of keeping this team alive. Remember, we're here to put a dent in the terrorist's operation; personal opinions have no place at the briefing table."

"You're right, Lieutenant. Everyone needs to chill out for a minute," T.C. made this comment to both Mac and Atwater. Atwater nodded and sat back in his chair. MacShane realized his attack on Atwater was entirely personal and had nothing to do with this mission. MacShane took a deep breath to clear his head and tried to get the briefing back on track.

"The Mafia ploy is probably the best chance we have. All we need is a name for the head guy in Acapulco. Any ideas?" MacShane resigned himself to the fact that the Mafia plan was the best he heard and wanted to start to fill in the blanks.

"How about Joey Parisi? He used to be my shop teacher in high school." Brody was trying to help the meeting get back on track.

"Works for me," commented T.C.

"Everyone else? Atwater?" questioned MacShane.

The group came to an agreement that the contact in Acapulco, a 'Miguel' introduced them to a Joey 'bag o' doughnuts' type guy, Parisi, and he put the deal together, including the asking price of the Tomahawk at a cool one million in U.S. dollars.

Chapter 26

After the briefing the crew members headed topside to get some fresh air and exercise. Atwater, as usual, went to his stateroom while T.C. went up to the bridge to relieve Holly. Stepping into the wheelhouse, he glanced at the twin-engine tachometers and noticed that the starboard one was starting to loose some rpm.

"Now what the hell?" he muttered.

"I swear I didn't touch anything T.C. I did as you told me; I sat here and watched the gauges and listened for alarms." Holly was still a bit gun-shy from her last encounter dealing with the ship.

"I know, it's not you. Throttle might have slipped some." T.C. gave the starboard engine more fuel however the tach hardly moved. "Shit!" said T.C. Pulling both throttles to the neutral position.

Rushing to the bridge window, he called to MacShane, "Mac, look over the stern and let me know if you see anything." The rest of the crew, realizing that the ship had come to a stop, walked over to the side and looked out at the clear, calm water.

Having inspected the stern, Mac called up to T.C. "We are trailing a bunch of shit behind us. Looks like something's hanging off the starboard prop."

"Damn, I'm going to have to go overboard and check the props. Holly, don't touch anything!" T.C. headed down to his stateroom and donned his bathing suit. Coming out on deck carrying an M-16, he met up with Mac and explained what he was going to do.

"You sure about this? Can't you try throwing it in reverse or something?" inquired Mac.

"No, I've got to go overboard and check this out; from the looks of it… we got something wrapped around there good." T.C. was referring to the scattered debris that lay floating around the ship. "Autopilot is great but it doesn't warn you of any floating hazards."

"Keep a watch for sharks, will you Mac?" asked T.C. of his buddy as he hands him the rifle. "I'm going to suit up in the engine room and use the outside hatch to get into the water."

"No problemo pal." MacShane checked the magazine, pulled the bolt and engaged the safety. Hefting the weapon to his shoulder, he tried out a practice bead on a piece of floating 2x4.

T.C. put on the diving gear, making a mental note to thank Spyder for leaving all this nice equipment. Opening the outside hatch, T.C. stepped off the side and was swallowed up by the clear, warm water. Swimming below the surface towards the stern of the ship, he gave thanks to the powers that be for having calm, flat seas for this maneuver. Looking down into the bottomless abyss T.C. gets a feeling of weightlessness as if floating in space. With the regulator exhaust gurgling behind his head with every exhale, T.C. scans the ocean from left to right. He sees nothing but the vast empty expanse of bright blue color filling his mask. Without a focal point, T.C. started to feel a bit queasy, needing something to focus his eyes on. He looks up at the hull of the ship. Thinking about how dangerous, if not impossible this would be in rough seas. One timing mistake and the whole weight of the Sequoia could come down on your head. He again gives thanks for the flat seas.

Swimming along the keel of the ship, he reaches the propeller shaft, noticing the problem immediately: huge sheets of Visqueen are wrapped around the shaft and prop. T.C. reaches down his leg and, unsheathes his Scuba Pro dive knife and started to cut away at the thin plastic.

Back on deck MacShane is keeping a sharp eye out for any type of movement in the water.

"What's that? I see something moving under the water," Connie yelled.

MacShane already had them in sight and said, "Relax Connie those are Mahi-Mahi. Not generally known as big man-eaters. But have been known to make the best dinner around, too bad we don't have the fishing equipment out."

"They're beautiful. Look at the colors: blue, green, yellow. How pretty!" Connie was getting excited at seeing the fish in their natural environment.

Brody was also looking over the side but suddenly disappeared below deck. Assuming he was seasick, no one thought much of it. In fact, the rest of the group started to imitate a barfing maneuver by puffing out their cheeks while covering their mouth with their hand.

T.C. finally finished getting the last bit of the plastic sheet off the shaft and was returning to the hatch. Swimming along the surface he gave MacShane the thumbs up sign indicating mission accomplished.

As T.C. removed his fins and flipped them into the ship, he heard a gunshot and saw a large splash about 50 yards away from the ship. Thinking MacShane was zeroing in on a shark, he hustled his ass out of the water right before the calm surface exploded in front of him.

"What the hell are you doing, you asshole!" MacShane was standing on the stern, yelling at Brody, who had now reappeared with an M-79 grenade launcher.

"Just doing a little fishing Colonel," replied Brody, acting if this was the most natural thing in the world. "Check it out. You said these fish will make a great dinner, didn't you?" he told pointing to where the explosive charge went off. As the water settled the crew noticed that there were four large fish floating on the surface.

"Secure that weapon soldier. Lieutenant, relieve Sergeant Brody of that weapon!" commanded MacShane.

As Lopez walked over to Brody, she asked him, "Now that you killed them, what are you going to do with them?"

"Watch and learn, Lieutenant." With that answer, Brody stripped down to his boxers and dove over the side to bring back some of the floating dead fish.

"What a fucking idiot!" Now MacShane was really pissed and shouted out, "Sergeant, get your ass back onboard this ship now!"

Brody either didn't hear MacShane, or he elected to ignore the order. Regardless of the reason, Brody was now too busy swimming out to the buoyant carnage to respond. MacShane was still shouting ordered when he saw swirling movements in the water moving closer to Brody's position. "Damn-it! Everyone stand back," shouted MacShane as he hoisted the M-16 to his shoulder and took aim. Though not the biggest Shark in the ocean, it was the largest Hammerhead MacShane had ever seen; he estimated it as a good 12-14 feet long.

MacShane took his time and steadied the M-16. With perfect marksmanship, he squeezed off three shots in rapid succession, hitting the large beast in the top of the head right between his t-bone eyes. The well-placed shots cause the grey predator to do a death roll onto its side and sink beneath the surface into the depths below.

Brody, thinking MacShane was shooting at him, managed to grab two dead Mahi by the tail and started making his way back to the ship. The fish in his grasp were still twitching as the last bit of life left their bodies.

When Brody reached the open hatch that T.C. had used, MacShane was there to meet him. "Get your ass in here!" MacShane was furious. He almost wished he would have let the shark take a small bit out of him just to teach him a lesson.

"Dinner is served," announced Brody with a huge smile as he whips the fish into the hatch.

"Get your ass in here now, or I'll let the next shark have its way with you," growls MacShane.

"Shark! A SHHHAARKK! Is that what you were shooting at?" blurts Brody now turning a pale white.

"What, you thought I was shooting at you? If that was the case, mister we wouldn't be having this conversation, you stupid bastard!" yelled Mac as he grabs Brody's arm and yanks him into the boat, damn near pulling his arm out of the socket.

"Consider yourself confined to quarters until further notice," commanded MacShane.

"But what about dinner?" asked Brody.

MacShane was at his limit and said, "We'll slide it under the door to you!"

After confining Brody to his quarters, MacShane and T.C. headed to the bridge to get the Sequoia back on her original heading.

Mac, puzzled by the plastic sheets, asked T.C., "How he thought they got all the way out here." And before T.C. could answer, Atwater entered the wheelhouse and demanded an explanation as to what all the excitement was about.

"What the hell is going on here, MacShane? I was trying to do my work when I start hearing gunshots, explosions, and a commotion with the crew." Atwater was now fuming, more about being disturbed than the cause of all the bedlam.

T.C. started to explain about the ship getting the Visqueen wrapped around the prop and how he had to go overboard to clear it when he noticed Atwater actually starting to crack a smile.

"Dopers. It's an old smugglers trick," said Atwater. "They use that stuff in case someone is chasing them, such as the Coast Guard, or someone is trying to pirate their load." MacShane and T.C. looked at Atwater, not knowing whether to believe him or not.

"You serious?" asked T.C.

"What did you think? Someone was painting their living room and it blew away?" answered Atwater sarcastically, then adding, "Yes, I'm serious. When dopers see someone chasing them, they unroll a sheet of that plastic stuff and throw it in the water. The pursuing vessel gets this crap wrapped around its drive gear, and it either stops them cold or considerably slows them down to the point that the smugglers getaway. They could keep ten to twelve rolls under the navigator's seat, unrolling and tossing as needed."

"You know way too much about this stuff Atwater," stated MacShane.

"It's part of my job," replied Atwater with a stare. "How far off course are we?" He continued, changing the subject without missing a beat.

T.C. answered and then started to tell Atwater about Brody's overzealous behavior when Atwater cut him off, saying "Brody's an asshole; let him sit in his cabin for a while; it will give the rest of us a break."

For once, MacShane was in complete agreement with Atwater.

Chapter 27

MacShane left Brody in his cabin for the next two days. During Brody's absence, the trip almost seemed peaceful. With calm seas and not much else to do, Holly went back to working on her tan and even talked Dixon and Lopez into joining her. Kim stayed in her undies while Connie followed Holly's lead and dared to go bare, working on her all-over tan. Drake, Mac, and T.C. went about the daily chores of the ship while Atwater stayed in his cabin, not even coming out for meals. They were placed in front of his cabin door, and by morning, only the dirty plates remained.

In the wheelhouse, Drake and T.C. checked their position on the navigation chart and put together an eta for Grand Cayman. "Better give Mac a call and bring him up to speed," spoke T.C.

Drake's voice crackled over the intercom, interrupting Mac who was up forward relaxing with a Monte Cristo#2 cigar while catching up on some reading. "Mac to the wheelhouse" was all MacShane needed to hear. He put down his copy of Mark Twain's 'Following the Equator' and hustled up to the bridge, Damn near tripping over Sargent Dixon as he reached the top of the stairs.

"Son of a bitch!" exclaimed MacShane as he leaped over the naked sun worshipers.

"Care to join us, Colonel?" chipped in Lt. Lopez, laying on her stomach and lifting her head in order to give MacShane a come-hither look. Mac had previously noticed that the Lieutenant was well put together, but he had no idea exactly how well until now.

MacShane made a growling sound as he stepped over the last bare butt and looked right at Holly, uttering, "This is your doing, I take it," as he entered the bridge.

Holly looked at the other two girls and giggled at MacShane's reaction. Lopez looked at Holly and said, "Well, he didn't say no." With that the girls burst out laughing.

"Do you know what's going on outside that hatch?" Mac questioned T.C.

"Yeah, Holly asked if the girls could lay out for a while and catch some rays. So?" answered T.C., perplexed.

"Do you know they're naked?" added Mac.

"Yeah, and?" replied T.C.

Drake perked up at this point. "You knew they were naked and didn't say anything. Some friend you are!"

"Dude, you know Holly, that's the only way she'll get sun," answered T.C.

"That's what I'm talking about; this is still a military mission. We need to keep some form of discipline," complains Mac.

"Hey bro, you're the one telling Connie we're not real big on formalities around here. Remember!" T.C. reminded Mac of a previous conversation. "Besides, I think she has the hots for you."

"What!" exclaimed Mac.

"Yeah, Holly told me. Last night," added T.C.

"You're one lucky dude," commented Drake, looking at the bridge window, taking in the view.

"Is this what you called me up here for, more nonsense?" Morgan was indignant.

"No, we wanted to tell you were here," calls out T.C. pointing to their position on the chart. "About 10 hours out of Grand Cayman. Mac, how about letting Brody loose? We need to go over our game plan once more before we reach land anyway," said T.C.

"I'll let him out in time for dinner, we'll have a refresher course while we eat," informed MacShane, walking over to the window to take a peek. "What time is chow?"

"About 18:00, I was just getting ready to go below and start working on the pork tenderloin," responded T.C. "I've got a new recipe I want to try out; it's an apple-raisin sauce made with Marie Bizard apple liquor. First time I'm making it, nothing better than testing it out on a captive audience."

"For joy! Only 4 more hours to go. I'm putting you in charge of the Follies Brassier out on the bridge wing. Make sure everyone is ready to go at 18:00 hours. I'm going below to check on Atwater and fill him in." Mac was getting into his command mode; giving ordered was second nature.

"Me! Why me? I've got a dinner to prep," whines T.C.

"Your woman, your problem. Carry on mister," stated Mac as he turned and left the bridge, going through the opposite door so as to not get involved with the bare-ass sirens waiting outside to tease him. MacShane was an excellent commander and knew when to put his mission first, no matter what devilish delights could be tempting to distract him from his objective.

Reaching Atwater's stateroom, MacShane knocked on the door. After waiting a sufficient amount of time, he knocked again and added, "Atwater, open up. It's MacShane, what the hell are you doing in there anyhow!" The door never opened; all Mac heard was Atwater saying, "Go away MacShane, I'm too busy for a social call."

"Atwater, open up. Were 10 hours out of Grand Cayman, I'm holding a briefing at 18:00 during dinner, so make sure you show up and are on time. That's all!" MacShane turned, heading back to the forward area to resume reading his book, when Atwater's door opened ever so slightly. MacShane turned back to the door and noticed it had opened only to the point of letting Atwater press his left eye into the crack between the door frame and the door, enabling him to peek out. Despite the small opening, MacShane did happen to notice that the rest of the room was dark, with only a faint green glow visible behind Atwater's head.

"Don't you start playing G.I.Joe with me pal," Atwater muttered. "I've taken this mission seriously from the start. Just because you're getting a case of the jitters, don't start taking it out on me. How dare you treat me like some runny nose boot camp recruit."

"Look here, spook, up until now, I've taken your shit and just blew you off as being a major asshole, but now it's getting down to crunch time, and I need to know where everyone stands. Be at the briefing! 1800 hours! Understand!" Atwater pushed the door shut without an acknowledgment which really pissed off MacShane.

Mac started forward again, rubbing his forehead, replaying the past half hour. Naked women sunbathed on deck, laughing. Brody, a loose cannon, was confined to his stateroom, and Atwater remained locked away, barely eating. The only normal ones, it seemed now, were T.C. and Drake, who only two weeks ago MacShane thought were the most unstable people he had met in some time. Oh, how one's view of the world changes so quickly.

Chapter 28

18:00 hours. The crew is assembled around the elegant dining room table, passing around a basket of freshly baked biscuits. T.C. was in the galley, carefully pulling his latest creation from the oven, making final preparations before presenting it to the group. Meanwhile, at the head of the table, MacShane began his briefing. "We're going to be in Grand Cayman about midnight. I contacted Customs over the radio but they shut down right about now, so we have instructions to anchor off until morning. At that time, a tender will bring out a customs and immigration official to check our paperwork," MacShane addressed Atwater. "Nice of you to join us this evening. I'm going to need all the documents showing our 'transgression' through the Panama Canal."

"You'll have 'em, don't fret none over me Colonel," replied Atwater, now sporting a two-day growth of stubble along with a stench of not having bathed recently.

MacShane let the slight go and gave his head a quick shake as if to blow it off. Morgan was preparing to begin his instructions of what needed to be done for the arrival of the Cayman officials when T.C. entered with his pork tenderloin concoction.

"WOW! That smells great!" exclaimed Brody, who has only been eating sandwiches for the past two days.

"Pull any more shit and that smell will be the closest thing you'll get for food until we return," MacShane warns Brody.

"Yes sir, I understand completely. From here on out, it's all business, I assure you, Colonel." Brody seemed sincere in his willingness to comply, but MacShane was hesitant in accepting his word at face value.

"Roger that. And if you'll pass that platter and leave some food for the rest of us we can get started." Everyone found a small bit of humor in MacShane's statement, except Atwater, he found it nauseating and a waste of time.

"Can we proceed with this 'briefing' so I can get back to work?" Atwater's sarcasm wasn't lost on the rest of the crew. MacShane gave him a cold stare and continued.

"We were instructed to drop anchor off the George Town docks approximately a half mile from shore. In the morning the Cayman officials are coming out to check our papers and do a routine inspection. Obviously, we can't show them our cargo or let them into the interior of the ship. So what I propose we do is have a table set up under the a/c port under the bridge. It's going to be a hot, humid day and those guys will want to get back to their office asap. I'll need everybody's passports so this can be a quick, smooth maneuver."

"Bullshit!" shouts out Atwater. "I don't carry any paperwork, and as far as you people know, I don't even exist. You keep them busy topside, don't worry about me, they'll never know I'm here. You people go on deck and make nice, and I'll do what I have to do."

"And exactly what is that Atwater?" This was coming from T.C., who had had just about enough of this crap. "What do you do all day and night in that stateroom anyway? You got the latest issue of Penthouse stuffed under your pillow?" T.C.'s last comment had the table smirking now.

"You'll find out when the time's right, mess boy. You just keep flipping those burgers, and we'll all be fat, dumb and happy, like the rest of the country. Always willing to let someone else do the dirty work. Don't interfere with the lust for bigger TVs or fancier cars. Making themselves numb to the plight of the rest of the world. That's the new America, alright. Instead of the motto 'Don't tread on me it should say 'Don't count on me.'"

"Enough, Atwater. Save your breath for a soapbox back home," MacShane cut off Atwater's tirade, steering the briefing back on track. "When we clear customs, we're going to have to take on fuel. After the ship is docked at the Kirk fuel dock, Drake, Brody and Dixon get off and mossy around the place, asking vague questions of the dock hands about ship movement in and out of the island. Try to find a local who doesn't mind talking to strangers. This rock is fairly small, and gossip is a way of life."

"That's your game plan? Asking some inbred natives about the activity in the shipyards? Man that's brilliant. You might even secure an office in the Pentagon with this plan." Atwater was being plane insubordinate and MacShane was at his limit.

"Enough Mister!" MacShane was still in charge and had to act accordantly, using all his willpower to keep from telling Atwater to 'eat shit and bark at the moon'. "This mission is going forward with or without you. Either add something constructive or restrain yourself from any further outbursts. You read me, Mister." This was the first time in years that T.C. had seen the look MacShane was giving Atwater. The last time he saw it, they were deployed in Iraq during Desert Storm. MacShane needed information on sniper locations; he wasn't about to waste any more of his men's lives trying to be politically correct. He sent for an officer of the Republican Guard they had in custody and started to interrogate him. Not liking how the information was coming across MacShane un- holstered his 45 and stuck it in the middle of the prisoner's forehead, right between his eyes and asked the questioned again. T.C. couldn't tell if it was the look in MacShane's eyes, the 45-caliber pistol pressing against the skin on his forehead, or a combination of the two. But whatever the reason, the prisoner gave up the much-needed information and MacShane got a reprimand and a commendation all in the same day for saving his men's life.

Atwater was enough of a professional to know when to cool it. He responded to MacSahne by slouching back in his chair and crossing his arms on his chest.

"Now to continue, you three find out as much as you can, stop in the storefront shops, and ask the clerks; maybe they overheard something that may help. We're only going to be here a short while, so don't waste too much time on one person. Cover as much ground as you can."

Chapter 29

Daybreak came and the Sequoia has been anchored off Georgetown C.I. for the past few hours. Since he was confined to his quarters for the prior couple of days Brody decided to stand the first watch. Sam gazes out from the bridge as a few Albatrosses leave the island to start their daily hunt for food. Below, he hears the beginning sound of a new day milling about in the galley. Drake emerges barefoot, wearing faded beige shorts and a paint-splattered t-shirt. Hair unkempt, rubbing sleep out of his eyes. "How's everything Sam, any problems?" Drake asked, scratching his bristly facial hair.

"Everything's good, only saw that little red light come on once," reports Brody, pointing to the instrument panel. "Stayed on for about 30 seconds and shut off. Didn't think it was all that important."

"Bilge pump light, let's ya know when it's kicked on and runnin'. No problem, it's normal. Any sign of life on shore yet?" asked Drake.

"Nope, pretty quiet so far. Hope those guys are on time, I'd really like to get my feet on land for a while," commented Brody

"Well, if they're anything like the rest of the Caribbean Islands, we might not see them for an hour or two. Go below and get some rest. I'll take next watch."

With a full cup of black coffee, Drake made himself comfortable in the large seat behind the helm. He reached up and turned on the ICOM vhf marine radio to channel 9 in case the officials tried to hail them. Two cups of coffee and an hour later, the radio's faint static was interrupted by a crisp message.

"Sequoia, Sequoia, this is customs agent Ebanks. Do you copy please." Hearing the message, Drake smiled to himself. He loved the sound of a Caribbean English accent. Picking up the mike, he responded. "This is the Sequoia; we copy Agent Ebanks, go ahead."

"Good morning, Sequoia, Officer Bodden and I will be leaving the docks momentarily. Please awaken your crew and have all appropriate paper work at the ready."

"Roger that Agent Ebanks, we look forward to your arrival. Sequoia standing by channel 9." As soon as Drake finished with Ebanks, he switched on the intercom and hailed everyone below.

"Attention all hands, attention all hands, that is except you Atwater. Grand Cayman officials are on their way out, let's get a move on, we have fifteen minutes, twenty top," Drake repeated the message once more to guarantee everyone is awake and moving. From the bridge, he could already see T.C. setting up a folding card table on deck under the a/c port connected to the cabins. Holly and Connie, still in their nightshirts, carried out a couple of folding chairs. MacShane, Brody and Dixon reinspected the tarps covering the cargo to make sure nothing was exposed and Atwater, true to his word, was among the missing.

As predicted, the Cayman officials arrived eighteen minutes after their transmission. A small tender pulled up to the side of the old freighter. Brody and Drake had already lowered the cargo net so the officials could make their way on board. After climbing up the netting everyone could see from the look on their faces that the officials were none too happy with the setup. T.C. walked out to greet them, extending his hand.

"Welcome aboard gentleman, I'm the captain, T.C. Allen; please follow me. I have all the necessary paperwork laid out on the table over here."

The two were dressed in crisp white uniforms, pressed with pinpoint accuracy. Their bright white shirts and shorts were a stark contrast to the dark brown bodies underneath, beige knee socks, white shoes, and a pith helmet topped off the ensonbo. T.C. knew that there was no way in Hell these guys were going to get themselves dirty first thing in the morning and he keyed in on it.

"This is an interesting vessel you have here, captain. Exactly what do you haul with it?" asked agent Ebanks, who looked more accustomed to checking in cruise ships than cargo tubs.

"Whatever we can, sir, we usually get hired by having the lowest bid. We try to keep our overhead low," answered T.C.

"Hey MacShane! Yo MacShane, get these officers some coffee while they look over the paperwork," commanded T.C. as he walks them over to the card table. "He's my first officer, a pretty good one most of the time, but I always have to keep on his ass. He's been working for me ever since I bailed him out of a Dominican jail for being publicly intoxicated. He was chasing goats around a field, calling them woman's names." T.C. looked at both officers and shrugged his shoulders then added. "He's a great sailor, don't get me wrong, just have to keep him away from the rum, if you know what I mean," T.C. pulled out a chair and offered Agent Ebanks a seat.

Ebanks looked down at the greasy cushion and decided that he and Officer Bodden would rather stand.

MacShane came out on deck without the coffee, and when questioned as to why, MacShane said, "The girls already finished off the first pot, but I have them makin' more Capt'n."

"Nonsense!" shouted T.C. "Get them out here immediately MacShane!" he ordered.

Morgan opened the hatch and yelled inside, "Capt'n wants you wenches up on deck, move it, on the double and bring your coffee!"

The two officials were looking at each other in total disbelief. Not knowing what to expect next.

As the hatch opened, Holly and Connie came out, still in their night shirts. T.C. barked an order, causing them to jump spilling a few drops of coffee on the deck.

"How dare you finish off the coffee before our guests can have any. Give them your cups, and you wait for the next pot."

Without hesitation, the girls replied, "Yes sir, Captain!" as they reached out, offering cups of coffee to the two officials.

"No! No thank you, mon! We don't want any coffee tanks anyway. We need to get all your papers stamped so you can be on your way. Don't be worrin' 'bout us," said Ebanks, who now seems to be in a hurry to leave this crazy ship before he ruins his uniform.

"Give me toes passports, mon!" spoke Bodden following Ebanks lead. "Captain call your crew out so's I can stamp their papers now."

T.C. walked over to the hatch opened it up, and yelled inside, "Everyone assemble on deck Immigrations Officer needs you."

T.C. and MacShane smiled at each other, knowing that their game plan was working. The crew dutifully mustered on deck. Officer Bodden quickly held up the passports to check I.D, satisfied that the pictures looked close enough, he stamped each one and set them in a pile on the dirty table. As soon as Bodden stamped the last document," T.C. asked. "Agent Ebanks where can we fuel up were pretty low after coming through the canal?"

"Ya, mon I bet you are. You dock over at the base of that big radio tower over dare, you see it? My cousin runs the fuel dock; I tell him your commin'. You're going to leave after you fuel up, yes?" Ebanks proper Caribbean English was starting to turn into a fast-talking island slang.

"Yea, we have to get going, got some supplies to deliver. You gentleman ready to see the rest of the ship?" inquirs T.C.

"No! That won't be necessary. Here are your papers, everything looks to be in order. I'll let my cousins know to expect you soon. Then you leave, right?" asked Ebanks again just to make sure he heard correctly the first time. As long as these crazy people weren't staying Ebanks figured it wasn't really his business what was on board and he truly didn't want to inspect or touch anything on this scow. He just wanted off as soon as possible.

"Yes sir, after we fuel up were out of here, many places to go many things to see," reaffirmed T.C.

"Very good captain, here are your papers, bon voyage. Come on Bodden lets go, we have more ships to do today."

"Thanks Agent Ebanks, tell your cousin to be on the lookout for us." T.C. was waving ever so cordially as the two men climbed over the rail and hopped back into their tender.

MacShane couldn't hold back his laughter any longer. He burst out with a full-fledged belly howl. "Did you see the look on their faces when they saw the grease all over the chair, I think they were afraid to touch anything at that point."

"That was one smooth act. See I told you living like this has its advantages," replied T.C, smiling from ear to ear, slapping Morgan on the back. "Ebanks eyes looked like flying saucers when I told the girls to give up their coffee to him, I nearly pissed myself! Damn I bet everyone in town will hear about the crazy crew on the filthy ship. It couldn't have been any more perfect!"

Atwater watched the whole episode from his vantage point in the cargo hold. "Laugh it up now, funny boy. We'll wait and see how funny it is when the shit starts to hit the fan."

Chapter 30

Tied up to the fuel docks in Georgetown T.C. supervises the fueling as the empty Sequoia gets a well-deserved drink. "Keep it commin' boys this is one thirsty girl," turning to MacShane he gives him the nod to disembark with Lopez to ask some questioned in town.

"Let's go Connie. Drake, Brody and Dixon have about a half-hour start. Since they went right towards town, we need to head off to the left and see what's up." MacShane led the way as the two exited down the gangplank.

North Church Street was alive with traffic. Jittneys, cabs and busses jammed the tiny streets of Georgetown. Pedestrians added to the mix crowding the narrow sidewalks. 'Watch when we cross, they drive on the opposite side here." instructed MacShane to Lopez.

"Thanks Dad! But I've been out of the country before," shot back Connie in a teasing tone.

MacShane cut his eyes at Connie before his eyes settled on a ramshackle hole-in-the-wall bar about fifty yards ahead. "Looks like a good place to start. Right across form the docks, somebody might know something."

"Man, you spare no expense when you're out to show a lady a good time, eh, Mac," said Connie as they stood on the steps of the dilapidated structure. "'The Stiff Conch' what a great name, wonder if we can buy the franchise rights for the Stated? Think about it a 'stiff conch on every corner. Kinda poetic don't ya think?"

"After you my dear," responded MacShane as he opened the squeaky wooden door. It took a few moments for their eyes to adjust to the low lighting. Inside, the place was even worse than the outside, damp and musty air, complete with the stench of stale beer. Despite the early morning hour, the bar had a number of people in it. The breakfast beverage of choice seemed to be a pint of Guiness, sitting in front of the majority of the men. Everyone sat at the bar minding their own business watching a cricket match on a black and white television set. Everyone except a drunken sailor who was arguing with the short squat bartender who refused to issue him credit for one more drink. MacShane and Lopez grabbed one of the two booths and couldn't help but overhear the two men bickering.

The drunk was pleading for another drink when MacShane heard him say with a heavy Spanish accent. "Listen my friend when I get back from Cuba, I will have plenty of money I will come back and promise to pay you double."

But the Bartender wasn't falling for that one. "You want rum you pay with money not promises. Now get out of here before I ring up the constable," he warns, waving a stubby finger at the drunk.

MacShane, sensing a chance to learn more stood up and walked over to the drunk putting his arm around him. "Oyja! Amigo! Como sta? You want rum? Come sit with us." The drunk turned and gave MacShane a big toothless grin. The light from the television gave Mac a good look at his glazed over eyes. This might be just what the doctor ordered he thought.

"Bartender, a rum for my friend and two beers for my woman and me," ordered MacShane. Grabbing the drunk around the waist and draping an arm around his neck, Morgan made his way back to the booth with the drunk dragging his feet on the dirt floor.

Connie didn't know what to expect when Morgan pushed him into the booth and sat next to him blocking the drunk in. "My god! He smells awful!" complains Lopez.

"Buenos Dias Senorita! You are very beautiful today," said the drunk to Connie.

"So my friend," started MacShane in perfect Spanish. "How did you come to be in such bad shape?"

"Those pendahoes! Bastards! They left me here! I meet a local senorita, we made big party, I fell asleep and when I wake up my ship is leaving. They don't wait for me! Cabrones!" cursed the drunk.

Stubby brought the ordered drinks and gave a disgusted look to MacShane for keeping the drunk in his bar. "Ya not doin' that lad any favor mon," quipped the barkeep as he placed down the drinks. MacShane waved a twenty in stubbies face and told him to keep the change. He left without another word. Seems like wherever you go, money is preferred over the need to take care of our fellow man.

For the next half hour, MacShane grilled his new friend about the goings on in Cuba, and the more rum that went in, the more information came out. That was until the saturation point occurred. Now the drunk could hardly keep his head off the table. With his words coming out badly slurred, the drunks' usefulness had reached its limit. MacShane looked at Connie and suggested they had better get back to the ship. Leaving the drunk face down on the table, MacShane walked up to the bar and handed the bartender another twenty. Mac whispered a few words in his ear and motioned for Connie to join him as he made his way out the door into the street.

"What on Earth did you tell that bartender that let him allow you to leave that old drunk at the table?" asked Lopez in disbelief.

"Simple, I told him that if he'd let me leave my friend in the booth till, I took you back to your hotel I would go to my ship and bring some of the crew back to carry him away. I gave him an extra twenty to keep an eye on him," answered MacShane.

"Damn! Your good MacShane." Connie was laughing now, thinking about the bartender's expression when no one came back to claim the drunk.

MacShane's look changed back to business when he commented on the information they had just received. "We would have been sitting ducks without this info Connie, that drunk might have just given us a chance at completing this mission and living to talk about it."

Chapter 31

With all hands back on board and the vital information obtained from the waylaid drunken Cuban in hand, the crew makes ready to leave Grand Cayman. Next stop Cuba, the Pearl of the Caribbean.

On the bridge Morgan, Drake and T.C. were laying out a navigational chart, plotting the next heading.

"What's our ETA?" Drake asked T.C. as he was laying out the intended course for the upcoming leg of the journey.

"Well, from my calculations, by this time tomorrow, we're going to be hip deep in authentic Cohibas and Cuban rum," replied T.C. as he closed his dividers and placed them in a drawer under the chart table.

"Damn! It's a short time now," said Drake.

Morgan, detecting a slight bit of apprehension in Drake's voice, said, "Yeah, we really need everyone to look sharp," he added. "There's no telling what we can expect from here on out."

Another beautiful Caribbean sunset was taking place as the Sequoia steadily made her way to her appointed destination. Sailing on the flat sea directly into the brilliant red, orange and purple hues, the ship is dwarfed by the huge clouds on the horizon. Morgan was up forward, leaning on the starboard rail, enjoying an H. Upman robusto while taking in the view. Lost in thought he didn't hear

Connie walk up behind him and was visibly startled when she put her arm on his shoulder.

"Man! Don't do that! It could be dangerous," alerts Mac as he regained his composure, lowering his arm and relaxing his fist.

"Dangerous for whom?" asked Connie.

"Lady it's a good thing for you that my reflexes are still in top shape or I might have come around and decked you," boasts Morgan.

"Mac there's a little thing about me you don't know." hesitating about what she was going to reveal. "I can take care of myself, don't worry 'bout poor lil ole me," Connie assures him.

"You mean if a big guy like me came up to you and tried to take advantage..." Mac made his move on Connie. He tried to put his arm across the back of her shoulders and one around her waist but Connie moved like lighting and had Mac face down on the deck with her right knee in the middle of his back and his left arm twisted in hers. Mac was in a mild state of shock, he couldn't believe that she could get the drop on him.

"Told you, big boy. Give up yet?"

Mac struggled but couldn't get free "Give up?" reiterated Connie.

"Ok! Ok! I give, but what the Hell just happened?" Mac was getting back on his feet, dusting himself off.

"Fourth-degree black belt Colonel, been practicing since I was ten. I started lessons after being shaken down for my lunch money at school. Been doing it ever since."

On the bridge, T.C. happened to catch the show and was howling over the loudspeaker. "Mac with moves like that, there's no wonder why you've never been married." MacShane looks up at the bridge window and flips off his old buddy. Commenting, "Don't you have a call to make?"

Morgan was referring to a link up with the Thetis to give them an update.

"Come on up and we'll call them together," answered T.C.

With Mac and Connie on the bridge, T.C. pulled out the portable communication device and powered it on. "Vatican City, Vatican City, this is Crusader. Do you copy." hearing nothing but static T.C. tried again. Vatican City, Crusader. Do you copy? Over!" T.C. looked at Mac and Connie, giving them a shrug. As he drew in another breath to hail the Coast Guard again, the speaker crackled to life.

"Crusader, this is Vatican City how do you copy?" came the reply in a slow southern drawl.

"Loud and clear, V.C. just thought we'd check in with mother hen to let everyone know we're a-ok. Pulled out of Grand Cayman just under two hours ago headed for destination you know where," answered T.C.

"Any luck in George town?" the voice now belonging to Captain Hathaway.

"Well the girls hooked up with some doctors who were in town for a convention, Drake and Brody made it with the twin barmaids at the Holiday Inn, Mac got a case of the crabs from a local working girl and Atwater got arrested for hanging around a grammar school trying to give candy to little girls. But all in all I would certainly endorse George town as a liberty port for your crew sir."

"PUT MACSHANE ON!!" booms the voice at the other end. Hathaway wasn't in the mood for nonsense. Mac grabbed the mike from T.C., giving him a disgusted look and answered the captain's request. "MacShane here Captain." And without waiting for a reply continued on saying, "We made contact with a waylaid Cuban sailor and got a ton of information out of him, some vital for the completion of this mission. Were on course for our designated destination. All is well, the ship and crew are in perfect order.

"Very well MacShane, keep us posted as to your progress. Vatican City out," the static returns and MacShane let out a deep breath. "Why did you have to fuck with him? He's our only chance of backup if we happen to need any. God! T.C., sometimes I really wonder about you."

"Relax Mac. He's just a bit uptight. A few more phone calls from me and I'll have him mellowed out just like I did to you. You were a real tight ass when you first came on board, remember?" T.C. was smiling, trying to get Mac to do the same. Connie was standing next to Mac and said, "You mean more than he is now?"

"Lady you've got no clue. I took this guy here and added at least twenty years to his life." T.C. put his arm around his old buddy's shoulder and gave him a little shake. "He was starting to really come around to, but then this shit happened and, you know, old habits die hard, what can I tell ya?"

"I know what I can tell you." Mac was speaking directly to T.C., "I'm taking the first watch, you two get below and get some sleep and make sure the rest of the crew does the same. Tomorrow is commencement day and everybody better be ready to graduate." T.C. and Connie went below, passing along Macshane's message.

Chapter 32

Captain Yakabofsky enters the command center of the B-51, a Foxtrot class submarine of the former Soviet Union. Yakabofsky looks at his watch, 19:00 hours and asked Lieutenant Commander Espisito, "What is our depth and speed?"

"Sir, as per your ordered El Captain were at 200 meters traveling at 3 knots. Heading 192 degrees," came the rapid reply.

"Very well, commander, give the order to surface, but slowly. I want to break the surface at sunset." Yakabofsky went around the control room checking his crews' stations, mentally grading each man as he went about their tasked. 30 years in the Soviet Navy made Igor Yakabofsky a wise and experienced sailor. After the collapse of his beloved 'Mother Russia' he found himself out of work and nowhere to go. Since he had no family to hold him, Yakabofsky took a job aboard a tramp steamer headed to the Caribbean, anywhere beats the winters in Leningrad he told himself. During his travels he met a few other officers of the former Soviet super power, some working for the drug lords of Columbia, others making their way into Cuba to work on some big project Fidel had going. Igor's luck changed when he was in an outside café in Curacoa, there he ran into a classmate from the Tikhookeansky Naval Academy, he told Igor he heard of a job in Cuba where they were looking for a Captian for a 'Podvodnaya Lodka' (Russian for submarine).

Igor was foaming at the mouth, waiting for the right chance to get off the tramp. He was at the point where a winter in Leningrad didn't look too bad. He took down all the information from his friend and put it away for safekeeping. The next thing he did was to find a ship going to Cuba and hitched a ride.

But now Yakabofsky loathes the day his "friend "gave him the information. Igor was stuck on a leftover, cold war, diesel-powered submarine that should have been used for target practice over a decade ago. Having served aboard the latest nuclear vessels in the Soviet fleet, Yakabofsky can't believe how he has lowered himself to the level of a paid mercenary on this antiquated sub and its crew of poorly trained Cuban nationals.

Built in the Sudomekh Shipyards in Leningrad, the B-51 was originally commissioned way back on October 26, 1967. Serving a tour of duty in the North Atlantic, the ship played a constant game of cat and mouse with the United Stated Navy. Getting as close as four miles off the northeastern coast of New Jersey where, the captain and crew ran simulated missile attacks on New York City and the surrounding suburbs. However, that was during the so-called "good old days"—a time when adversaries were clearly defined, and their actions, though hostile, were at least predictable.

Now, the tired old B-51 patrols the southern coast of Cuba, keeping a watchful eye for any unwanted intruders.

"Ventilate the boat and charge the batteries, Lieutenant. At daybreak, we'll submerge to 45 meters and continue our patrol." Captain Yakabofsky gives a half-assed salute to the Lieutenant Commander and retires for the evening.

"Aye, aye, El Captain." And then under his breath muttered, "pendajo."

Chapter 33

The night passed quickly, and rest was uneasy for the crew of the Sequoia. Showtime was now only hours away causing a mild case of the sweats among them.

First light brought out the crew, and even Atwater decided to show up. "Hey, look! The groundhog came out to check his shadow." Wise-cracked Drake, who was getting ready to relieve Brody on the Bridge.

"Fuck off, civilian!" comes the gracious reply from Atwater.

MacShane, Holly, Kim, and Connie were at the galley table watching the confrontation, finishing a gourmet breakfast prepared by T.C., who was still stuck at the stove cleaning up.

"Want breakfast?" T.C. asked Atwater.

"I'll make it myself!" grunted Atwater.

"Suit yourself, dude," answered T.C. in his low-key fashion, clapping his hands over the stove reminiscent of a blackjack dealer leaving his table. "It's all yours buddy."

Atwater stepped up to the range, grabbed a pan from the overhead rack and dropped it on the burner. Next, he slopped in a glob of butter, letting it melt and sizzle. The butter was boiling as Atwater used two hands to crack open three eggs on the side of the pan, leaving egg whites trailing down the outside of the skillet.

Atwater used a fork to shuffle the eggs around as they splattered, popped and bubbled in the hot liquid. Using his fingers, he tried to remove some of the unwanted shells.

All T.C. could do was stand there with his mouth agape, seeing but not really believing. He hadn't seen such a poor display of cooking since his first day of culinary school.

Atwater continued to 'cook' and was now taking a spatula to his creation trying to flip the eggs. The eggs fell apart and broke into about a dozen pieces. Taking the pan off the burner a few seconds later, Atwater scraped the eggs onto a plate leaving a good portion of the eggs stuck to the pan.

T.C. couldn't take anymore. He reached for his pan, shouting," heathen! You uncivilized, uneducated shoemaker! That's no way to treat my equipment! Who the Hell ever told you that you could cook?!"

Atwater sat down, unfazed by T.C.'s commented. He salted his eggs and, in a nonchalant matter-of-fact way, said, "I'm eating, ain't I? What else matters?"

T.C. was outraged."YOU DICK! I've seen guys right off the boat make a better meal than you. That's the last time you'll ever use my stuff again, G-Man!"

"Fine with me pal. Now don't bother me while I'm trying to eat." Atwater stared at his plate, slowly moving his fork around the broken pieces of an egg as the rest of the crew went up on deck, leaving Atwater to his own devices.

Chapter 34

As per Yakabofsky's ordered, the B-51 is exactly 45 meters below the surface, holding the appointed course and speed when, at 07:30, an ear-piercing alarm goes off. Lieutenant Commander Esposito gives the command to attain periscope depth. The boat levels off, and the periscope is raised as Captain Yakabofsky arrives on the bridge. "Status Esposito." Yakabofsky had a certain disdain for the Cuban crew. He felt they were arrogant, hot-headed, trigger-happy pirates who had problems with discipline. At times like this, he much preferred Leningrad in the winter.

"El Captain, we have a freighter entering Zone 7. Sir, we have no ships scheduled for that area; all ships are to use Zone 1 today. Shall I give the order to load the torpedoes, Sir?"

"At ease Lieutenant, have a little patience; maybe this guy didn't get the memo? Eh. We don't want to sink one of our own, now do we?" the captain looked at the crew, who were now snickering at the Lieutenant's rash comment. Reversing his hat, Yakabofsky leans up to the periscope and said, "Let's take a look and see what kind of threat we have here."

A few moments later, Yakabofsky lets out a laugh. "This is what you wanted to waste one of our expensive torpedoes on? Give this tub a couple more days, and it will sink by itself."

The crew now taking turns looking through the view finder and laughing at the old rust bucket in the periscope.

"But Sir, why is it in Zone 7? We must make contact and find out," stated Esposito.

"Yes, yes, Lieutenant, and so we shall make ready to surface so we can interrogate this menacing scourge of the high seas."

Chapter 35

With Drake at the helm, the rest of the crew assembled on deck to do some morning calisthenics. Stretching and bending, the group was working up a sweat when Drake hit the p.a. system, calling all hands to look off the port bow. Atwater even came out to see what all the commotion was about while T.C. headed up to the bridge. A huge swirling, foaming maelstrom was forming in the ocean as everyone stared. MacShane was the first to speak, "Girls get below and stay out of sight; looks like we're going to have a visitor."

As soon as the woman were below deck a conning tower of a submarine pierced the surface of the water, a huge Cuban flag painted on the side. A few moments later, the sub was fully surfaced and the pressure hull was cutting a course right for the Sequoia. MacShane looks over to Atwater and said, "What do you make of it?"

Atwater answered in his flat, dry encyclopedia style, "Old Soviet Foxtrot class, Fidel probably got a Hell of a deal on it. Haven't seen one of those in years. 300 feet long, 24' 7" beam and a 20-foot draft. Diesel, electric engines capable of reaching 16.8 knots, usually carries a crew of 78 and has an armament of 22 torpedoes when fully stocked, with 6 tubes in the front and 4 tubes aft, it was originally equipped with nuclear warheads on the torpedoes during the cold war. And besides having a maximum diving depth of 985 feet, there's not much else I know about it."

"Well mister, it seems like your knowledge of this particular Foxtrot is going to get a lot more personal. See that blue and yellow check flag he's hoisting? That's the Lima flag, an international signal to 'stop instantly,'" replied MacShane.

"Mac, he's hailing us in Spanish. I need you on the bridge," calls out T.C. from the bridge window.

"And so it begins. Let's hope we can bullshit our way out of this one," MacShane told Atwater as he double-timed it up to the bridge, leaving Atwater at the rail checking out the sub.

The submarine was now alongside the Sequoia, a mere 150 feet off the port side. Atwater could see what he believed to be the captain and some of his minions checking out the Sequoia with binoculars. Atwater noticed that the man he thought to be the captain was uniformed slightly different than the others. Then he realized that the jacket and hat were of a Russian naval officer.

Atwater was going to take a gamble, hoping that this captain didn't just happen to find some of the belongings left over from the previous crew. Atwater made his move and shouted over to the sub in Russian, "Comrade! You Ruskie?" and waited for a reply.

Atwater didn't have long to wait as the answer came back in Russian, "Da Comrade, Captain Igor Yakabofsky Soviet Union North Atlantic Fleet, retired."

Atwater had lucked out; he still might be able to pull this out of his ass and get the mission back on track. Communicating back to Yakabofsky in Russian as if happy to see a fellow countryman, Atwater bursts out, "Finally a civilized human being! I'm Vladimir Sokolov KGB and I, like you, am a retired Captain. Now I am forced to babysit a crew of misfits on a broken-down ship. How we got this far without sinking is a miracle."

Captain Yakabofsky smiles and nods his head in agreement as he motions his arm to look at his ship. "Yes, my friend once we had the best of the best, now we have to settle for purgatory." His expression shifts as he eyes the unknown vessel. "But why are you in this area today? All shipping is to use zone 1?" Yakabofsky still the professional doing his job and interrogating the unknown vessel on its intent.

"You can thank our incompetent radio man for that. In his haste to take down the instructions, he knocked over a glass of water on his notes, causing the ink to run. The idiot said we were to use these coordinates for our approach," explained Atwater beginning to believe that his story is being bought.

"What do you have on board, Sokolov anything good?" asked Yakabofsky.

"I've acquired a few items during my tenure with the KGB that I now need to cash in, heard the market is open and the prices are right," informed Atwater, trying to be as vague as possible.

"Da. Da. How...," Yakabofsky was interrupted by Esposito, who was giving a command to lower an inflatable boat and send a crew over to investigate the ship. "Belay that order mister, no one is going anywhere." The crew, looking at both Esposito and Yakabofsky, wondering what they should do next.

"You men stow that gear and get back below, Esposito. You will check with me before giving any ordered for the men to leave the ship." Esposito left the conning tower and retreated down below after the captain's tongue-lashing. Looking back at Atwater, Yakabofsky shakes his head and continued his conversation. "As I was saying, how long will you be in port Vladimir, I am starving for an intelligent conversation and a decent game of chess."

"Only a few days, or until I get all my goods unloaded, when is your patrol over, Igor?" Atwater now getting chummy with his new friend.

"Three, maybe four days. They never let me know for sure. One day, they call us in and change crews, depends if they remember that we're out here or not," commented Yakabofsky laughing.

"I will see if we can wait, my friend. I too yearn for a good game of chess," replied Atwater, knowing that he was up to his neck in a high-stakes game now.

"You can tell your crew they can be on their way; you don't want to miss the first rounds of trading. Fare well, Vladimir, see you soon," said Yakabofsky.

"One more thing Igor, since the fool ruined all the instructions, can you give me the code word for the dockmaster? I hate to call in again and ask, it's bad enough I have to be seen on a tub like this without letting everyone think we're all blockheads." Atwater was going out on a limb, figuring that an installation of this magnitude would have other safeguards.

"Of course, my friend, it's 'Machete,' but you didn't hear it from me! The head security man at the docks is named Escobar. He's a good man, a decent chess player look him up when you get in. See you soon; good luck at the auction." Yakabofsky gave Atwater a snappy salute and headed below. The B-51 submerged moments later.

From the bridge, T.C., Drake, and MacShane couldn't believe what they had just witnessed.

"What the hell is going on Atwater? One minute the Commander is giving us ordered to prepare to be boarded, and the next thing we're being let go. What gives?" asked MacShane, watching the conning tower disappear below the surface of the bridge.

"Too bad you didn't learn Russian instead of Spanish, MacShane. Now we can head into port without being hassled," gloats Atwater. "Don't everyone thank me at once."

MacShane and T.C. were back on deck; they wanted some answered from Atwater. "Just what the hell did you say to him?" asked MacShane.

"We had a nice chat, told him I was former KGB, found out that he is a retired Soviet sub-Captain stuck on an old piece of shit boat with a ragtag crew, much like myself." T.C. cut his eyes at Atwater over the last remark. Atwater ignored it and continued, "And like anyone else, he was happy to see a fellow countryman so far from home."

"That's it?" asked Morgan.

"Pretty much, oh by the way, did that drunken Cuban sailor tell you about the password at the docks?" T.C. and Morgan looked at each other. "No? Didn't think so. Good thing I thought about it. Now we can go on and at least get into port without getting blown to pieces. I'm going to my cabin; get me when we get close, ok boys?" Atwater left T.C. and MacShane on deck as he headed below.

"Com'on Mac, I'll get us something to eat," T.C. remarked to his old buddy, thinking food is the answer to everything.

"No thanks, I've lost my appetite," MacShane muttered, gazing out at the sea, wondering what else Atwater found out or gave away. Snapping back to reality, MacShane headed up to the bridge to radio in their encounter with the old Soviet sub. "Vatican City might find this bit of information interesting," Morgan thought to himself.

Chapter 36

Entering the Monterrey passage, MacShane gave T.C. their bearings: "Stay on a heading of 48o 30' until we reach the first buoy at Cayo Cruz, there we adjust the compass heading to 63o until the next buoy, then change course to 90o and follow the channel markers. This should take us right into the installation, and let's pray that drunken sailor didn't get his directions mixed up."

"Yeah sure, you make it sound easy enough; wonder how many other surprises we have in store," answered T.C.

"Speaking of which, Drake get Atwater up here, will ya?" MacShane requested.

Plying through the protected waters of the Ensenoa De La Broa, the Sequoia is making good time. Mountains on each side of the bay make for a beautiful tropical backdrop, one that could almost be used for brochures advertising A honeymoon cruise. Wild green parrots fly overhead, their squawking voices adding to the soothing sounds of water lapping against the side of the ship. Only this time, the serene beauty is a mask, concealing the death that lies beneath. This wonderful island has now turned into an instrument of destruction. Connie is on deck watching the mountains as they pass by when Holly walks up to her; seeing tears in her eyes she asked. "Connie, what's the matter?"

"Nothing, it's personal," she replied.

"Was it MacShane? Did he do or say something to upset you?" prodded Holly, adding, "If he did, just let me know and I'll—" Connie interrupted Holly, who was shaking her fist.

"No, no, Morgan's the best, it's the fact of just being here. My family used to have a farm over that mountain. My parents would tell us stories of the green fields and cool winds that came down from the hills. Of what a beautiful country Cuba used to be. Now that I can see it for myself, it's a bit overwhelming," explained Lopez.

"One day Connie, one day Castro will be gone, and maybe then everything will get back to normal." Holly didn't know what else to say. She was trying to take her friend's focus off the present and direct her attention to a hopefully happier time.

"It just tears me up to think that Castro is using this beautiful land for such a heinous purpose. My family's homeland, a safe house for all the wretch of the world! Pa-tuie!" Connie spat over the side, getting a direct hit on a floating coconut, imagining that it was Castro's eye. "That's the main reason I volunteered for this mission, to see what it will take to stop this madman." Connie was opening up now and was starting to feel better.

"Com'on time to get below and find Kim, see if there is any ice cream left, I have a feeling the shit is about to hit the proverbial fan, and we girls need to get in as much comfort food as we can before that happens," points out Holly bringing a smile to Connie's face.

Back on the bridge, Atwater arrived with Drake, "Must be close to Showtime," blurts out Atwater. "How close are we to port?"

"I was actually thinking you might be able to tell us," responded MacShane.

"What heading are we on?" asked the CIA man

"Made our final course correction and were following a steady 90o, straight up center of the channel markers," answered T.C. standing at the helm.

"Great, now all you have to do is follow the yellow brick road, and we should see OZ in about 45-50 minutes. Even you can manage to do this one *Captain*. Mocked Atwater. I've got to get back below and finish up a few things. Next time you get me, make sure the dock is in sight!" exclaimed Atwater as he turns and heads back to his cabin.

"Man! That guy! What an asshole!" commented T.C. "After this mission is over, I'm going to bake him a special going away chocolate cake. And the only thing else I'm going to say is that he better have an enormous amount of toilet paper with him."

"Relax, I'll take over. Go below and let everyone know what our status is. Things might start happening fast, and everybody needs to be ready. Even I can keep this tub between the markers." instructed

MacShane. Adding. "Have Kim finish up on the Tomahawk. And T.C., make sure Brody doesn't have any weapons on him. We don't need that nut to start shooting up the countryside."

"Gotcha. Mac. Call out if you need anything." with that T.C. disappeared below decks, leaving MacShane alone on the bridge. Finally isolated in the peaceful confines of the wheelhouse, Morgan inserts a Jackson Brown CD, lights up an Arturo Fuente cigar and savors the sweet aroma in his mouth. Exhaling the smoke, he can't help but puff out some smoke rings. Trying to get in the last bit of me time before it breaks loose. With a light knock on the door frame, Connie waits to gain permission before entering. "Com'on in, no need to knock were all one big happy family. What brings you up here?" asked Mac.

"Just wanted to see what it looked like from the driver's seat," answered Connie. "Nice view, you can see all over from here."

"Yeah, we're on top of the world. T.C., tell you what our status is?" questioned Morgan.

"Sure did, told everyone to be ready for anything. He even patted down Brody to see if he was packin'," snickered Connie.

"Just doing what he's told, he's a good man," replied Morgan.

"How's your book coming along? There seemed to be plenty of time to work on it," said Connie, changing the subject.

"Not bad, I kinda like it. Don't think anyone will ever believe it," answered MacShane.

"I bet they make a movie out of it," remarked Connie, openly flirting with MacShane.

Mac was ready to give a witty reply when a loud boom interrupted his thoughts, and a large splash appeared off the starboard bow. "Son of a bitch! They're shooting at us!" Mac picked up the p.a. and addresses the crew, "We're taking fire, we're taking fire! All hands on deck!"

Atwater came busting onto the bridge, "Belay that order, Colonel! It's only a warning shot, they could have sunk us if they actually wanted to. Have they tried to make any communications?"

"No, the radio has been quiet. I pulled us out of gear and we were starting to drift. Maybe they expect us to make first contact," said MacShane.

"Your Cuban friend forgot to mention that too? Damn good intel work, MacShane. Go ahead and try it; all they can do is blast us out of the fucking water," replied Atwater.

MacShane turned off the CD player and picked up the mike. In perfect Spanish, he announced, "Attention, attention we are here to attend the auction. Do you copy? Over."

Almost immediately, a deep Spanish voice was heard over the radio and in more of a command than question came the request.

"Password!" and the voice was gone, causing a mild case of the sweat on the bridge of the Sequoia.

MacShane looked at Atwater, "Well?"

Atwater stood gloating for a moment, reveling in the fact he knew something no one else did before giving up the password. "Machete," smiled Atwater.

"Machete! You sure?" MacShane had a quizzical look on his face and couldn't believe it.

"Trust me, I'm in no fuckin' hurry to be blown up, how about you?" shot back Atwater.

MacShane keyed the mike and uttered the word Atwater had given him, "Machete."

Again, the same deep voice immediately replied, "Pass," and the radio goes silent.

Back in gear, the Sequoia was plying a course through the still water. Up ahead, the channel started to narrow. The crew stands on high alert, each member assigned a specific area to watch. MacShane was keeping the old freighter on a straight course when T.C. lowered his binoculars and informed, "Looks like we're getting an escort. A couple of patrol boats coming down on us pretty fast, .50 caliber machine guns on the bow."

"Perfect! Get the woman below; I'll try to raise them on the radio," added Mac to the bridge crew.

"Attention, attention, we are here for the auction and request docking instructions," Mac transmits, waiting for a reply.

"You will follow us!" came the almost immediate reply.

MacShane saddled the microphone in its holder and informed the crew of the situation. Brody was the first on the bridge. "What a set up! First the lookouts with the howitzer and now some speed boat jockeys. Looks like they got it all covered," he said.

"You best remember it all mister," commanded MacShane. "We have to get back out past all this security if you ever want a eat a Big Mac again. No tellin' who could be driving this tub on the getaway!" Brody shut up and started to make a mental picture of the surroundings.

T.C. was back on watch, in the distance, he could make out the secret installation. He let out a low whistle as he lowered the binoculars. "Damn! There are a lot of ships up there."

"How many do you guess?" asked Mac.

"50 to 75, somewhere in-between. All shapes, all sizes. This is some major shit!" answered T.C.

"How soon to the docks?" inquired MacShane again.

"Half hour, forty-five minutes. Looks like the Columbus Day Regatta in Biscayne Bay. Minus the drunks," stated T.C.

"Well we better start playing the role said Mac as he picked up the mic and hailed the dockmaster. "Attention dockmaster, this is

the Sequoia we are requesting docking instructions; do you copy?"
The silence was lingering, MacShane picked up the mic and was
ready to repeat his request when the speakers barked to life.

"This is Security Officer Rojas. What do you want Sequoia?"
came the mundane sounding voice.

"I repeat, we request docking instructions so we can participate
in the auction," reiterated MacShane.

"Look around you Sequoia, get in line and wait your turn,"
stated an unimpressed Rojas.

"Rojas, tell Senor Escobar I have a message for him." replied
MacShane now going over Rojas's head.

"Senor Escobar is a busy man you can tell him yourself when
you dock next week," responded Rojas.

"Man this guy is tough. He should get a job as a New York City
bouncer," Mac told T.C.

"What now? We can't wait that long to dock," inquired T.C.

"We'll get in now and watch this," MacShane keyed the mic and
spoke. "Very well Rojas, I guess the message I have for him from
Captain Yakobofsky will have to wait."

Almost immediately, a gravely raspy voice came over the
speakers. "This is Escobar. Who are you and what message do you
have for me from that Russian pirate?"

"This is Captain Felix Delgatto of the cargo ship Sequoia. Captain Yakobofsky sends his regards and said he hopes you have been practicing your chess game. He's eager to sit down and stimulate his mind. He also suggested we contact you directly for docking instructions."

"And what makes you so special that you need my help Delgatto?" quizzed Escobar.

"We have goods for the auction," answered MacShane.

"Look around Delgatto; you and 65 other vessels want to dock. Again, what makes you so special?" demands Escobar.

MacShane looked at T.C. "Damn he's going to make us pull down our pants on an open radio."

"We don't have much choice, Mac. We need to dock, and we can't leave him hanging. What else can we do?" asked T.C.

"Try to stall. "Mac picked up the mic. "We have munitions and electronics."

"So does everyone else. Go get in line Sequoia," ordered Escobar in a dismissing tone.

Mac now had his back against the wall and figured he had to drop trow or lose the opportunity. Picking up the mic he declares, "Yes Senor Escobar, everyone has that, but how many Tomahawk missiles do you have on the block for this auction?" asked MacShane proudly.

The speakers came alive with chatter, voices shouting out all kinds of languages. Escobar's voice finally prevailed and with a loud exclamation, he goes, "Conyo! A Tomahawk on board that bucket of merde. This I need to see for myself. Follow the escort boats. We will give you a nice spot right up front."

MacShane looks at T.C. and spoke, "Well we're in for it now. Make sure Dixon is finished with her work on the Tomahawk. We can't afford any screw-ups now."

"Roger that Mac," replied T.C. as he heads off the bridge.

Escobar comes back on the radio and announced, "DelGatto, you will follow boat number 15. He will lead you to your docking area. I want you to tie up in front of the Shackazulu, a coastal tanker under refit. It will be a good place to show off your goods."

"Thank you, I look forward to meeting you comrade." MacShane took a deep breath and gathered his thoughts. He needed to start devising an escape route if they were going to make it back. He started making a mental picture of all the vessels tied up and where the escort boats were docked. What he saw, he didn't like. A tight knot forms in his gut, and a sheen of sweat begins to gather on his brow.

MacShane got on the intercom and summoned T.C. and Atwater to the bridge. Arriving at the same time, Atwater spoke first, "Well, you finally called me at the right time. We're almost at the dock."

"Shut up and listen Atwater. They're giving us front row center, said that way we would have a good place to show off our stuff."

T.C. blurts out, "Dude, there's no way those monkeys can come aboard. We're fucked if they get on, we've got to keep them off somehow."

"Yeah, that's your problem. I've got some of my own. How did you let them put us right up front like that? Damn rookies!" bitches Atwater.

"Screw you, Atwater, like I had a choice, we're all in this together. T.C., take over and dock this tub. We're going to tie up in front of the Shackazulu. I need to get on deck and habla with the dock hands. Have Brody meet me on deck and tell him to keep his frigging mouth shut," commanded Mac leaving the bridge before T.C. takes control of the wheel.

Chapter 37

T.C. waved off the escort boat when he had the Shackazulu in sight. Atwater was still on the bridge, and both men were in awe as they took note of the coastal tanker. The Shackazulu was registered out of Libya and was being fit with a surface-to-air missile launching system. The deck was cut down in the middle. It opened like a giant clam of death, exposing the launching rail and surface-to-air missile. "God! These people are vicious!" uttered T.C.

"I was briefed about this, but they said it was only in theory. No one thought they actually had completed one of these. We need to find out how many more ships like this one are floating around out there," said Atwater, now more somber than ever.

MacShane whistled up to the bridge while making a hand gesture to slow it down and move the ship in for docking. T.C. came back from his short trip into "I can't believe what I'm seeing land" and maneuvered the ship into port. The short Cuban dockhands were whirling the mooring lines over their heads to gain enough momentum to launch them up to MacShane and Brody to make fast so they could pull the ship in.

The gang of men pulled the Sequoia into the dock, and she came to rest against the dirty old tires hanging off the seawall. After the ship was secured, the pack of men ran down the dock as one of the other ships were making ready to depart. As MacShane and Brody were putting out the gangplank an old Willy's Jeep pulled up to the dock, painted with a very bad camouflage job. Before it came to a complete stop, a tall man with a dark complexion, wearing a tan uniform hopped out and yelled up to MacShane, "Ola! Captain DelGatto!"

Morgan leaned over the rail and answered, "Si, I am DelGatto, Senior Escobar?"

"Si, I am Escobar Director of Port Security. I need to come aboard and view your goods Captain."

Brody was now next to MacShane and was giving him an inquisitive look. MacShane said under his breath without looking at Brody what Escobar had asked and told him to get inside and to keep everyone in there. Brody was gone in a flash.

MacShane waved to Escobar and motioned him aboard, hoping that something would present itself to delay him. MacShanes luck was not that good, and Escobar walked up the ramp. When he arrived on deck, he had a look of disgust on his face due to the condition of the ship. "You have a Tomahawk on board this piece of merde?" scowled Escobar.

"Si Senior Director you want to see it for yourself?" offered MacShane.

"Si, Sibut quickly we have papers to fill out Captain," said Escobar.

"Follow me Senior." MacShane led Escobar over to the covered Tomahawk and lifted off a corner to give him a tesase. "What do you think amigo? We make some good denaro tonight eh!"

"CONYO!! How did you get this? I thought you were lying to get a good spot. I can't believe my eyes," said Escobar as he reached out to run his hand over the metal body.

MacShane was quick to change the subject and said, "Amigo you mentioned something about some paperwork. What do you need."

Escobar still slightly in awe of this deadly machine, said, "Of course, the paperwork. Castro wants to have a record of all the ships and captains who come through here. He recently got a laptop computer and is still playing around with it. Come Captain, get your first mate and follow me to the jeep. I will personally take you to the registration area. A man with this kind of power deserves special attention. Quickly, I will wait for you in the jeep." While Escobar was walking down the gangplank MacShane went inside to inform the rest of the crew of what just transpired.

"Brody, I need you to come with me. T.C. get Drake when he gets out of the engine room, then take Holly, Connie and Kim and keep watch on deck. Put on side arms; everyone here is packin', so try to fit in. But whatever you do, don't let anyone on until we get back. I'm going to try and pick this guy's brain on our way over to the registration office. Atwater, you do whatever it is you do. We'll be back as soon as possible. Let's go Brody, and keep your mouth shut until I can figure out how to get you to fit in." MacShane and Brody left the safety of the Sequoia and climbed into the jeep with Escobar headed to the registration area.

In the jeep, MacShane didn't have long to wait before Escobar started to hit him up with questions. "So Delgatto you a Cubano?"

"Si, I was born here; my parents both left for America when I was very young. They said that when they get to America, they will send for me and we will live in a big house and have many things. My old man's daydream. They left and I never heard from them again. I don't know if they made it or not and now, I don't care. I lived with my grandmother. She died when I was 14; after her funeral, I went down to the dock and hid on the first ship I found. An old tanker out of Russia, the crew was nice to me and dropped me off in Spain, and I've been out to sea ever since.

"We ran some ganga and iiliio but now the real money is in weapons," said MacShane, hoping Escobar bought his brief overview of his life.

"And this one," asked Escobar, pointing to Brody. "What's his story?"

"Who Brody...? We found him off Jamaica 4 years ago; he was smuggling dope out of Port Maria. One morning, on his way to

Miami with a loaded-down sailboat, a Coast Guard chopper started chasing him. He healed the boat over and slipped over the side unnoticed with a half-full scuba tank, the sailboat was five miles away before they finally stopped it and arrested the remainder of the crew. They never rolled on Brody, thinking he had fallen overboard during the night and was already dead. He was floating around for three days before we spotted him and picked him up. He's been with us ever since. He's a good man, but his Spanish is very poor," laughed MacShane. Escobar looked at Brody and Brody just gave him a stupid dumb smile.

Escobar looked back at MacShane and started laughing himself, "With a crew like this, how did you ever get such a weapon?"

"Connections amigo. Over the years I've made many friends in many different ports. Now it's time for them to start paying off," replied MacShane with a large grin.

The jeep continued on for roughly a half mile, MacShane and Brody taking in the sights as they passed small portable buildings and makeshift tents, most covered with large netting and palm fronds. When the jeep came to a stop, it was in front of a large olive-green tent. On either side of the entrance were sentries who snapped to attention when they saw Escobar.

"Come gentleman we will fill out your papers and maybe have a drink of rum," instructed Escobar as he put his arm around MacShane's shoulder, walking him into the tent.

"Some command post you have here amigo, all the conveniences," smiled MacShane as he looked around the inside of the tent. From the dirt floor to the old-style communication system, the place was a dump.

"From the looks of your ship, this is really first class si?" remarked Escobar getting a dig back at MacShane.

Brody was eyeballing the whole setup. On the radio were two overweight older men jabbering in Spanish to someone in parts unknown. At the desk in front of the radios was a young man sitting on a stool with three large binders in front of him.

"Come DelGatto, your paperwork. This is my nephew; he will get you processed quickly," informed Escobar.

MacShane walked up to the desk and laid out his paperwork that was given to him on the Thetis. The young man studied them and said, "You came through the Panama Canal? What was it like?"

MacShane brought his attention back to the young man and answered, "It's a very unique experience, an amazing sight. When the big gates close behind you and the water starts to fill up... it's really a... something to see..." Macshane's thoughts were interrupted as he overheard a radio broadcast from Yakobofsky on the sub.

Escobar went over to the radio table and replied, "Yes captain they arrived; we gave them a slip right up front."

"Make sure you remind them not to forget who their friends are!" shouted the captain. "And Escobar you have a Syrian freighter coming in. He wants to trade some opium for Korean missiles. See if Captain Phong is still into that. My guess is he'd rather have the cash, Yakobofsky out."

Escobar handed the mic back to the operator and sauntered over to MacShane and Brody.

"You men had already made some powerful friends here, we hope you remember them AFTER the auction," added Escobar.

MacShane knowing a shakedown when he hears one reply. "Amigo, know this about Captain Felix DelGatto when he profits all who help him profit. DelGatto remembers his friends."

Escobar, now displaying a huge smile, waves off his nephew's protests about the paperwork being completely filled out and walks MacShane and Brody out of the tent door. "Si DelGatto, remembering your friends will make you go a long way in this business."

MacShane, looking at Brody and then back to Escobar, said, "Nothing will make me and my crew happier than to get a long way from this business."

Escobar now getting in the jeep, didn't pick up on MacShane's answer.

Chapter 38

Escobar's driver pulled the jeep up in front of the Sequoia where Brody and MacShane jumped out. "See you tonight at the auction amigo, then we party after, yes?" said the security director as he commanded his driver to pull away.

"What was that all about?" asked Brody.

"Seems we have a few more partners to divvy up our take with. Everybody's got their finger in the pie," said MacShane.

"Great! And who do you complain to? Castro?" said Brody.

"Exactly, these guys can shake down anyone and get away with it. What a setup!" said MacShane. "And now the drug trade is getting involved; wait till this news gets back to Vatican City. Time to get aboard and fire up the com link."

As the men started up the Gang way, a dirty security guard called out to them. "Ola, you men work aboard the Sequoia?"

MacShane turned to face the old tired-looking man. "Si, it's our ship. What can I do for you, amigo?"

"Tell Captain Carlos that his old amigo Lupe Rios wants to see him. Tell him I am ready to be cut in on his action. He's a good man. I work hard for him," said the dirty guard.

"Amigo there is no Captain Carlos; the ship belongs to me, Captain Felix DelGatto. Carlos got shot by a jealous husband in

Panama, he died a while ago," replied MacShane, trying to get rid of this guy.

"So amigo maybe I work for you like I did for Carlos. He used to use me in Columbia to load ganja and cocaine. Many a night I loaded this old ship for the CIA; they made many dollars to help the Contras," said the man.

"So you've been onboard before eh?" asked MacShane.

"Oh, si Captain, so beautiful inside, she still look good?" asked the guard.

"Why don't you come on board and take a look, I love to show off my ship," replied MacShane.

Brody stared at MacShane when he saw the grubby guard start to follow them on board. MacShane gave him the wave off and kept speaking Spanish to the guard. On deck, MacShane led the guard to the water-tight hatch and opened it up, allowing Lupe to step inside into the air conditioning. "Si, Just as I remember, so nice and cool in here, so—" That was his last words before MacShane conked him on the head with a steel bar laying Lupe out on the cold iron floor.

"What the hell MacShane!!!! We can't keep him here. What are we going to do with him?" asked Brody.

"Well, we can't let him go; he basically tried to shake me down. He used to load this tub in Columbia for the CIA to run covert drug running to finance their black ops!" explained MacShane. "Bring him below we'll keep him in Atwaters room."

"Shit! This could blow the whole deal! Now what happens?" asked Brody.

"We tie him up and hope nobody misses him. Grab his ankles," instructed MacShane.

Carrying the un-conscience Lupe down to the staterooms, they stop in the Galley to grab a drink. T.C. is making lunch and drops his Hinkle chef's knife on the floor as he sees MacShane and Brody with a limp body. "WHAT THE HELL!!! Who's that???"

"Unexpected guest, sit him in the chair and try to bring him around; I have a hunch," suggested MacShane.

While T.C. was trying to revive Lupe, Macshane went below deck towards Atwater's room.

"Who's there?" questioned Atwater from behind his door.

"Com'on out Atwater, there's something you need to see in the galley," answered MacShane

"Get lost, MacShane. I've got to finish up my work," replied Atwater.

"Bring your ass to the galley or I'm going to drag you there by your friggin' neck." McShane was getting tired of Atwater's crap.

The polished door opened, and Atwater came out. "What the hell do you want now?"

"This won't take a minute. Follow me!" said MacShane.

As the two men entered the galley, Atwater was visibly startled at seeing the old Cuban guard. "Why is this guy here? Are you some kind of a fucking idiot or what?!!"

Lupe, having gained consciousness, looked up. When he saw Awater, a big grin appeared on his face. "Senior Nixon! Remember me!! It's me! Lupe Rios, I help you load this ship many times in Columbia, remember?" Atwater stood there, not believing that this ghost from his past was getting ready to blow his whole deal.

"Senior Nixon... now that's original," remarked T.C.

"Com'on Atwater out with it; what's all this shit you've been up to, and how do we fit into all this?" asked MacShane.

"This guy has to die, plain and simple. Too many people have worked way too long and hard to let this derelict ruin everything." Atwater picked up T.C.'s Chef knife and started towards Lupe's throat when MacShane intervened.

"How about telling us why this guy has to die first?" interjected MacShane.

Atwater was about out of options. "Alright, here's the deal: 6 months ago, we had intel that Castro was getting into the big leagues. A doctor on his staff found out Castro had cancer and knew the end of his regime was coming up fast. The doctor made a connection with a local who worked at the base in Gitmo; the two started to talk; they figured that this type of information would be very useful to the Americans, and we would be willing to pay plenty for it. And rightly so, Cuba has been a pain in our ass since the 1950s."

"That's great, Atwater, so you're here to give Castro a get-well-soon card," replied MacShane.

"Listen asshole, when Castro found out he had cancer, he felt that he had to finish the job. He started against us back in the fifties. He called the leaders of Syria, Libya, Iran, Iraq, and North Korea. It was these guys that gave Castro the funds and manpower he needed to build this base right under our noses," explained Atwater.

"And where are you in this whole master plan?" inquired MacShane.

"My job, Colonel, is to infiltrate the countryside and work my way into Havana. Along the way, I'm to set up a network of informers that reports any and all movements of troops and supplies from all the countries that move through here. The last thing this administration needs is foreign troops from North Korea, Syria or Iraq staging here in the mountains, waiting for a signal to cross a short ninety-mile stretch of water to the Florida coast. Once there, they scatter throughout the Country and implement their plan to conquer us from within. And you, Colonel, you and your crew of misfits were to transport me here where I would slip off the ship and disappear into the jungle. But now, true to form, you have us right up front under the scrutiny of the head of the port security," spewed Atwater.

"Don't even try to pin this on me! This wasn't my idea to cruise into Cuba with a Tomahawk on board!" shot back MacShane.

"Look dude, we can still pull this off," said T.C. "These guys build this base right under our noses I'm sure we can get a single, smelly, dirty CIA agent off a ship without being noticed."

"What have you got in mind, surfer dude? You have an old halloween costume on board? Maybe I just dress up as Chewbacca and walk into the jungle? Damn rookies!" ranted Atwater.

"No dude, much better," replied T.C. "We put Holly on stage. She does her act, and I guarantee that all eyes will be on her. You will be able to walk a brass band through the base, and they won't notice."

"What the hell are you talking about?" questioned Atwater.

"Holly! She's a professional dancer. We put music over the PA system and turn the deck into a dance floor. Holly comes out acting kind of drunk and starts to dance, there you have it... instant distraction. From the looks of things, these guys have been here for quite a while," explained T.C.

"Damn good idea T.C., and what if these guys want to get a little too friendly?" asked MacShane.

"Simple, I come out, throw her over my shoulder and cart her back inside. By that time, Atwater is long gone; the locals have had a free show and were locked up below decks, ready to book out of here," stated T.C.

"Might just work at that," commented MacShane.

Atwater was standing there with total disbelief on his face while looking at the old Cuban now tied up to the chair. T.C. and MacShane were standing behind him, waiting for an answer. "You guys are Fucked up! My life and the security of our Country depend on a stripper doing a dance on the deck of this broken-down tub?!!"

"Yeah. That about sums it up," T.C. concluded.

"And when will this grand performance take place?" asked Atwater.

"Tonight, after the auction, we act like we're partying with our new-found fortune, and it gets slightly out of hand," answered T.C.

All Atwater could do was resolve himself to the fact. He grunted and started to turn back to his cabin when MacShane called out, "Atwater, how about taking your cousin back with you?"

Atwater just turned, scowled and flipped MacShane off before heading back to his cabin.

"Well amigo," MacShane said, realizing that Lupe was going to be there awhile, "you want something to eat?"

Chapter 39

The auction time was getting close. MacShane, T.C. and Dixon were getting the Tomahawk ready to be lifted off the Sequoia to take its place on the viewing stage. A camouflaged crane was making its way down the dock. "Here comes our boy now," announced MacShane, spotting the slow-moving crane.

"Kim, how close are you?" asked MacShane.

"Few more minutes, just finished entering Langley's code sequence, now I'm uploading the continuity test pattern and self-diagnostic run. If anyone here knows anything about tomahawks this will convince them that it's the real deal," answered Sergeant Dixon.

"T.C., get on the other side. Let's get these lifting straps in place while Kim buttons this baby up," instructed MacShane. The two men fastened the straps around the tail section and in front of the wings, estimating where the center of gravity might be and cinching the straps together with a lifting ring over the center fuselage.

"That should do it. Now tie a few guide lines around her to help stabilize the lifting process," ordered MacShane. "Don't want anything to happen at this point."

Mac and T.C. guided the crane's cable down and connected it to the lifting ring. Once secure, T.C. gave the crane operator the thumbs-up signal, and the Tomahawk slowly started to rise up off its wooden bunk. "Grab that guide line, she's starting to spin," yelled MacShane.

Dixon, being the closest to the line, grabbed it, stretching the line to its limit. Kim strained and pulled. The tomahawk was headed straight for the bridge and would have slammed hard into it if not for Dixon's quick response. T.C., watching all this in what appeared to be slow motion, signaled the crane operator to stop lifting. "Damn, that was too close!" remarked T.C.

Mac yelled over the side at the crane operator, telling him to slow down or the profits he lost would be taken out of his hide.

Now a crowd was gathering. The rumors were true; a real tomahawk was being unloaded right in front of their eyes. The crowd and commotion were growing when Escobar pulled up.

Jumping out of his jeep, the director of security started to give the crane operator an abusive tongue-lashing. "You Idiot, I told you not to move that tomahawk until I was here to supervise! Another move like this, and you'll be sent to a prison farm, picking tobacco ten hours a day!"

The driver, realizing his mistake, hung his head and said nothing. He sat there, waiting for his next instruction.

Mac had joined Dixon on the guide line and told T.C. to give the operator the lift signal.

With Morgan and Kim on the one guide line and T.C. and Brody on the other the crane operator ever so slowly lifted the massive weapon and brought it over the side. As it hung suspended in space, Mac and Brody tossed the guide lines over the rail to some of Escabar's men waiting on the dock; it was their responsibility now, and the crew of the Sequoia took a long, deep breath.

MacShane started towards the gangplank. "I'm going with them, see where they're going to secure her; we don't need to have any more mishaps. T.C. get Drake, use whoever you need and get this tub ready to depart on a moment's notice."

"Roger that Captain," answered T.C. as he saluted and turned to go below deck to see what Drake was up to. Entering the engine room, he found Drake laying on top of the large engine with a bucket of tools.

"What are you doing? Mac said we need to get this tub ready to go on a moment's notice, and you got half the engine torn apart. What gives?" asked T.C., now starting to get worried.

"Man it's only a quick inspection, relax! One of these injectors was starting to hang up, nothing major," responded Drake.

"Well, you better get it back together quick. They unloaded the Tomahawk, and Mac went to see where they were taking it. Now we need to stand watch on deck, so hurry up! Man! What if we had to book out of here?" T.C. was cut off by Drake.

"Dude, have I ever let you down? No! And you know why? It's because I know what I'm doing. If we had to "book out of here," like you say, then don't you want both engines working at their max? Of course, you do, and how does that happen? By leaving me the hell alone and letting me take care of my babies." Drake hated to be interrupted while he was working. "Now how about you go keep watch and let me finish."

T.C. stood there for a moment and watched as Drake went back to turning wrenches. It was pointless to argue, so T.C. left the engine room and headed topside, hoping he would get more cooperation from the rest of the crew.

Chapter 40

MacShane followed the slow-moving crane and watched as the dockhands lowered the Tomahawk onto the stage into some make shift holders. Auction time was slated to begin at 1900 hours; all the merchandise for that night's auction was to have been numbered, lined up and inspected by then. MacShane and crew had three hours to wait for the festivities to begin. When it seemed like all eyes were on the Tomahawk, MacShane nonchalantly wondered about looking at what the others had to offer. Even for a seasoned vet, the list of goods was somewhat impressive.

Cases of AK-47s with ammo and boxes of night vision goggles, both in newly sealed Soviet packaging. Racks of RPGs, crates of Vietnam-era AR-15 rifles, Chinese made hand-grenades, hundreds of pounds of C-4, stacks of North Korean surface-to-air missiles, Soviet-made RPG's, land mines from Syria, boxes of cell phones from India and, barrels of ball bearings manufactured in Germany, twenty 500 pound bombs with Chilean markings, the different types of equipment and the amount of carnage that can be delivered with such weapons was mind-numbing to MacShane.

"So, amigo you brought the Tomahawk, yes?" came a question bringing MacShane back to life. It was asked by a big burly one-eyed man a few inches shorter then MacShane who appeared to be of Mid-eastern decent.

"That's right, Felix Delgatto, Captain of the Sequoia," answered Mac.

"Yes, I saw that bucket come in. You docked right in front of me. I am captain Musa Amed of the Shackazulu," said the old salt.

MacShane knew he had a prime opportunity to get some great intel and started a conversation. "Yes Captain, I saw your ship, but just what is being done to it?"

"No Captain it's not my ship. I am but the lowly hired help. I transport these ships for others who own them. This one is having a portable rocket launcher installed in the cargo hold. Once it is finished, I am to take it back to Syria and from there, who knows, it will be someone else's problem. I just bring them here and take them back; really quite boring after a few runs, but the pay is good, and the work steady. How about you? I never saw you here before."

"This is our first time; I heard about this place in Panama City from an old Russian sailor I knew. He said a fortune can be made for the right kind of stuff." Morgan was making it up as he went along; he only hoped his new friend was buying it.

"You're swinging a pretty big dick for your first time here, Captain?" The old man was starting to get suspicious about MacShanes story. "Tell me how did you get this Tomahawk?"

"Like I told Escobar, I have many friends. We not only ran ganja and cocaine, but we also did some white slavery trading in Europe.

One of my associates in Turkey had, shall we say, a customer that had some very different kinds of needs. He also happens to be in a very high position at the NATO base in Izmir. People will do all kinds of things to feed their addiction," spelled out MacShane, hoping this would get some of the heat off him.

Amed glared at MacShane with his single dark eye, sizing him up. Then, after a few seconds, Ahmed scratched his chin and spoke. "White slavery? I ran women for the Russian Mafia and traded them with the Saudis for opium. Maybe we know some of the same people Delgatto, what you think?"

MacShane was feeling backed against a wall. There were too many witnesses around to make Musa disappear, so Morgan did the only thing he could think of: he started to laugh. "Maybe we do, captain; we have a few hours before the auction; let's go back to my ship and drink some rum."

MacShane put his arm around the crusty man's shoulder and started back to the Sequoia when he heard a jeep horn beeping. Turning around, he saw Escobar waving him over.

"Delgatto, come with me. Someone wants to meet you, my friend!" shouted the security chief.

"I was going to have a drink with my new amigo here," answered MacShane.

"With Amed!? You should hang out with someone more your style. Besides Captain Amed has to leave, his bosses radioed and want him back as soon as possible. Come my friend! These are some very important people," said Escobar.

MacShane felt relieved that he didn't have to complicate matters by taking out another person, especially a ship's captain. "Sorry amigo maybe we meet again on our next trip." MacShane patted Ahmed on the shoulder and got into the jeep.

"Dirty man that Amed, you shouldn't trust him. He will turn on you like that. Nobody around here likes him and besides he smells bad. Come I will introduce you to some nice people. People who can help you," suggested Escobar as the jeep turned around and headed away from the auction stage.

A short way into the hills Escobar stops the jeep in front of an old adobe building, bigger than a hut but smaller than a house. From the look of it, the building had seen better days; patches of dried mud were falling off, laying right where they had fallen. "Come, Delgatto, now you meet some real players," with that Escobar opened the wood-slatted door and stepped inside; MacShane was right behind him.

"Gentleman!" started Escobar, "This is Captain Delgatto."

MacShane's eyes were still adjusting to the darkened room when a round of applause rang out. Now seeing better, MacShane could make out five figures sitting around a rectangular table on wooden chairs. The room was much cooler than the jungle heat outside, but that didn't stop MacShane from breaking out into a light sweat.

Escobar moved MacShane forward and started the introductions. "First, we have Saeed Shaheed representing the Syrian government. Next, we have Colonel Kwan Yang Keon from North Korea; this is General Nicolai Zuberoff, former Soviet Union. From Iran, Overlord Habib Hassim representing Mahmoud Ahmadinejad and finally, my good friend General Lorenzo Cortez from Venezuela, who speaks for President Hugo Chavez. These are the men who made this place happen. Many dollars have been invested here so we can disrupt the West." While Escobar was still beaming, MacShane made the rounds shaking hands and memorizing faces.

"Gentleman, this is a great place you have. An installation like this will advance your cause tenfold," spoke MacShane, now trying to play the game and walk away with his skin.

"Thank you, captain. You must realize that a place such as ours needs tight security, don't you agree? " General Zuberoff said.

"Absolutely General," answered MacShane, wondering where this was leading.

"Good! And since I am in charge of who comes and who may go, then you won't mind a few simple questions, eh, Delgatto?" continued Zuberoff.

"Of course, not General were all here for the same purpose. Ask what you will." MacShane's mind was in overdrive; he knew he'd better sound convincing, or the only way he was going to leave was in a box.

Zuberoff looked over at Colonel Kwan as if yielding the floor. "Captain," began Kwan, "this is a great piece of equipment. Now tell us exactly how you acquired it." Kwan's voice was no-nonsense, so MacShane did the same thing he did to Captain Amed: He laughed.

"You find this humorous, Captain?" snapped Zuberoff. "In the old days, I would shoot you myself for such disrespect."

"Then you would never know how I, Captain Felix Delgatto, came up with the best item ever to hit this auction." MacShane was pushing it to the limits. "I will tell you what you need to know, General, but if you were any kind of Security Chief, you would already know by now. And that's why we are having this meeting, aren't we, General? That's why I'm not face down, floating out to sea with the outgoing tide." MacShane was playing a huge wild card, hoping that this panel of death merchants had run the serial numbers on the Tomahawk and only wanted to confirm their reports.

"You have Iron for guts, Delgatto. I give you that. Now tell us what we ask of you." Zuberoff calmed down.

"With connections all over the world, I was able to pick this up in Acapulco from a guy who took it as payment for a drug deal gone bad," started MacShane, sticking to the story the crew came up with.

"Go on Captain, and how did he come up with it?" prodded Colonel Kwan as the others concentrated their attention on MacShane.

"My contact? That's my information. I give you him, and I'm out—no deal. Escobar, get that crane and reload my Tomahawk back on board. I don't think I like the service here." MacShane started to walk out, and Escobar, realizing his cut of the deal was flying south, interjected.

"Wait, my friend, General, let's be reasonable about this. This is Captain Delgatto's first time at the auction. He must know somebody, or he wouldn't be here. Come, let's be gentlemen about this. Here, Captain sit." Escobar was working overtime not to let this deal go bad.

"Escobar is right, sit Delgatto, maybe we shouldn't be so hasty." Zuberoff wasn't used to such independent behavior and tried a different tack. "But we need to know a few more answers. First, tell me where this Tomahawk originally came from?"

"My sources told me it was taken from the United States Navy in Turkey, from the Nato base," answered MacShane, adding, "My source said the mafia was involved, like I said before, something about a drug deal gone bad."

"And how did you obtain it?" Kwan asked, as the rest studied MacShanes's facial response.

"Well, colonel, me and my crew were eating the best cheeseburger in the world at MiMi's in Acapulco when in comes an old associate. He saw our ship in port and started looking for us. We had just sold our load of cocaine and were celebrating when he made us this proposal. Seems like he had this problem he needed help with. Long story short, we made a deal, and here I am."

"What was this associate's name?" shot Zuberoff.

"Alright! His name is Joey Parisi, we know him as Joey bag o' doughnuts. Maybe you can send him a Christmas card. Now how about you, General, where do you people come from?" It was now MacShanes turn to ask some questions.

Zuberoff looked at the group, and they nodded their heads in unison. Then Zuberoff spoke, "Okay, Delgatto, your story filled in a few blanks for us, so you deal with the Mafia, eh?"

"What a man's politics are or where he gets his money is no concern of mine, General. My crew and our profits are what's important to me, they tell me the big money is now in weapons, I deliver a top-of-the-line Tomahawk, and this is the treatment I get. I walked your auction, General, some AK-47s big deal, I can get all

I want in Honduras. Cell phones? Are you selling weapons or opening a telephone exchange? So far gentleman, I'm not too impressed." MacShane was giving an Oscar-rated performance. Now things should start to get interesting.

General Zuberoff was fuming, "Listen to me, you third world monkey! You come in here on some broken down wreck with a weapon like a Tomahawk and were supposed to give you the royal treatment without any kind of interrogation? You think we're playing games? The Shackazulu tied up behind you belongs to Saeed here; remember that name because the Shackazulu will be in all the history books. She and her sister ships are going to be stationed throughout the Caribbean and Mediterranean, and on a given day, they will destroy and sink 10 luxury cruise ships full of Americans. Think about it Delgatto, 30,000 people taken out in one day, that should send a message.

MacShane couldn't let on that this plan bothered him, so he fired back, "Listen, Zuberoff and the rest of you, I don't care about your politics, who you blow up or why, as long as it's not me. I want the money. You think I want to spend the rest of my life in that tub. It's a means to an end for me; nobody cared about Delgatto when I went to sea at age 13. No! All I want is my money and if I can't find it here, I will go somewhere else."

MacShane stood up again. Zuberoff looked at his partners and said,"Delgatto, you speak strong words. Step outside and let me and my partners talk this over. Escobar, take our guest outside for a walk." Zuberoff dismissed MacShane as if he were a puppy dog.

MacShane led the way with Escobar on his heels.

Back inside the adobe shack, the talk was heated. "Zuberoff you think we can trust this man? You told him my plan, what were you thinking?" shouted Seead.

"Yes Zuberoff, you put a lot of trust into this new man," came the remarks from the rest.

General Zuberoff didn't let the talk phase him. "Listen my colleagues, a man like this can be very useful. He's got balls of steel; his allegiance is to himself and his pocketbook. I already ran the serial numbers of that Tomahawk through my Soviet connection. His story checked out about the Tomahawk; I was testing him to get his reaction on the Shackazulu operation. Did you notice his eyes? They didn't flinch; all he cares about is his money. This is one cold-hearted bastard! Bring him back in."

Back inside the shack, Zuberoff started to lighten up a bit. "Tell me, Delgatto, do you like our operation here?"

MacShane still felt he was being set up, so he cautiously replied, "This place is ingenious. All you need is someone like me to bring in some real nice stuff, and then we can get down to making some serious money."

The board of death merchants started to laugh at MacShanes remark. Then Cortez spoke. "You have only seen a small section of this place, my new friend. My government and Saeed's government spent a combined amount of over one hundred and twenty million U.S. Dollars to have this place built. Castro was only too happy to cooperate; he's old and dying and finds a perverse humor in all this. After he dies, we keep Raul in as a figure head, but we will be the ones who really run this country. That maricon is happy to sit back in the palace and collect our checks, he really doesn't want to be bothered with anything."

"So how much more is there to this place?" asked MacShane.

"Let us say that all the major weapons and equipment are in a separate area for what the Americans call High Rollers. What you saw out front is only a small bit of what goes on here. That is mainly for the small fry. That load of AK-47s you saw, those as well as the M-16, will probably go to one of the Somalian traders; they like to buy automatic weapons, which makes them feel important," added Cortez.

"But what about the phones, how do they fit in? Is there any money in it?" asked MacShane, trying to get as much information as possible without seeming to pry.

Habib spoke up, "Those phones are used by the insurgents in Iraq. They also use them for suicide missions. Sometimes, the bomber backs out at the last minute, and if that happens, we can trigger the bomb remotely. One way or another the mission is completed," laughed Hussim.

"So that's what the ball bearings are for?" said MacShane.

"You are a quick study, Delgatto. Now come with us and see where the real money is made," said Zuberoff, taking MacShane by the shoulder and walking him out through the back door.

Behind the mud hut, Zuberoff reaches into his pocket and takes out a small remote-control device. "Now you will see where all the big boys play Delgatto. Watch this." Grinning from ear to ear, Zuberoff presses a button, and the dense jungle slowly parts.

"What the hell?" said McShane, watching the moving plants.

"This way, I'll give you a private tour before the action starts," commented Zuberoff.

The jungle foliage started to move aside, opening to reveal a football-field-sized warehouse buried halfway down into the surrounding landscape, completely obscured by the thick brush overhead.

"Payday!" thought MacShane as he stepped into the hidden warehouse.

Arranged in neat, orderly fashion were weapons beyond his wildest expectations. Scud missiles from North Korea, portable rocket launchers on flatbed trucks, components for the missiles used by Hesbala and then he noticed the finely machined parts sitting by themselves. MacShane had to find out what they were for.

"General Zuberoff, those canisters and other parts, what are they for?" asked MacShane.

"You have a good eye, my friend. Those are going to be the most expensive things here. And I happen to own them," said Zuberoff proudly, then continued. I have a cousin back in Russia who is supplying me with nuclear reactor parts. Habib's people will pay plenty for these!"

MacShane was overwhelmed. He felt his jaw tighten and his fist clench. He wanted to take Zuberoff apart with his bare hands, but he thought of the circumstances and took a deep breath to regain his composure. Having come this far, he can't blow it now. Exhaling, he said, "I think I see another way Delgatto can make a few more dollars. "How's that, my friend?" asked Zuberoff.

"Making special deliveries, General, these things have to have a ride to somewhere. Maybe my crew and I can make some pocket change delivering some weapons to their new home," offered MacShane.

"On that old tub?" laughed the General.

"And who will stop an old tub like that? Think about it: We came through the Panama Canal, took on fuel in Grand Cayman and made it here, and no one wanted to put a foot on my ship. I call that a special delivery system. What do you think?" MacShane gave him a toothy smile. He saw the wheels turning in the General's head.

"Maybe you have something Delgatto. I will pass on your proposal and see what the others think. Come, you need to get back to your ship and I have much work to do." Zuberoff called up Escobar and motioned for him to bring the jeep. "See you at your auction Delgatto, good luck, we'll talk later.

MacShane couldn't wait to get back to inform the others of what he had discovered. "Man, Vatican City is going to blow a gasket over this one," he thought to himself as Escobar drove him back to the Sequoia.

Chapter 41

Back on board, MacShane gathered the crew together to share his discovery; after making sure their new guest was secured out of earshot, Morgan said, "Listen, these guys need to be stopped and fast. I was shown an auction place with enough weapons to start another world war. Everything from scud missiles to reactor parts, there's a huge underground warehouse up in the hills chock full of stuff." MacShane was visibly excited.

"Great work, MacShane. Just report what you found and don't worry about the rest," said Atwater dryly.

"We need to do something; this place was built with funds provided by the Iranians and the Venezuelans. Even the North Koreans, Russians, and Syrians are involved. They have a board of directors that run the place!" continued MacShane.

"Get that link to Vatican City fired up," remarked T.C.

"No good! They have a tracking station up in the hills. We can't take a chance on being discovered. We're on our own," responded MacShane.

"That's right, you're on your own, because as soon as that auction is over and Miss America over here does her thing, I'm off this crazy tub and into the hills. You people just better stick to what they told ya!" quipped Atwater.

Drake, T.C., Brody, Holly, and the rest sat there in silence for a minute. Each one thinking about what Morgan told them and what Atwater said. Each one knew that these people must be stopped. But how?

MacShane was the first to speak. "Sergeant Dixon, what will it take to bypass the link to Langley and give us the capability to detonate the tomahawk from offshore?"

Kim thought for a second, noticeably taken back. "My orders were to get it ready to be activated from Langley," she told.

"Sergeant, I know what your orders are; I'm asking you a question," said Morgan.

Atwater jumped up. "You can't do that, MacShane. Those orders came from the top. You were only supposed to reconnoitre and report—nothing else!"

"Nobody's asking you, Atwater. As far as you are concerned, you're out of here, remember?" shot back MacShane.

The rest of the crew watched the two men. MacShane repeated his question to Sergeant Dixon, "Can it be done, Sergeant?"

"Yes, Colonel, it can, but it will take some time," replied Dixon.

"Then you best get started Sergeant. Drake, how are we set mechanical-wise?" inquired Morgan.

"My babies are ready and able, Colonel; just give me the word, and we'll be flying out of here like a fat kid playing dodge ball, " Drake said.

"Lieutenant, you and Brody get the small arms ready and start securing the ship. I think we might have to leave unexpectantly and Holly..."

"Yeah, I know; get ready to do my act and stay out of the way."

"You're learning," remarked MacShane.

"You people are nuts; you can't take on the whole island. That's not the plan!" Atwater was starting to go off.

MacShane looked at him and said, "Why don't you go back to your room? We've got work to do."

Chapter 42

17:00 hours and the auction was getting underway; MacShane and Brody were towards the front so they could get a good idea about who was who. As predicted, the Somilians bought all the automatic weapons. They were acting like little kids at Christmas, jumping around the stage waving AKs in the air, hooting and hollering. "Damn, this is some scary sight!" whispered Brody to MacShane.

"Too bad we're over here. I would really like to see who was bidding on the stuff at the big auction," commented MacShane.

As the next item came up for auction, MacShane heard the ship's horn blasting. Turning around, he saw the Shackazulu making steam and getting ready to put it out to sea. "There goes another big problem," stated MacShane. "Hopefully, when we get clear, we can contact Vatican City to take care of her."

The auctioneer slammed the gavel down to close the sale of the RPGs to a small Mideasterner with a toothless smile. "Here we go, looks like we're next," expressed MacShane anxiously.

The bidding was fevered; the price was at 50,000, then 75,000, then all at once, the crowd got quiet and from the back came a bid of one million dollars in gold. The bid was from a tall thin fellow dressed in black robes, he was a Saudi and all his fingers had gold rings on them.

"Who the hell is that?" asked Brody.

From the corner of his eye MacShane spotted Escobar "Don't know but I'm going to find out, stay here." With that MacShane pushed his way through the crowd making his way to Escobar.

You see my friend!" said Escobar as MacShane walked up next to him. "You see, I told you we will make good money tonight."

"Yes amigo, but who is that? Can he really pay us in gold?" probed MacShane.

"What? You don't know Prince Siad? It is a great honor to have him here. You should feel very fortunate that the brother of Osoma bin Laden is buying your Tomahawk. Yes, amigo, he can pay that and 10 times more." Escobar was elated.

"Osoma bin Laden's brother..." MacShane thoughts were interrupted by Escobar.

"Come," the auctioneer slammed his gavel. "Prince Siad is calling for us to come over quickly—he doesn't like to wait!" Escobar had a death grip on MacShanes' elbow, and he wasn't about to let him get away as he pushed his way through the crowd.

"Prince Siad, this is Captain Delgatto. It was his Tomahawk you bought," introduced Escobar.

"Captain, I will be taking this back with me as a souvenir of my trip to the tropics; my crew will make arrangements to have this missile sent to one of my ships for transport," replied the prince.

"And what about my payment? When do I get my money?" questioned MacShane.

Escobar's mouth fell open, he couldn't believe he was talking to the prince like that. "Captain Delgatto, the Prince is a very good customer here, you can be assured that you will get your money."

MacShane was going to push it further. "He said I was going to get gold. Where is this gold he talks about? How am I going to get it?"

The prince was becoming upset. Never had anyone talked to him like this and lived. "Insulant dog! I should take this Tomahawk and give you nothing!"

"Do that, and you won't get the firing codes to activate the electronics; all you'll have is a million-dollar paperweight," said MacShane.

Siad stopped. He looked MacShane dead in the eye. From the second their eyes locked, MacShane could picture nothing except the burning Twin Towers and wondered what part this man may have had to do with it.

"You are a strong-willed man, Delgatto; I like that in a business associate. You will have your gold. I will bring it myself to your ship. Escobar will show me the way," declared the prince.

Brody approached MacShane as the Prince turned to leave. "You made a new friend, I see?"

"That guy is the brother to Osoma bin Laden," MacShane responded flatly.

"Dude! No way!" was all Brody could say.

"Yes, way, let's get back to the ship. We're going to have a visitor."

Pushing their way through the crowd, well-wishers were patting them on the back and rubbing their heads until they reached the dock.

"Man, if you ran for mayor of this dump, they would elect you hands down," said Brody as they approached the Sequoia.

"Never mind, we've got a shit load of work to do before we start to celebrate," stated MacShane

Onboard, MacShane gives the rest a quick briefing of what transpired.

"Really! His brother!" exclaimed Lopez.

"Yea, really, and he's coming by to pay us. So no celebration until he leaves. Sergeant do you have us connected to the Tomahawk?" asked MacShane.

"Yes, sir, but I want the record to show that I did this under protest," informed Dixon.

"Relax Sergeant, it's all on my ass. There's no way we can let this business continue any further. We'll wait until we get paid, then haul ass out of here. Now, let's get ready for our company."

Chapter 43

Below, in Atwater's stateroom, MacShane made sure Lupe was secured to a chair before laying out his plan. "Here's the deal Atwater, like it or not, the Prince is going to come by and pay us. We start to party and Holly does her act after he leaves. You slip over the side and disappear. We're going to fire up the engines and get the hell out of here. I can give you 15, maybe 20 minutes to get into the jungle before I set off the Tomahawk," said MacShane.

"You're really mad; you think these Cubans are just going to let a ship leave without proper clearance?" asked Atwater.

"Let me worry about that. Do you think you can get far enough away by then?"

"You let *ME* worry about that, Colonel," answered Atwater.

"A real asshole right to the end, aren't you?"

"Yeah, but my ass isn't going to be swinging from a yardarm when I get back. Good luck, MacShane."

"Same to you."

The intercom barked to life. "Mac big hubbub on the docks, better get up here!" announced T.C.

"On my way," replied Mac. Giving Atwater a salute he turned and headed out on deck.

The prince and his entourage were coming down the docks with Escobar and his staff as escorts. MacShane smiled at how Escobar wasn't going to let any spare change fall between the cracks on this deal. "I'll go down and meet them. T.C., wait here, let's see what happens," informed MacShane.

The convoy stopped in front of the Sequoia and outstepped the Prince. Peering up at the old vessel, he had a look of disgust on his face. MacShane had seen that look before and capitalized on it. "Prince, nice to see you come aboard and have something to eat."

Siad's sour puss told the story. "You live on this! I wouldn't let my camels defecate on something like this." Waving his arms to one of his minions, he added, "Here, give him his money, maybe he will buy a new boat."

Out of the back of a truck came burlap sacks full of gold coins. "These sacks of Krugerrands are in 100,000-dollar increments. Go ahead, open them if you want," boasted the Prince.

"Escobar said you were a good customer; his word is good enough for me. Give him the first two bags; he's earned them," ordered MacShane.

Escobar was beside himself; his eyes were popping out of his head, and his mouth was wide open. Stammering, he said, "Thank you, Captain, you are most generous."

"I told you Escobar when Delgatto makes money, all that help him, make money!"

"Now the codes, Captain, you have them, don't you?" asked Siad.

MacShane reached into his shirt pocket and pulled out a piece of paper, handing it to the Princ. He asked again, "Please Prince, come aboard and eat with us. We celebrate our good fortune."

"When you get a new vessel Delgatto then maybe I will visit. Until then I have many things to do," stated the Prince as he got back into his jeep. "Enjoy your money, Captain."

The last of the Prince's men came down the gangplank and loaded back up into the truck. MacShane turned to Ecsabor. "This is a great set up I have to come back soon. Now my new friend how about you come aboard and celebrate with us?"

MacShane already knew that answer. "Thank you, captain, but I need to get these bags to a much safer place. Maybe I come back later. Thank you again, Captain," Escobar told him as he sat on the sacks of coins in the back of his jeep and told his driver to take off.

MacShane boarded the Sequoia and gave T.C. the high sign to start the music.

T.C. looked at Holly she was dressed in her stage costume, a big blonde afro wig and seventy's style clothes. He asked if she was ready. "As I'm ever going to be," came her nervous reply.

"Remember, act like you've been drinking, stagger around the deck for a few minutes, pretend you're drinking out of this bottle of Bacardi, and then when you have everyone's attention, start your show. I told Atwater to wait for your second song before slipping over the side. I'll be out after he's over the side and drag you back in. Good luck baby. Knock 'em dead!" were T.C.'s words of encouragement.

T.C. had Holly's CD already cued up and turned it on. Out of the water tight hatch staggered Holly. Moving around the deck to the sound of Wild Cherry's 'Play That Funky Music White Boy.' The lights from the overhead rigging and ambient light from the complex gave Holly plenty of light to be noticed. Staggering up to the rail she leans over and starts waving to the work men on the dock, *'Get down and boogie and play that funky music til you die.'* Once noticed, it didn't take her long to attract a crowd. As the men started shooting up from the dock Holly began her routine. First, she threw the bottle of Bacardi over the side and barely missed the crane operator. This had all the other men laughing and then she started to peel off her shirt. Atwater could hear the cat calls and cheering in his stateroom below decks and was anxiously awaiting her second song.

Holly was a pure pro. She had every man's attention for blocks around. Taking off her shirt, she twirled it above her head and threw it to the crowd, leaving her in a rip-away bra. As the shirt floated over to the dock, a gust of wind picked it up and kept it from making it to shore falling into the water. Two chubby dock hands tried grabbing for it, lost their balance and landed in the canal. This brought tons of laughter from the rest. Holly quickly got their attention back as she skillfully removed her bra and let her 36 Ds breathe. Now the men were really cheering. When the second song started, Atwater was in position. He couldn't believe that this plan had a chance. As Holly stood up on a crate, she gyrated around to the sound of Donna Summer's classic 'Love to Love You.' With all eyes on her, she grabbed the sides of her slacks and tore them away from her body, leaving her dancing around topless in only a bright red g string caressing her body to the erotic song *'Ohhhh, love to love you babe.'* This was Atwater's cue to bail, and over he went, disappearing into the darkened water.

MacShane was watching everything from his vantage point on the bridge with Lopez and Dixon. He waited a few seconds to make sure Atwater was well on his way before he signaled T.C. to stop the show. Holly was working it hard, giving it her all, hoping that their plan was working. As T.C. stepped out on deck, he could hear the boos coming from the crowd. MacShane was on the intercom with Drake in the engine room. "Drake, we'd better get these things spooled up, we're going to have a very hostile audience in about 30 seconds."

"Roger that Mac, these babies are ready when you are!" came the answer from below deck.

T.C. was chasing Holly around the deck, really putting on a show. The crowd was laughing and booing at the same time. T.C. finally caught Holly and threw her over his shoulder and brought her inside.

"Man! What a show!" was all Brody could say as Holly passed him on her way to her stateroom.

"Next time, it will cost you junior," was Holly's reply.

MacShane turned the keys and fired up the big diesel engines. Next, he gave the high sign to Brody to cut the mooring lines. Brody ran down the length of the Sequoia with his Kabar, cutting the ropes that were securing the ship. By now, T.C. was back on the bridge. Picking up the intercom he calls below to tell everyone to hang on.

"Mac, stand by the radio; I'm not real sure how our sudden departure is going to be received," ordered T.C. as he maneuvered the Sequoia away from the dock.

No sooner than the words were out of his mouth, then the radio came to life. "Sequoia, Sequoia, this is security control; what are your intentions?"

MacShane and T.C. looked at each other, sweat starting to form on their foreheads. "Stand by, let me try something," suggested Mac.

"Sure, what else have we got to do?" answered T.C., now piloting the Sequoia past the mid-channel marker, trying to pick up a little speed.

"Security, this is Captain Delgatto, I need to speak to Senior Escobar immediately!"

There was a pause, the dead air increasing the already high tension level on the bridge. Seconds were dragging on with no response. MacShane picked up the mic again and reiterated. "Security, this is the captain of the Sequoia. I need to speak to Senior Escobar now!"

This time, MacShane didn't have to wait for an answer. "Yes, Captain, we are getting him now, please stand by."

"That's more like it, maybe we're getting somewhere now," commented Mac.

"Yeah, but where is it taking us?" asked T.C.

"Anywhere but here, my friend, anywhere but here," said MacShane.

As the Sequoia makes its way up the main channel, T.C. and Mac anxiously await the radio call from Escobar. With in the next few minutes the two men hear the graveled voice.

"Delgatto! What is going on? Where are you going? We have a business to discuss."

"Sorry my friend, but one of my crew got a little out of hand celebrating our good fortune. I thought it best to leave quickly. You have 200 horny men on your docks, and we are a small crew. We decided to ship out before something got out of hand, and we have a big problem," explained MacShane.

"Yes, I heard about the show. I'm sorry I missed it myself. Leaving was a very wise decision, Captain. I really couldn't afford to lose any of my men to such nonsense. But where are you going, and when will you be back?" asked Escobar.

"Columbia amigo, I have an old debt to pay off. Don't worry, you will be hearing from me again real soon," remarked MacShane.

"Good enough Captain; I will pass on your clearance to leave with the artillery guard post in the mountains. Smooth sailing amigo; we will see you soon. Escobar out."

"Man that was almost too easy," commented T.C.

"We just gave that guy 200 grand in gold. At least we got something for our money," replied MacShane.

Chapter 44

"This is the point where we made contact with that Howitzer on our way in," stated MacShane. "We can give Atwater a few more minutes; I want to make sure we're out of range just in case."

With the wider expanse of the waterway, T.C. stepped up the throttles. "A few more knots won't hurt anything either," commented T.C.

"Sergeant Dixon, the firing codes please," said MacShane.

Dixon apprehensively handed the remote firing mechanism to MacShane. "Colonel, I still want my protest noted to this action," answered Dixon.

"So noted Sergeant. Now, are the codes imputed?" asked MacShane.

"Sir, all you have to do is flip the yellow switch and press the red button," replied Dixon.

Back on the docks, Prince Siad was supervising the loading of the Tomahawk onto his transport ship. The crane operator was concentrating on lifting the metal beast, being very careful not to damage the valuable cargo. He totally blocked out the honking horn of the semi-driver trying to pass him with a trailer load of 500lb bombs.

"Be careful with that Tomahawk, you dog, or I will have your head nailed to the bow of this ship," shouted Prince Siad to the crane operator. Little did he know that that was the last insult he would ever utter.

MacShane's timing couldn't have been more perfect. The Tomahawk was being lowered onto the ship when MacShane pressed the red button. The explosion was so great that the crew of the Sequoia could see the white-orange flash and, a few seconds later, heard the telltale rumble.

The devastation was immense; Siad's ship was vaporized along with the missiles, he also had on board, barrels of black powder, and pallets of ammunition in the hold. On the dock, the semi was engulfed in the fireball, detonating the 500-pounders on the trailer. Five ships, three in front and two behind Siad's, were also blown up. Flying debris and flaming projectiles were landing on the other vessels moored at anchor.

A mile away in the Security bunker, the whole building shook from the explosion. "What happened? Someone find out and give me a report!" Escobar was yelling out his orders.

"Sir! The tomahawk! It exploded!" came a voice over the radio from the guard tower across the compound.

"Are you sure, we're not under attack?" answered Escobar, whose whole world was just turned upside down and shaken.

"Yes sir, the tomahawk, it just exploded! I was watching with my binoculars... it was hanging there... and it exploded. Prince Siad's ship is missing, the two ships that were in front and the three behind his are sunk at the dock, and more are on fire in the harbor. It's hell come to life, sir. Many are dead; bodies are floating out in the channel. We need help—" Then the radio went silent.

"Delgatto!" shouted Escobar. "Get that rats nest on the radio and order him back... immediately! Give me that other head set I need to contact the artillery out post, see if they can stop them."

"Sequoia, you are ordered to return to dock. Repeat, return to dock immediately!" the radioman kept trying; however, all he heard in his headset was static.

"Sorry sir, they're out of range," came the reply from the outpost. Escobar was fuming but knew he still had a chance for the sub to stop them.

"Yakobofsky, Escobar, we have a major situation here. I need you to intercept that scow and have it return to port. Yakobofsky do you copy?"

Nothing.

"Yakobofsky! Do you copy? Answer me!" Escobar was quickly losing his composure.

"This is sub-B-51 Executive Officer Esposito, reporting security chief."

"Where the hell is the Captain? I need him at once!" yelled Escobar.

"He's on the conning tower, sir, we're recharging our batteries. One moment, I will get him."

"Listen Esposito, you need to stop that rust bucket Sequoia! Do you hear me? Turn her around and sent it back to port! Immediately!" Escobar sounded like he was going to jump right out of the speakers.

"One second, Security chief, here's the captain." Esposito only too happy to hand the mic over to the captain.

"What is it Escobar? Someone short you a half of percentage?" laughed the Captain.

"Listen to me, you wise ass prick! Intercept that rust bucket... the weapon they sold detonated and demolished three-quarters of the base! The place is in ruins! If they don't heave to, you have my permission to blast her out of the water!" ordered Escobar.

Esposito looked at the Captain as if to say now, who's the idiot.

"We understand, Yakobofsky out!"

"Prepare to dive, Mister Esposito; radar get a fix on our target." The Captain was now in full attack mode.

"We have plenty of water in front of us and underneath us, give it all she's got Drake," said T.C. over the intercom to the engine room.

"Look up ahead, ships lights. That's got to be the Shakazulu," commented MacShane. "Can you catch her?"

"Catch her, I'll blow right by her," responded T.C., patting the helm.

"We've got to stop her or disable her somehow. I'm sure they saw the blast and are calling in to find out the damage," suggested Mac.

"Stop her? With what? This ain't no battleship, ya know." answered T.C.

Mac thought for a moment, "Brody's grenade launcher! That should do some damage."

"I guess that should do something. Alright, I'll get us close enough so we can try. I'll head her off at the pass partner!" said T.C. as the rest stood and watched, not believing what they were hearing.

"There they are captain, 15,000 yards and closing. They are coming right for us!" announced the radar man on the B-51.

"Excellent, now the radio. Sequoia, this is Captain Yakobofsky you are ordered to return to port immediately! Repeat, return to port immediately!"

The crew on the bridge of the Sequoia heard Yakobofsky's order. "Yeah, I'll get right on it," T.C. shouted to the speaker.

"We need to ignore him; he could be bluffing, floating around miles from us," replied Mac to a less enthusiastic crew.

Again, the speakers crackled. "Sequoia, we have you on our radar. If you do not return to port, I will fill your hold with a few torpedoes, and the sea will ingest that sorry example of a ship!" declared Yakobofsky.

"Sorry example of a ship!? That bastard! Who blew up who?" T.C. was taking the Captain's words personally. He picked up the mic and answered, "Screw you, Ivan! Come and get me!"

"Are you asking for trouble? He could be sitting off our bow as we speak!" MacShane was now the one worried.

On board the sub, the radar man gives his latest report. "Closing Sir, now at 12,000 yards."

"Good, it seems that we're going to get some target practice boys. Make torpedoes one and two ready to fire."

T.C. was now fired up. Picking up the intercom, he calls Drake in the engine room. "Drake, we have a bit of a dilemma up here, seems like that Russian sub we encountered on our way in now wants to sink us. We need to engage the unit."

MacShane looked at T.C., not knowing what he was talking about.

"Don't know bro. We only tried it out once. I think we should wait," responded Drake

"Look dude, we need to use the unit now, or we're going to be catching torpedoes with our teeth. We have to try it now!" shot back T.C.

"Alright, but you make sure everyone is holding on to something," answered Drake.

"Give me a minute to get ready, and I'll call you right back," said T.C.

"What's going on?" asked Lopez noticing the blank look on MacShane's face.

"Steady as she goes, Mister Esposito. Radar range."

"10,000 yards, Sir."

"Excellent. Mister Esposito, you may have the honors," instructed Captain Yakobofsy as a sort of an apology to his junior officer.

"Thank you, captain." Esposito took his place at the periscope. "Steady…, steady…, Ready! Fire one! Fire two," with that order, the torpedoes were swimming on their way towards the Sequoia.

"What do you want to do about the Shackazulu? We're just going to watch her sail away?" asked Lopez as they were fast approaching the converted vessel.

"We can't take the chance of having that sub zero in on us. We'll have to just file the report and hope one of our guys can intercept him somewhere else before he makes it back home," replied MacShane. "We just can't take the chance."

***

"Captain, the torpedoes are running true and steady," reported Esposito.

Yakobofsky was timing the run on his stopwatch. "Any time now..."

***

MacShane was watching T.C. as he flipped a bank of switches, and he thought he felt the ship Lerch. "What the hell is going on here!?"

"Hang on... here we go!" exclaimed T.C. as he picked up the mic and hailed the engine room. "Drake, let it rip!"

Suddenly, the Sequoia started to shake, the cavitation coming from the props had the whole ship vibrating. Then, just as quickly, the vibrating stopped, and the ship felt as if it was rising out of the water. The increase in speed could also be felt, and now the Sequoia felt like it was flying.

"Shit! What the hell is happening?" asked MacShane.

T.C. flashed him a smirk and answered, letting out a nervous laugh. "I guess the unit's working."

"What is this unit?" asked Lopez.

"It's a special modification the dopers added. Better known as a hydrofoil," explained T.C. "Drake and I only tested it once before and were a little scared when all the vibration kicked in. So we shut it down." T.C. shrugged his shoulders and added. "Guess we should have stayed with it a while longer."

***

"The torpedoes are late; what is going on, Esposito?" asked Yakobofsky.

"Sir, this is impossible! Come see for yourself," answered Esposito.

Yakobofsky took his place at the periscope. Not believing his eyes, he rubbed them and looked again. All he could think of was how is he going to explain that he missed a broken-down freighter that should have been in the scrap heap because it lifted out of the water and the torpedoes passed underneath it.

As the Sequoia is making tracks, the crew is watching as they pass right by her and head directly to Shakazulu! The crew of the sub wait anxiously knowing that they can't do anything about the track of the explosive fish right now. As Captain Yakobofsky watches on his periscope the night sky lights up as a huge fireball shoots skyward as the Shakazulu explodes and sinks to the bottom. Leningrad now looks better than ever.

"Damn! Look at that!" shouted Lt. Lopez, pointing to the burning wreck.

"Torpedoes!" shouted MacShane. "Those were meant for us! They must have passed underneath the hull when the hydrofoil lifted us up! Man, I love this old tub!" with that said MacShane leans over and kisses the bulkhead.

"Well, there goes one less problem," remarked Sergeant Dixon.

"That sub will never catch us now. We're hitting about 46 knots. Next stop America." Said T.C. as the crew on the bridge burst out in cheers.

***

"Yakobofsky! Report!" came the sharp sound on the sub's radio.

Yakobofsky reluctantly picked up the mic. "We missed them Escobar." was all he said.

"Missed them. How did this happen? You are supposed to be the great Russian sub-commander."

"And Escobar, you better tell Saeed he's going to need another ship; the Shackazulu is a complete loss." Yakobofsky cradles the mic and picks up the ship's intercom. Knowing that his time of command is near the end, he makes this announcement to his crew, "Gentleman, this is the Captain. There was an incident at the auction compound; at least three-quarters of the facility has been destroyed. We are to proceed to Nicaragua under radio silence and await further

360

instructions. Captain out." Leaving the bridge, Yakobofsky heads towards his cabin, hoping he will be able to buy himself enough time to get a good head start on the death squad that will be sent after him for letting the Sequoia getaway. He was tired of Cuba anyhow.

Escobar was livid. He had one more ace up his sleeve, and he was playing it now. Tuning the radio to the helo pad on the other side of the mountain, Escobar calls in a favor.

"Helo station alpha, this is Security Chief Escobar, do you copy?"

Almost instantly the speaker had someone at the other end.

"Go ahead, security chief, this is Helo Station alpha," came the rapid reply.

"I need to speak with comrade Colonel Domingo. As soon as possible."

"Yes, Security Chief, right away."

Escobar sat down to wait; he wanted his revenge, and this was going to be the only way to get it. Moments later, a new voice came over the radio.

"Escobar, is that you? What can I do for you this time?" asked Domingo, accustomed to Escarbar calling only when he wanted or needed something.

"Domingo, I have a major problem. The base has all but been destroyed. Someone got through our systems and must have planted a bomb in our mitts. The sub missed them, and now I need your Mi-24 helicopter to intercept and sink them.”

“Hold on! Your base is gone!?” he asked.

“Yes, yes there is incredible damage; the only thing that will keep me alive is that I can say that the persons that did this are dead! I need your help... I will pay for it!” Escobar was getting desperate. “I will give you 50,000 dollars in gold coins.”

Domingo would have normally told Escobar to pound sand, but 50,000 is 50,000. He didn’t have to fly the mission, just assign it to someone, sit at his desk and wait for the helicopter to return with his money. “Exactly what is the target, and where might it be?”

Chapter 45

MacShane was in the library with the sat phone; he wanted some peace and quiet when he gave his report to Vatican City. He knew it was going to get ugly. "You did what?" came the booming voice of Commander Hathaway.

"We had no choice; the place needed to go. You weren't there to see what we were up against." MacShane knew his argument was sounding weak, but he was sticking to his story. He was too tired to get into it, knowing he would only have to repeat this story about five more times. "You'll get a full report when we make port. By the way, since we have a prisoner on board, where would you like us to dock, Commander?" MacShane asked sarcastically.

"Since you are probably going to have the entire Cuban fleet chasing you, I want you to meet up with the aircraft carrier John F. Kennedy and her carrier group. They were down in Columbia doing a drug deterrent mission and now are headed to the Key West Naval Station, you'll come in with them. Give me your coordinates, and I will have them set up an intercept course. And MacShane, you and that band of misfits better enjoy the voyage; it may be a long time before any of you see the ocean again. Hathaway out!"

In the wheelhouse of the Sequoia, the crew was cutting up, releasing some of the nervous energy from the previous 24 hours. It was a beautiful night as the ship cut through the water at 44 knots.

The three-foot swells were hardly noticed as the hydrofoil kept the majority of the vessel out of the water and on a smooth ride. The moon was half full, glimmering off the water. Stars were twinkling and the warm night air almost made them feel that what had just happened took place long ago. MacShane was finally on deck finally getting ready to enjoy a Macanudo when Connie walked up next to him and started up conservation.

"You haven't had much me time since we left Grand Cayman, have you, Mac."

"None of us has, except Atwater. Hope he got out alright. He was a major asshole, but I guess he has to be to do what he does." Morgan took out his lighter and lit up. Taking a drag, he holds it in his mouth for a moment savoring the tasty smoke. Exhaling, he tries to puff the perfect smoke ring. Unfortunately, the speed of the Sequoia tears the fragile ring apart.

"Do you think you're going to catch Hell about setting off the Tomahawk at the auction?" asked Connie.

"Already started, guess the rest will depend on how much damage we did," answered Morgan.

"What's this we stuff? You pressed the button remember; Sergeant Dixon gave it to you under protest," said Connie.

"Yeah, time...will... te... You hear that? Quick up to the bridge. Move it!" ordered Mac.

"What? What's the problem?"

"Helicopter, Russian Mi-24 Hind. Move it!" answered Mac, tossing his cigar over the side.

Double-timing it up to the bridge, MacShane points to a silhouetted outline of the Helicopter coming for them at sea level. "Turn off all the running lights, start evasive maneuvers," instructed MacShane.

"Think they're looking for us?" asked T.C.

"No doubt, since their sub missed us. Didn't see this guy on our way in, they must have a base somewhere else on the island," said Mac. He then added, "He'll probably give us the once over before he shoots to make sure it's us. That only buys us a few minutes at best."

"Can we shoot him down?" asked Holly.

"I wish, the Russians call those things the flying tanks. They're heavily armored and carry 12.7 mm Yakushev-Borzov multi-barrel machine guns, 4x AT-6 spiral anti-tank guided missiles, 4x 80mm S-8 rocket pods and 4 external fuel tanks. The thing does 208 miles an hour, so we're not going to outrun it. In other words, Holly, no!" answered Mac.

"How do you know so much about them?" questioned Holly.

"Had to train on one in Louisiana for adversary training; the fuel tanks on the wings would have been our best chance. But..." He let the conversation drag. The Mi-24 Hind was slowing down to give them the once over.

At this point Brody left the bridge and headed below without a word. When MacShane saw Brody leave, he suggested that the girls get below decks and don life jackets, just in case. T.C. and Mac stayed in the wheelhouse, watching as the copter flew overhead about 100 feet above the deck. The copter went about a quarter mile and turned to do another fly-by.

"Now he's just screwing with us," commented MacShane.

"Yeah he's got us dead to nuts. What's he waiting for? Do it already!" shouted T.C. out the side window of the wheelhouse, giving him the finger.

"Probably a young crew getting their jollies before blasting us," answered MacShane.

"Mac! Look!" T.C. was pointing to the deck; there was Brody with an RPG, and he was pointing it at the copter on the darkened deck of the Sequoia. Brody lifts the Russian-made Rocket Propelled Grenade launcher to his shoulder and waits for the opportune moment. Carefully he aims; Brody has a good sight picture; he squeezes the trigger and off blasts the projectile. Headed straight for the copter. Seconds pass as the track of the tiny missile glows in the dark, streaking towards its target. The copter never moved as the grenade made contact in front of the port wing tearing a hole in the top engine intake. Smoke and fire started coming out the top sides of the copter as it turned and tried to make a run back to base. Three minutes later, in the distance, the crew of the Sequoia stood on deck, watching as the copter went down in a ball of flames only to be extinguished by the sea. What the crew would never know is that the only reason Brody's grenade brought down the chopper is that a piece of flying shrapnel tore a hole in the fuel line. A fuel line that was supposed to be steel braided but was hastily replaced by the maintenance crew with a plain neoprene type II fuel line. If not for that fortunate mistake, the grenade would have only been a nuisance.

MacShane walked up to Brody and said. "What did I tell you about running around my ship with weapons?"

"But Sir, I—"

MacShane couldn't keep a straight face as Brody start to stammer; he gave him a smile and asked, "And exactly where did you get that RPG, Sergeant Brody?"

"At the auction. I bought it from an Egyptian for two hundred bucks. I always wanted one of these. And I still have two grenades left," answered Brody.

The crew broke out in laughter. "T.C., can we please get something to eat and hit the rack? We've had a very busy day, haven't we children?" remarked MacShane. "I'll take the first watch; would anyone care to join me?" MacShane was looking directly at Connie, who nodded her head and gave him a sly smile.

"Com'on T.C.," added Holly. "I'll escort the rest of these nice folks to the galley, where you can whip us up something special. You two keep your eyes open now ya'hear."

"Keeping our eyes open is exactly what I had in mind," replied Connie.

Chapter 46

Tying up at the Key West Naval Station, the crew onboard the Sequoia was getting prepared for the insults and comments about being aboard the old girl. But now, it didn't bother them; they owe their lives to that rust bucket. Setting up the gangplank T.C. was caught off guard as two crewmen passed by and offered him up a salute. T.C. returned their salute haphazardly, not quite knowing what to think of it. MacShane steps out of the hatch and walks over to T.C.

"We're all set inside; all we have to do now is wait," suggested Mac.

"You won't believe what just happened. I was setting up the walkway and two sailors came by and saluted me. They didn't bust my balls or anything. Don't you think that's a bit odd?" asked T.C.

"Who knows, they might be new guys, hell they salute everybody," responded Mac.

At that point, a Chief Petty Officer drove by in a jeep, looked directly at them and gave a snappy salute. "See, I told you. What gives?" asked T.C.

"Beats me. But get ready; here comes our company now," remarked Morgan, referring to the procession of town cars headed their way. "Might as well get this over with. Go ahead inside; I'll bring our guests into the dining room. Oh yeah, make sure Lupe is finished with his breakfast before they take him away. He really turned out to be a nice guy."

"Roger that Colonel," replied T.C., giving MacShane a salute.

"Beat it!" was the reply.

The line of cars came to a stop in front of the Sequoia. Out stepped Major Chandler with his right arm in a cast and a neck brace looking kind of beat up. Next was General Kane, already burning a cigar, behind them was the rest of his staff and Commander Hathaway. "Well here we go," expressed MacShane.

"Good morning gentleman, would anyone like breakfast?"

"Let's get to it Colonel, we have a lot of ground to cover. Word of your exploits has already started to circulate around the base," explained General Kane.

"Yes sir, this way gentleman," answered MacShane.

MacShane watched the faces of the men as they entered the hatch and were taken to the dining room. The looks were more than he expected. He was actually taking pride in the fact that this was his home, and he really didn't care of what other people thought.

The General and staff took their seats around the table, and the debriefing began. One by one, the crew was brought in to tell their story of what led up to the destruction of the base. General Kane was shaking his head when Holly told him about their diversion plan to get Atwater off the ship. "And it worked?" he asked.

"You bet your ass General, when I'm working, the whole room watches!" she said proudly.

After everyone had a turn, General Kane had the whole crew back as one unit. "I didn't know if I should lock you all up or give you commendations, but after hearing all these different points of view and from the intel we received from Cuba I have to give you all a well done! There was so much damage to that facility that Castro closed it down. It seems that his backers weren't ready to take another multi-million dollar hit to rebuild a facility that they couldn't control. The devastation you caused can be seen in these pictures taken from a source we have on the island.

"Atwater!" said the crew in unison.

"What was that, folks?" asked the General.

"Nothing sir... we… uh..." stammered MacShane.

"That's correct people, nothing! There's no such person, understand?" said the General, not really asking a question or expecting a reply.

The crew looked over the pictures and couldn't believe the damage. Ships sunk at the dock others on fire in the water, buildings leveled. To the crew of the Sequoia, it was a beautiful site.

"Excuse me General, can I get some 8x10 glossies for my portfolio?" asked T.C.

Giving T.C. a look that said it all, the General started to pick up his papers and put them back in his briefcase. Standing to address the crew, General Kane said.

"MacShane. You and your crew deliberately disobeyed a direct order to observe and report. Your blatant disregard for that order probably saved a countless number of innocent lives. For your quick thinking and courageous effort, there will be no formal charges leveled against you or any of your crew. Colonel, you have the gratitude of a thankful nation." Then the General saluted the crew and continued on to say.

"Well people that just about wrap it up, everyone will be getting a letter of commendation for their file. Since this mission never took place that's about all the government can do. However, you have the satisfaction of knowing it was your heroic duty that help take a huge bite out of the terrorist pipeline. Oh! MacShane we still have the small detail of the gold. I believe it was 800,000 after paying off Escobar."

"Well it's more like 700,000 after Atwat— I mean, after no one left our vessel, on our way out we were stopped by a patrol boat before Escobar could get us clearance, so we threw them a bag as a payoff to let us go on our way. At the time we didn't know if Escobar was going to play ball or not and thought it a wise investment. The patrol boat took the money and headed the other way wide open.

General Kane looked MacShane dead in the eye and asked, "That's the real story, Colonel?"

"General, at that point, I would have thrown one of the women over to them if the money didn't work. But yes sir, That's the real story General; I couldn't make up anything this crazy even if I had to."

The General asked the rest of the crew if this was in fact the case. Drake said he was in the engine room, Holly, Kim, and Connie said they were below decks putting on life jackets. Brody stated he was below decks standing guard over Lupe; T.C. was the only one who could substantiate Mac's story.

"Sir when that patrol boat pulled up alongside us, I thought we had it; only Mac's quick thinking kept us from getting caught. Yes sir, sure as the sun rose in the east, Mac threw that sack of coins over the side smack dab onto that boat. I think it split the deck when it landed. But those guys took off so fast they didn't even say thanks," testified T.C.

"Well then, good job of improvising Colonel, that will be mentioned in your commendation also. Great job everyone! Now Colonel, please show Major Chandler where the gold is so he can make arrangements for its removal and safekeeping. Excuse us gentlemen and ladies, I need to get back to Washington with Commander Hathaway, since this mission was a success we're going to put together a combined task force for future operations."

After Kane and Hathaway took their leave Chandler was being given the tour by Mac.

"What happened to you?" asked MacShane.

"The day I dropped you off, a van cut me off, and I skidded into a pole. You had to pass it on your way to the airport," answered Chandler.

"That explains the traffic jam... I was too busy getting my gear together to pay it any attention," remarked Mac.

"Well, be that as it may, I'm damn glad to see you Mac. And, oh yeah, I have something for you." Chandler reached into his coat pocket with his good arm and took out an envelope. "A bet's a bet, here you go, pal two grand! This is one, twenty-to-one shot I don't mind paying off."

MacShane was hesitant to take the money, especially since Chandler was all beat up.

His hand was almost on the envelope when he pulled it back. "No Tony, I can't your money. Especially since you're all banged up."

"No really take it, I did what you suggested and asked the General to bankroll the bet. He said if MacShane can pull this one off, he deserves it."

"Well in that case! Come to Papa!" MacShane opened the envelope and, took out five crisp Ben Franklins and handed them to Chandler. "Well, if the Generals buying let us not be greedy and spread it around. When MacShane makes money everyone around him, makes money!" then Mac started laughing.

Damn! Thanks Mac, that was too kind. I'm going to take the wife out for a nice steak dinner."

"My pleasure Tony, here's the gold. Get your boys down here and offload it. We need to get on our way. Me and my crew still have a date with some lost treasure."

Epilogue

"T.C., when the waiter comes by, please have him bring me another pina colada? Thanks doll," said Holly as she got up from her lounge chair and dove into the pool.

"Man, I love Nassau, the weather, the hotels and the restaurants, this place is heaven on earth. What you think, Mac?" asked T.C. as he stretched out in the shade.

"You know, I think you're on to something. But I really feel like I'm finally starting to relax," commented Morgan sipping on a Bacardi Black and Coke. MacShane's thoughts were gently interrupted by a low moaning voice.

"Morgan, do my back again, especially up around my shoulders. Ok?" asked Lieutenant Connie Lopez lying next to Morgan.

"Sure thing baby. Think about it you still have two weeks of furlough left. How about we take the Mako over to Rose Island for a picnic, just you and me," asked Morgan.

"But that place is deserted. There's nothing to do there," replied Connie.

Morgan was one big smile when he replied, "I know!"

Connie sat up and returned his smile, now eager to get moving. "I'll go to the lobby and call ahead for a picnic basket lunch. I'll meet you back at the ship."

"What a romantic you turned into," commented T.C. as he and Morgan watched the lieutenant walk away in her new bikini.

Then T.C. turned to Mac and said in a quiet voice. "Do you really think they bought that story of the sack being tossed over the side?"

"Must have; they let us leave the country, didn't they?" answered Morgan.

"100,000 in gold. The authentic coin of the realm. Spend it, trade it, hell you could even make bullets out of it. What better way to fund our expedition," replied T.C.

"What, not that Jamaica story again!" wailed Morgan.

"Ya see, we take your half and my half, and we buy some more equipment. We fly Spyder and Bonbon over to help us out—"

MacShane cut off T.C.'s tirade in mid-thought. "You know we have other partners to consider. And from what I can tell, it's going to be some time before these girls are ready or willing to take another trip. We need to go into town, pick out a bank and get a couple of safety deposit boxes. Then I'll feel better. But for now, I'm taking my tired ass back to the Sequoia, bringing Drake a nice pizza so he will help me get the Mako ready and then I'm going to spend the rest of the afternoon with a special lady."

T.C. sat back, thought about his friends' words for a moment, nodded his head in agreement and spoke. "See, didn't I tell you that this was the wisest investment you would ever make! Remember, be back early. I'm making pot roast for dinner."

The End!

To My Dearest Reader

I want to offer you a a hearty thank you for your purchase and reading of "One Drunkin Monkee," I hope this story has sparked your imagination and maybe added a desire to go out to explore and enjoy the sun and the sea. If you do partake on an adventure of your own please do not do what I did. Always use sunblock, sunscreen and UV clothing along with wide brimmed hats. The sun is enjoyable but can be hazardous to your skin, having experienced numerous Melanoma and removal of pre cancerous spots from not using the above mentioned precautions I can tell you the sun is some serious business.Take precautions when you venture out, if you are a sun worshiper already please schedule yearly dermatologist visits. I want you to be around and healthy to enjoy forth coming stories.

All the best!

W.C. Beattie